# THE LORD BEHIND THE LETTERS

---

CLEAN HISTORICAL REGENCY ROMANCE

EDITH BYRD

STARFALL
PUBLICATIONS

# GET EDITH'S EXCLUSIVE MATERIAL

Visit the author's website to get your free copy of Edith Byrd's bestselling books!

Just visit the link below:

http://edithbyrd.com/

# ABOUT EDITH BYRD

Edith Byrd comes from a long line of Ohio natives. She left her little Ohio only for educational purposes to study geography at Montreal where she also met her husband. Upon their marriage they both returned to Ohio where they've been living for the better part of the last two decades.

For Edith, writing didn't come naturally, and she never had the strong urge to publish her thoughts. Her creativity sprung when her second-born son was diagnosed with Asperger's, so she had to come up with alternatives for him to focus on any subject. This constant practice in creating stories for her son and her interest in literature pushed her to eventually write books.

In her free time, she volunteers for people with disabilities, studies Ohio's history, and enjoys long walks with her husband and two dogs.

# THE LORD BEHIND THE
# LETTERS

# CHAPTER 1

*"PROFITLESS USURER, why dost thou use*
*So great a sum of sums, yet canst not live?*
*For having traffic with thyself alone,*
*Thou of thyself thy sweet self dost deceive.*
*Then how, when nature calls thee to be gone,*
*What acceptable audit canst thou leave?*
*Thy unused beauty must be tomb'd with thee,*
*Which, used, lives th' executor to be."*

"It is beautiful," Fiona said softly, still drinking in the words even as she spoke.

Kendrick stared out the window of the carriage a moment, the words moving through his mind. Yes, it was quite beautiful.

"Did you write that?" she asked. He almost wanted to laugh at the very thought of having written something so achingly wonderful, but of course his mother did not recognize that it was absurd to even think such a thing.

"I could only wish to have written something so lovely," he replied, and she gave him a small smile.

"Your poems are lovely as well, Kendrick." She always did believe in him and he gave a smile in response. The last time he had read her any of his own poems she had been extremely pleased with them as well. In fact, she had not even realized they were ones he had written rather than ones that were already published.

"I thank you, however this is a level to which I ascribe but cannot achieve. Perhaps someday I shall be able to write something as spectacular as these words. It is a dream I continue to seek." It was a dream that he focused on each day when he sat down at his desk to write. Some days he felt closer to it than others, and his diary could certainly attest to that, with a multitude of poems of varying skill levels.

"Soon, Kendrick. Soon you shall be able to achieve your dream." All he could do was smile, as he knew he was still quite a distance from such a goal. To be able to write anything even close to as marvelous as Shakespeare was a feat in itself. But he would continue to try for it. As yet, however, his own poems paled in comparison.

"We shall be arriving soon, Mother," he said instead, glancing out the window toward the street. They were indeed approaching the front stoop of the duchess and the Deighton Estate.

"Ah, yes," she straightened in her seat, brushing out her dress and smiling even more serenely. The blue color of it was her favorite, though their father had always said she looked best in green. Still, this dress looked elegant and the floral print was a testament to the fact that the weather was finally starting to warm in a way that called to mind summer and all the wonderful things that went along with it.

Though the duchess was quite above the station of his mother, as a countess, the two women were close as anything. They had grown up together and even at their age they bandied about practically like schoolgirls when they were together. Kendrick could not help but smile at the thought of it. They would come together quite often, and his mother always wished for Kendrick to accompany her, though often before he had been too busy to do so.

Each time that they would plan to meet, his mother would ask him to come, and occasionally he would accept. The two women seemed to enjoy having his company when he did come, at least as much as he enjoyed being there. Though often they would fall to gossip and stories that held no interest for him. When that happened he would settle into a chair beside the window to write or find his way to the library that Rose always told him was 'available whenever he liked.'

"My Lady," the groom opened the door and reached inside to assist her from the carriage and Kendrick followed after.

"Thank you, Gregor," his mother said gently as she waited for Kendrick to alight and take her arm. The groom nodded his head with a smile and climbed back onto the carriage to take it around the back while Kendrick and his mother approached the estate. Gregor would see to the carriage and horses and then wait in the stables until they were ready to leave. Though Kendrick was quite certain there was a certain young maid in the duchess's household who would see to it that Gregor had something to eat while he waited as well.

"Ah, My Lady, Her Grace is expecting you," Markus informed them as they entered, gesturing them toward the front parlor. A maid, one Kendrick had not seen before, stepped forward to lead them into the parlor where the duchess was indeed waiting for them.

"Fiona! There you are. I have been waiting and waiting. You know it is not good manners to keep the duchess waiting, don't you?" The tone was serious but the sparkle in her eye said she was jesting at their expense. Fiona laughed in response and the two women embraced warmly.

You would never guess that they had seen each other already once this week. And twice the week before. They always greeted one another as if they had gone months apart. Kendrick could only wish he had a friend whom he was so pleased to see each time. But there were none even close. In fact, his brother was his closest friend and even Edgar was not so much his friend as that.

"And Kendrick, it is nice to see you as well." The duchess finally turned from his mother to notice that he stood still at the door.

"The pleasure is mine, Your Grace," he replied, stepping forward to take her hand. She really was a pleasant person and she had been a part of Kendrick's life for as long as he could remember. As it was, she treated him nearly as well as a son, and he thought of her as a loving aunt. Though she certainly looked like a high-class dowager. Her hair was always styled just so, pulled up to frame her elegant face and to complement the lovely gowns she always wore.

Rose always preferred to wear darker colors, and while some said it was because she was still mourning her own mother, Kendrick knew that it was because she felt she looked better in those dark colors, though through the occasional comments she made it was obvious that she did indeed miss her mother as well.

The deep green of her current dress was exactly the style that she wore most often, with a full skirt but none of the hoops that many of the younger girls had taken to wearing for special occasions. Rather, her gown draped elegantly about her, filling the chair but in a more graceful manner.

"Now then, Eliza, bring us the tea things, would you?" The maid, who Kendrick now realized had settled herself into a corner, likely to wait for just this instruction, now curtsied and showed herself out of the room. "And what has transpired since I've last seen you?" the duchess asked, and Kendrick could not help but laugh.

"I cannot imagine much has happened. It has only been a few days since we have been here last." The two women gave him indulgent smiles.

"Ah, but a few days can feel like a lifetime when separated from your loved ones," the duchess replied and they all could not help but laugh. Fiona had settled into a chair quite close to the duchess, and for now Kendrick relaxed onto the couch near them both.

"Kendrick has just been reading me a lovely poem. Have you brought the book with you, Kendrick?"

"I left it in the carriage," he replied and his mother sighed.

"Well, it is too bad. But perhaps you could bring it along the next time we visit," Rose said instead.

"I do love a good poem," the duchess replied and he promised to bring a book of poetry with him to read to them the next time he visited. By then it would likely not be Shakespeare, but there were a number of other poems that he could bring along with him instead.

"Perhaps in two days' time?" he teased and the women both laughed at him before falling into their own conversations. For a time he remained nearby, but it was clear that the women had already forgotten about him. Kendrick was left to his own devices and began strolling about the parlor a moment before settling before the fire where he could still hear their conversation and step in if needed.

"There has been news from London, have you heard? The Crown Prince has been betrothed," Rose announced.

"Ah, yes. That princess from Spain, I do believe?" his mother replied, leaning closer with intrigue.

"Aye. She is a lovely thing, from what I hear of her. Quite accomplished." Talk of betrothals between those he had no direct knowledge of was of no interest to Kendrick and he found himself gazing absently into the fire until the conversation turned to books.

Unlike many women of the ton, both his mother and the duchess loved to read and spent hours pouring over books when they were not busy with other matters. Not to mention the hours they could spend discussing such things. But this time the duchess did not seem to have her heart in the conversation and Fiona finally mentioned it.

"There seems to be something the matter, Rose. Whatever is it?" Her concern was evident in her furrowed brow and the way that her voice dipped lower.

"There is nothing of consequence," Rose replied, shaking her head slightly.

"You seem to have something on your mind. Whatever it is has you distracted and that means it is of consequence," Fiona replied firmly.

Kendrick turned toward the women again, concerned himself. Or at least curious as to what might be the matter.

"You do seem quite distant, as if something were troubling you," he added

"Troubling me? No, it is no trouble. However, I have been thinking on something for some time and perhaps now is as good a time as any to see how you feel on it," Rose finally admitted.

"Of course. You can tell me anything at all, Rose," Fiona obviously thought it was something difficult or perhaps something sad as she seemed to brace herself slightly, though her main focus was concern for her friend.

"Well, I have been...scheming at something," Rose replied with a sparkle to her eye. "And we shall see whether you approve." Fiona was immediately interested, and also very much more at ease, while Kendrick found himself intrigued as well. Whatever it was the duchess was very keen on it because her eyes were sparkling again and her voice sounded quite animated.

"It is about my daughter."

"Hazel? Is something the matter?" Fiona looked concerned immediately and Kendrick shared in the emotion. He had not seen Hazel in some time, ever since she was sent to Bath to continue her education at the finishing school there, but he was still concerned for her.

"Oh no, nothing is the matter," Rose reassured them with a wave of her hand, "But she is getting older now. Of an age to be married."

"Is she that old already?" Fiona asked in surprise, "It seems no time at all since she was born."

"She shall be 21 before the winter. It is high time that a suitable match be found for her,"

"Oh!" Fiona was immediately interested and had plenty of thoughts on the matter. The Earl of Rochester has a son of a good age. Just 30 I believe. An accomplished young man. Or perhaps the Baron of Kingston's eldest son. He is a little older at 36 but he could be a good match."

"Nay, I have no interest in either of those boys for my future son," the duchess replied with a shake of the head.

"Certainly not the earl himself?" Fiona exclaimed in shock. "Though he is a widower he is far too old for your daughter. He must be near on 50."

"Oh goodness, no. I should not even consider such an old man for my girl," it was clear that Rose was thinking of something, or rather someone, specific and both Kendrick and Fiona leaned in closer as she continued. "I had thought that your eldest son, Edgar, should be the perfect match for my Hazel."

"Oh!" His mother seemed very excited at the prospect and Kendrick was pleased as well. Hazel had been his closest friend when they were children and he very much liked the idea of having her as part of the family. Though, on second thought the idea of her marrying Edgar gave him pause. From what he had always known of Hazel before she was as different from Edgar as night and day.

Hazel was sweet and fun-loving, and gentle. His brother...well, Edgar was kind and would certainly treat her well, but he was not the free spirit that Hazel was. Though Kendrick realized with a start that he did not know if Hazel was still the same as she had been. It had been quite some time, after all, and perhaps she had changed as a result of her schooling, though he hoped not.

"Your son is of a good age to be wed as well, is he not?" Rose inquired and Fiona nodded.

"Yes, of course. He shall be 26 just next month."

"Then he is perfect. Of course, I know that he will be good to her. I may not know as much of Edgar as I do of Kendrick," she paused here to smile at him, "but I do know that he is your son and as such he is a wonderful young man. He will be an excellent husband. And an excellent duke one day."

"We would be most honored by the match, of course," his mother replied quickly, her smile growing even wider. "I had always hoped that one day our children would wed, but I never dared to ask."

"Of course, it would make sense for our children to wed," Rose admonished gently. "Whyever should you think that you should not ask it?"

"The daughter of a duchess could do well better than the son of a countess," Fiona acknowledged.

"Oh posh," Rose scoffed with a flip of her hand. "Titles and things. There is nothing wrong with the son of a countess for the daughter of a duchess. There is nothing to these titles. And even if there were there is nothing that any can say of such a match. It is a good one for my Hazel and it shall be a good match for your Edgar as well."

"Indeed it shall," Rose agreed and Kendrick laughed.

"Well, I congratulate you both on making such a match. I am sure it shall be a wonderful exhibit of your matchmaking skills." The two women seemed quite pleased with themselves and

Kendrick laughed again. "Perhaps, however, the two of you should discuss the match with Edgar and Hazel before you set a date?"

"Oh, it shall be perfect," his mother waved off his concerns with a literal wave of the hand. "There is no need to involve either of them at this stage. Only to begin the preparations."

"Yes, there is much to do and I should like to have done with it as soon as possible. It is hard to imagine my girl already 20, but I should very much like her wed before she is 21," Rose replied firmly.

"There is a great deal to do for a wedding so soon!" His mother seemed nervous but excited at the same time and Kendrick could not help but catch some of their enthusiasm.

Yes, the wedding of Hazel and Edgar would be the social event of the season. It would no doubt be a true spectacle and he could only hope that it would be everything that they all believed it would be. But would the two really be a perfect match? Kendrick certainly hoped so for both their sakes...but as he listened to the two women begin to plan the entire affair...he wasn't so sure.

# CHAPTER 2

"Oh, Louise, have you ever been so tired in your life?" Hazel asked with a barely concealed yawn.

"Perhaps not," Louise agreed, stifling a yawn of her own. The recital was today, however and there was nothing to be done for it. Hazel had not felt ready and was certain that she had made the right decision in practicing late into the night. So long as she could stay awake at the bench when the time came. Or even through the rest of class.

Hazel yawned again as she glanced into the looking glass to check her hair and gown. Louise was struggling to keep her eyes open as she gathered up her textbooks. Still, they hurried out of the room and down the hall just in time for class.

"Oh, however will I manage to stay awake until it is time to perform?" Hazel asked quietly.

"How about if I tell you a joke?" She waited and Louise launched into not just one joke but a series of them. Jokes that were guaranteed to make her laugh, which wasn't such a good thing in the midst of class.

"Mademoiselle?" She stifled a laugh and looked up at the teacher. Madame looked quite angry and Louise and Hazel both apologized quickly, doing their best to look contrite until Madame turned away and continued the lesson.

As Louise continued telling stories and jokes under her breath, Hazel could not help but think of another person who used to do the same. Another person who would always make her laugh and smile, no matter what was happening around her, or how she was supposed to be behaving. Ah, it had been so long since she had seen Kendrick. Yet she wondered just how he was doing.

Of course it would have been inappropriate for him to write to her. A young man writing to a young lady would have been frowned upon in the best of circumstances. But the fact that they had fallen out of contact even before would have made it even more strange. Not for the first time she found herself wishing that they had remained as close as they had been as children, and that he could have written to her while she was away.

With everything that had happened since she had been away at school it would have been nice to have someone from home to talk to besides her mother. And of course she wished that they could still share so much with each other as they had always used to do.

"Hazel?" she realized then that she had drifted away with her thoughts of Kendrick, and Louise was giving her a concerned look.

"It is nothing," she replied and Louise let it go, though she still looked uncertain. Hazel felt her mind drift back to Kendrick. Kendrick. The boy she had once known everything about. The one she had been certain she was someday going to marry when they were ten and she had known nothing of titles or even what marriage truly was. She had only really known that Kendrick made her laugh and that he was the best friend she had ever had.

A smile crossed her face again and Louise was just about to speak up again when class ended. It made talking much easier and Louise quickly fell into step beside her.

"What is it you are smiling about so much?"

"I was thinking of a friend," she admitted and Louise looked even more interested.

"Oh? And who is this friend?"

"His name is Kendrick. And he was the best friend I ever had, before you of course," she added and Louise laughed.

"A boy?" Louise sounded shocked, though part of that was teasing.

"A man by now. Our own age."

"And yet he was only a friend?" There was more of the teasing tone to her voice now, as she struggled to keep up with Hazel.

"Yes. Only a friend," Hazel insisted. "We were but children when we were so close. And children know nothing of romance and love but what they see of their parents," she laughed. "And at that age our parents are so very old.

"No, Kendrick and I were friends in an age when being a boy and a girl meant nothing at all. Oh, but I do miss him. It has been so long since I have seen him," she added and Louise gave her a sympathetic look, though the glint in her eye said she still didn't quite believe that there was nothing more between the two. "It won't be long now that I will be returning home. And I do hope that I will see him again."

"And what if you find that he has become betrothed to a lady? Or perhaps that he is already married to one?"

"I would be happy for him," Hazel replied automatically, though she was a little surprised at the feeling that came over her at the thought of Kendrick being betrothed or wed. "My mother and his mother are the best of friends so I would always rejoice at his happiness. And besides, she would have written it in one of her letters if Kendrick had married." Of that much she was certain. The thought made her feel a little better, but she did not tell Louise that.

"You have heard nothing of him since you came to school?"

"Only a few passing remarks from my mother," was Hazel's response. There had been very little in any of the letters her mother had written about Kendrick, though she could not blame her for not realizing Hazel wanted to know more. "But I shall return home soon and have a chance to see him again. Perhaps we will not feel so drifted apart once we have reunited again." She had returned home several times since first going to Bath and had not seen Kendrick any of those times.

She had not even thought of him any of those times except on the occasions when she had seen Fiona. Even then she had merely asked the obligatory 'how are your sons?' and then changed the subject, or rather, allowed her mother to change it. There seemed to be always something for her mother to discuss with the Countess.

"It is always this way with friendships. Distance makes it much more difficult to maintain the friendship." Louise fell silent a moment. "You will not allow that to happen to our friendship when we return home, shall you?" she seemed concerned but Hazel quickly denied it.

"Of course not," Hazel insisted and Louise smiled again, though it was clear there was still some concern in her eyes. "Kendrick is a boy, and so of course it is different."

"Indeed. He is perhaps not just a friend after all," Louise's voice was teasing but Hazel shook her head firmly.

"Absolutely not. Kendrick is only a friend. He always has been and he always shall be. Nothing more." Her tone was resolute as she stated the facts. After all, how could he be anything more when she had not even spoken with him for nearly a decade?

They ambled into piano then and Louise was forced to stop speaking as Hazel was immediately directed to the front of the classroom. This was what Hazel had been concerned about all the previous night. Though if she was honest with herself she had been concerned about this for several weeks now. Ever since she had first set out to play the extremely difficult piece.

Louise gave her a bright, encouraging smile, which was better than the sea of very calm and blank expressions staring up at her from the rest of the class. But this was what she had been practicing for all this time. She could do it, right?

Hazel took a deep breath, smoothed her skirts, took her seat behind the piano, and began to play. As soon as her fingers touched the keys it was like they knew what to do entirely on their own. In fact, as her fingers raced across the keys she found herself wondering if she had even needed to practice as much as she had if her hands knew what to do. Though the thought was fleeting before the music swept her away.

Her red hair reflected the light as she sat at the piano, her amber eyes flashing with excitement as she played. It was always this way when she sat down at the piano. She felt as though she was in her own world. Her cheeks would flush with the joy of it, making the freckles fade slightly as they were hidden behind the deep pink that covered her face.

When she played, she did not need to worry about keeping a demure look on her face — soft but not 'dim' — or keeping her hands folded gracefully — but not gripped together — in her lap, or keeping her legs just so — at the edge of the chair, not out in front of her or under her seat. She could simply...be. Perhaps that was part of why she enjoyed it so much.

By the time she had finished there was complete silence. She had thought the room was quiet when she sat down, but it was even more so now, and for a moment she worried that it had not been as good as she had thought it was. At least, until her teacher beamed and stood, clapping her hands together.

"Ah, Hazel, it is beautiful. Absolute perfection." The entire class dissolved into loud clapping and bright smiles covered every one of the previously impassive faces.

"Thank you." She smiled in response and rose, curtsying to the rest of the class and taking her seat beside Louise. Louise did not have a performance today, though several of the other girls did. So they both sat silently as one by one the other girls performed their pieces. Each was beautiful and very accomplished, though Louise assured Hazel that none were as beautiful and flawless as her own performance had been.

It was not until they had returned to their bedchamber,

however, that Louise finally acknowledged how tired she was. She had, after all, sat up with Hazel all night to help her practice.

"Goodness, I did not know if I would make it through that." Louise told her, sinking down onto the bed. "I was certainly exhausted."

"Me as well," Hazel agreed, flinging herself down onto the bed beside Louise, in a most unladylike manner. They had just started to get more comfortable for their free period when a knock sounded at the door. With a groan, both rose to a seated position and then Louise went to answer it. Luckily it was not someone who wanted to come in and when Louise closed the door and turned back, Hazel allowed herself to sink back onto the bed again. "What is it?" she asked, distractedly.

"A letter for you, Hazel."

"A letter? From whom?" She looked up, surprised.

"From your mother," Louise replied, looking at the postmark.

"She always sends her letters on Friday," Hazel replied confused, and Louise shrugged.

"It was just sent this morning. She must have sent it off in a rush. Do open it. What does it say?" Hazel was just as keen to find out as Louise was, nervous that there might be some bad news contained in the letter for her mother to have rushed it along so much. But as soon as she began to read, she knew that it was nothing the matter.

*My Dear Hazel,*

*I have excellent news, Darling. I had intended to keep the secret until you returned home in two weeks' time, however I could not seem to find anything else to write to you except to tell you the news and so I decided it would be best to do so now.*

*I have found a match for you, Darling. And you are now betrothed and set to be married to Edgar Anderton. He is the son of the countess, Fiona, you well remember. I am sure you well remember Edgar's brother Kendrick. Well, Edgar is the Earl of Aethelred now, following the death of his father some years past. I believe he is an excellent match for you.*

*In prestige he is, of course, well within the realm of your equal. And in mannerism I am sure he shall be much more. He is most certainly an excellent young man and he shall be an excellent husband for you, I am certain. I am quite excited for the match, Dear, and I know that it will be an excellent one for you.*

*Well, now that I have imparted this information I shall conclude this letter. There will be another for you on Friday, of course, but I wanted you to know the news immediately. I am certain that you and Edgar shall*

*be a perfect couple. And, of course, your wedding shall be the biggest event
of the season.*

  *Much love,*
  *Mother*

Hazel sat in silence a long moment after she had finished the letter. Betrothed to Edgar? Was it truly such a perfect match as her mother said? She was not sure. Though to be sure she did not truly remember Edgar.

"What is it about?" Louise stared at her with her brow furrowed in confusion and no small amount of concern. But Hazel could not bring herself to speak about the contents of the letter. Could not even decide just how to say the words.

It was not that she was upset. It was that she was not sure how to process what she had just read herself. There was no way to express it to Louise if she was not even sure whether she approved or disapproved of the situation in the first place.

Of course, it made sense that her parents were searching for a match for her. She was already twenty, after all. But there had been no talk of it and she had not realized that they were already so close to making a decision on such a thing.

As Hazel did not seem inclined to speak, finally, Louise simply snatched the letter from her hands, her eyes skimming over the contents quickly as she read. Her eyes widened in surprise as she did and then she beamed in excitement.

"Betrothed? Oh goodness, Hazel! This is most exciting!" Louise seemed more excited about the prospect than she was, though she was still in somewhat of shock about the entire thing.

It did not surprise her much that her mother had found a husband and that she was now betrothed. She had always suspected as much would happen while she was away. But she had never stopped to consider just who she would be betrothed to. Or when that announcement would come.

If she were honest, it was a long time coming that she should be betrothed. And the idea of being betrothed to the son of a woman whom her mother considered to be her best friend... well, it was a wonder the betrothal had not been set before the two were even born. And yet... she had never even suspected. Had never even considered the thought. Now, however, she was attempting to remember any little thing she could of Edgar.

"Well, tell me all about him," Louise finally urged, sinking down onto the bed beside Hazel. There was very little to tell. Though Hazel was certain that Edgar was a wonderful man, just as his mother and his brother Kendrick were, there was little she could remember about him.

"There is not much to say," she hedged, and Louise looked at her incredulously.

"You have met him, certainly? Your town is not so large as all that, is it?"

"No, it is not over large," she replied. "And Edgar is the eldest son of my mother's best friend, Fiona. But it has been quite a while since I have seen him."

"Well? Is he handsome? Is he funny? Kind?" Louise pressed eagerly.

"I do not remember much," Hazel admitted finally. "He is older than I. Where Kendrick and I used to play together, Edgar was much older. There were very few times when he played with us. By the time I can really remember he was away with a tutor while we would play."

"You don't remember anything at all?" Louise seemed disappointed and Hazel attempted to remember some small detail about him.

"Well...I do believe he was quite handsome. In a different way than Kendrick. And he loved to travel. Kendrick told me once that when he was not with his tutor, he would travel a great deal. And often his tutor would travel with him so that he could spend even more time abroad. He began to travel earlier than most because he was so interested in it.

"Kendrick remained at home most of the time. At least, he did for as much as I remember." She found herself wondering if Kendrick had also begun traveling at some point after the two had stopped being so close.

"A traveling man. That is even more exciting. You will be able to travel the world as well, Hazel. Could you imagine it? All of those places we have learned about and you will be able to visit them." It was an exciting prospect. While she did not know much of Edgar, she was not worried. After all, the countess was a lovely person and she had raised Kendrick. So, of course Edgar must be much the same. And if he was then he would suit her just fine.

There was certainly no danger of his being a cruel man or an unfortunate husband. Fiona would have raised him well and her mother would certainly never have arranged the match if she thought Edgar anything but a good man.

And the idea of traveling with him, going abroad, seeing so many amazing things...it was certainly exciting enough. So she took the letter back from Louise, scanning over it one more time to see if she had missed anything. No, her mother had not said a word about Edgar aside from that he was Fiona's son. Had not given her any idea of the man he might be. But now that Hazel thought it over, she was less concerned and more excited at the prospect.

She was to be married. And soon if her mother's letter was any indication.

"I am so happy for you, Hazel. But this will not separate us. We shall continue to correspond. And I shall come visit you when you are settled." Louise pressed her hand with a bright smile.

"I am not married yet," Hazel laughed. "And even when I am set to be married you shall be there with me. I should want you to be there for it."

"I would be most honored to attend," Louise replied, her smile growing brighter still. "I am sure it shall be quite the occasion."

"That it shall," Hazel agreed, glancing back at the letter one last time before she placed it carefully in the bottom drawer of her jewelry box. Now she had only to wait and try to find out more about the man she was set to marry. And to hope he would be everything she could hope for in a husband.

# CHAPTER 3

TODAY WAS the day he had been waiting for. The day they had all been waiting for. Edgar was finally returning home from his travels. This had been one of the longest trips he had gone on, though it had also taken him the furthest from home and Kendrick was more than a little excited to find out more about his brother's travels, and to share the news of home.

He picked up the letter from the edge of his desk, where it had sat for the last several weeks since it had arrived.

*Dear Ken,*

*I write this letter to you, knowing that you shall share it with our mother and I flatter myself that you both shall be inordinately pleased to hear that I am set to return home. This trip to Africa has been truly remarkable and it is one that I cannot wait to share with you both. You would not believe the adventure I have had.*

*The date for my departure from Johannesburg is set for two weeks hence, and I am told the ship shall arrive in London on the 15th of June. You shall have little warning of my coming from that point as I plan to fetch a horse to ride home and to have my things sent after by carriage. After a lengthy sea voyage I am sure that I shall be more than ready to stretch my legs and riding such a way in a carriage shall not suit me.*

*Until we meet again,*

*Edgar*

He and his mother were in fact, 'inordinately pleased' to hear that Edgar was returning home and his mother had immediately set a person in London to inform them of the moment the ship arrived such that they could be prepared. The man had notified them a few days back and today was the day they were certain Edgar should be arriving.

Kendrick set the letter back down on the desk and dressed hurriedly, going downstairs to wait alongside his mother. Though it was early she was also dressed and waiting, both of them too excited to sleep any longer, though his mother's excitement was somewhat tempered by her concern over whether or not Edgar would be pleased with what she had done on his behalf.

"Oh, to have your brother returned home again shall be so wonderful," she told Kendrick. "It has been far too long this time."

"The trip to Africa is quite long on its own," Kendrick informed her. "He has likely not been there as long as it seems to us."

"Perhaps not, but for him to travel so long is certainly too much for his poor mother." Kendrick smiled, knowing that their mother worried every time Edgar traveled, especially as he was always going to such obscure places in search of new trades. She was always concerned that something would go wrong and they would not know of it. "And I cannot wait to tell him of the betrothal. Hazel is a wonderful match. She truly is a lovely young lady and I am sure that being at that finishing school has only made her more so."

"I am sure she is quite accomplished," Kendrick agreed and his mother practically beamed at him.

"She shall be an excellent match for your brother. Don't you think so?" She had seemed quite pleased with herself ever since the match had been set, and so had Rose. In fact, Kendrick had gone back to visit Rose with his mother twice since they had set the match and it seemed all they could talk about.

"I am sure she shall," he reassured her, though he was a little nervous about the prospect. Would Edgar actually be happy to be betrothed? It would certainly mean a change to his way of life and all of his travels. While some men would continue to travel just as much after being married, Kendrick knew that his brother would feel some obligation to remain home with his wife. Even if they did not suit.

Still, if the match did not seem quite perfect the pair would still do their utmost to make it a success. In fact, he was certain that they would have a happy marriage if for no other reason than they would both wish it to be so. And what he knew of both made him feel slightly more convinced that their marriage should be pleasant if nothing else.

"Do you think that your brother will be pleased with the news? Will he see it as a happy surprise?"

"Edgar will be pleased," Kendrick replied, though again slightly uncertain. There had never been any news that his brother was in love with another or that he was to return with a young lady. As such, Kendrick was certain that there would be no qualms from Edgar as to the betrothal. He must suspect that something of the sort would happen at some point. After all, since the death of their father and his succession to the earldom, Edgar had always known it was his responsibility to provide a worthy heir to take his place someday.

As such, it was his duty to marry and to marry well such that he could have that heir. And he could hardly expect to do better than the daughter of a duchess. Hazel possessed an excellent title for his wife and was likewise a perfect lady. With the temperament of both, the union should be a relative success. Of that he was sure...mostly sure, he acknowledged.

"My Lady, breakfast is ready in the dining room,"

"Thank you," his mother replied and, as there was no reason to wait, the two headed in to enjoy their meal. It would do just as well to wait for Edgar with a full stomach as an empty one, after all.

However, Kendrick and his mother had barely sat down to begin breakfast when the butler entered, announcing that the Earl had arrived, and followed almost at his heels by Edgar himself.

Edgar's hair had grown a little longer in the time he was away, though that was to be expected as he had been quite out of the way in Africa and then at sea. But the blonde color was as striking as always and he seemed to have grown even more muscular during his time away.

It was clear that he had been on horseback for nearly the entirety of the last few days, as his clothes were wrinkled and somewhat dusty from the road. But none of them cared about these meager things. Edgar was home. Standing before them right now with a smile that broke through all of the dust and the scrapes that he could see on his face and arms.

"Ah, Mother, you are a sight for sore eyes," Edgar seemed inordinately pleased himself to see them, reaching out first to hug his mother, who burst into tears at the sight of him, and then his brother, his green eyes shining at them both. "And Kendrick. Goodness Brother, you have gotten taller still since last I saw you."

"It has been a good while that you have been gone," Kendrick replied with a smile and a laugh. Edgar laughed along with him.

"Aye, that it has. I see you are just to sit down. It seems I have come at the perfect time."

"That you have. Just in time for breakfast, as usual," Kendrick teased and Edgar laughed again. Yes, it was nice to have his brother returned and as they sat back at the table he was more than pleased that it all felt so normal again.

"Are you quite all right? Whatever has happened to you?" Their mother asked, taking in the scrapes and cuts.

"Ah, this is nothing. A few marks from working on the ship the way back. And perhaps a few from the trip home," Edgar brushed off the injuries and after a closer look that revealed they were quite minor Fiona relaxed.

"Tell us about your adventures," their mother urged, knowing that Edgar would be more than eager to talk and tell them a great deal of what he had seen and done. It was likely best to allow him the time to speak first and then to share the news that they had for him.

"You know, of course, that I went to London over twelve months past. Well, the trip there was no difficult feat, but the voyage to Africa...well, that was quite something," he began. "I have traveled by sea a great many times and yet I have never experienced anything quite like this past trip. The seas were rough, to be sure. Rougher than I had bargained for. And I felt quite certain that I would fall ill. Even more so when the scurvy set in. Nearly everyone else traveling was afflicted, save the sailors, of course."

"Oh! Were you ill? Did the seas calm at any time in your travel?" Their mother looked very concerned, and Edgar waved it away.

"Nay, I did not fall ill with the scurvy. Though I did have my fair bout of trouble with the rough water. But the seas did not calm either. In fact, two of the crew were blown clear from the deck during our voyage. It's a good thing these large vessels travel with plenty of crew or we could have very well been stranded in the middle of the ocean. Two crew short and we could have been in a great deal of trouble. But as it was there were enough men to cover the slack."

"Those poor men," their mother said sadly and Edgar sobered a moment.

"Aye. They were good men, both of them. But with the storms there was nothing to be done. By the time it was noticed that they had been lost it was far too late to attempt to rescue them. They were gone." He fell silent a long moment, as did Kendrick and their mother. No doubt Edgar was remembering the men that had been lost. Kendrick was quite certain, however, that their mother was thinking of how easily it could have been Edgar who was lost at sea in such a way.

"I should hope that things got better after that," Kendrick

added, attempting to pull them all out of their melancholy thoughts and after a moment of thought Edgar continued.

"Oh, the seas did not get better at all. Not until we had nearly arrived. Then the skies parted and everything seemed perfect. It was as if the storms we had just traveled through had never even happened. And my first glimpse of Africa was under a beautiful sky. More lovely than I could have pictured.

"I have brought back trinkets, of course, but they shall come later, with the coach. However, I could not stand to be confined in a coach for several days, and to take the extra days before I could see the both of you. Ah, I have missed you a great deal." He smiled at them both again and their mother pressed her hand to his. Kendrick reached for another helping of fruit while Edgar took a pause to enjoy the sausages before him.

"We have missed you," their mother replied. There was another moment of silence and then Edgar continued.

"Once we arrived in Johannesburg there were men at the docks waiting for us. They had been notified of our arrival before we had even set out, so they knew to expect us at the beginning of the shipping season. And so we were most welcomed right from the start. But it is very improper to begin negotiations too early while in Africa. They prefer to get to know their guests first and then do business with them after." Another pause for Edgar to eat a little more, and then he continued.

"On our first night there we had a grand feast in welcome, and there was no talk of business. It was not until two nights later that we were finally able to speak on the business that had brought us there. To do so earlier would have been to insult our hosts," Edgar told them.

"And you found a great deal to trade?" Kendrick asked, interested.

"Aye, there is a great deal of tradeable goods in Africa. Such beautiful things as you could not imagine. Ivory is the main bit you hear of, but there is so much more. In Johannesburg in particular sugar is their main crop, and it is the best you've ever had," he promised. "But also wait until you see the things I have brought back. And they are only a sample of what I found there."

"You are not planning to return, are you?" Kendrick asked.

"Not for a great while. Not unless it is necessary," Edgar replied, but it was clear that he would certainly like to go back. So perhaps his words were meant only to appease their mother, who seemed oblivious to any evidence to the contrary.

"Is the trade all that calls you there?" Kendrick felt obliged to ask and Edgar started as though he had been in a trance.

"Whatever else could there be?" He seemed genuinely confused and Kendrick merely smiled and shook his head. He could tell that their mother was also pleased with the response because it meant that Edgar had not lost his heart to another just before his mother was set to have him married off.

"So, you've brought us back ivory, have you?" Kendrick changed the subject and Edgar allowed it.

"Small pieces, yes. It is quite valuable in London and throughout the world, though it is rather ubiquitous there. And tobacco likewise is of a high quality. The likes of which you have likely never seen."

"I should hope that neither of my boys would know good tobacco from bad," their mother admonished, and Edgar shook his head. She had always been opposed to smoking, even managing to convince their father to stop carrying a pipe with him wherever he went, though Kendrick knew he had smoked it when his mother was not around up until he passed, and their mother had pretended that she did not know it.

"I have not smoked it, Mother. But one can certainly tell the difference in the two. Most especially when those around you choose to smoke it. The smell of the two is quite different, after all." She seemed at least slightly appeased and Edgar continued on with his stories, now interspersing his tales with bites of food, as though he had not eaten in some time.

Kendrick had never thought that he wanted to travel, but as he listened to the rest of Edgar's stories about the people of Johannesburg and the trades that they had negotiated and the beautiful things they had seen, he wondered if perhaps travel might be an exciting prospect for him as well.

"Let us retire to the drawing room," their mother finally interjected, once they had finished breakfast and still continued nearly an hour in the dining hall. Edgar and Kendrick allowed her to lead them from the room, settling into their usual places in the drawing room.

Kendrick retired to the couch, where he often reclined while he read to her in the evenings. The book of poems they had been enjoying was still sitting on the table beside his seat, though this time he sat upright on the couch as Edgar claimed a large chair near the window that seemed always to have the very best light. Not to mention a view out the window that he always enjoyed. And their mother claimed a daintier chair closer into the room, while the large, overstuffed, green chair remained empty. Their father's seat, which had never been moved since his death.

"There is a great deal to tell, of course. Wonderful adventures and wonderful people," Edgar began.

"Do tell us more," their mother urged and Edgar did not need to be asked twice. Rather, he began his stories with renewed vigor as he reclined back in his favorite chair. None of them seemed to notice the time that went by. But when he took a pause their mother interjected finally. "You must be tired. Perhaps you should retire to your chamber and freshen up."

"Nay, I feel more energized than I have in some time. I could talk for hours."

"You already have," Kendrick teased and Edgar laughed loudly.

"Aye, perhaps I have. But I do not need to freshen up. Unless that is your way of telling me that I smell of the road and the sea," he told them and his mother quickly reassured him that was not the case.

"I had only thought perhaps you might like some rest. After all, it has been a very long voyage and a long trip here from London."

"A long trip, perhaps, but one with family waiting at the other end and so it is most worth it. I have long looked forward to seeing you both again."

"As have we," Kendrick replied. They were silent for a few moments as Edgar looked out over the grounds. It seemed he had finally run out of stories. Or at least he had run out of the ones that he felt more important to share.

"Now then, what is it you have to share, Mother?" he asked finally, and Kendrick waited to see what she would say.

"Whatever do you mean?" she hedged and both boys turned to look at her.

"There's certainly something that you want to talk with me about," he replied, finally acknowledging the distinct sparkle in her eye that had nothing to do with his finally being home. Not to mention the way she kept wringing her hands together "Has some-thing happened since I have been away? Are you both well?" He looked between the two and their mother rushed to assure him that both were healthy.

"But there is something we should talk about," Kendrick replied, looking to his mother to begin the conversation. She seemed a little uncertain still and both boys waited, watching her.

She was silent another long moment as Rebecca entered the room, bringing the tea. They were all surprised to realize that they had talked away most of the morning and it was now time for tea, but thanked her as she curtsied her way out.

Kendrick helped himself to a cup of tea and a biscuit, while he waited for their mother to continue. Edgar seemed inclined to wait and see a little more before he decided to join in with tea. Their mother, on the other hand, set about preparing herself a cup and very studiously staring into it for several moments before she finally broke her silence.

"I have made a match for you, Edgar. You are betrothed to be married." Kendrick had not quite expected her to be as direct as that, but she looked up to meet Edgar's eyes with an unreadable expression.

"Betrothed," Edgar repeated the word a little cryptically but Kendrick was pleased to see that he did not appear angry. He did not appear upset in the slightest, in fact. All he seemed was...surprised, perhaps. Of course, it would make sense that he would be surprised seeing as, as far as Kendrick knew, nothing had ever been discussed about finding Edgar a wife.

"Yes, she is a lovely girl. And you know her already. Hazel Tumbler."

"Hazel? The name is familiar; however I cannot say that I remember anything about the girl," Edgar replied, and Kendrick could tell he was wracking his brain trying to think who Hazel might be. Finally he turned to Kendrick. "Who is she?"

"Hazel is the daughter of the Duke of Deighton," Kendrick supplied and understanding dawned in Edgar's eyes.

"The duke? Duchess Rose then, mother's friend?"

"Aye, the same," Kendrick agreed and he could tell that Edgar was pleased to at least have a small idea of who the girl was and to remember even the slightest bit about her. Now that he seemed to recall at least something he collected his own teacup and a scone from the tray before settling back into his seat.

"She was a friend of yours, was she not?" Edgar asked, turning toward Kendrick again.

"Indeed. We used to spend a great deal of time together," Kendrick added.

"I remember seeing the two of you together. Playing quite a bit." Kendrick nodded and their mother chimed in.

"She is grown now. And quite ready to be married. She has been in Bath this last three years completing her education."

"A finishing school then," Edgar replied and their mother smiled and nodded.

"Yes. She is a perfect young lady. And an educated one at that.

Her mother has missed her something terrible, but it is for the best that she receives a good education, of course." The boys acknowledged her comments but both were still thinking of Hazel. One trying to remember anything, and one remembering everything.

"Well, it is good then that she is a good match." Edgar seemed comfortable enough with that, relaxing into his chair as he had been before the conversation began.

"Oh it is indeed," their mother agreed. "She is a perfect lady, and beautiful as anything. Isn't she Kendrick?"

"I have not seen her at all these last three years, Mother," Kendrick protested. "And only barely in the last decade." And when he had last seen Hazel he had not been inclined to think her beautiful or otherwise. He had not thought anything of her looks. She had been merely his friend. That had been quite enough.

"Well, she is a beautiful girl. And she shall be a wonderful compliment to you, my son."

"I am glad to hear of it," Edgar replied, and he did look at least somewhat pleased, though Kendrick could not say that he looked exactly happy at the news. "I only wish that I knew more about her."

"Kendrick can tell you a great deal. He knows her so well." Edgar turned to look at him and he shook his head in protest.

"I have not spoken to her since she went to Bath. I know nothing of her now. I am sure becoming a true lady has changed her and I would not presume to know anything of who she now is." Edgar seemed a little disappointed that Kendrick could not tell him anything more but Kendrick was not sure that any of his memories were accurate to the girl that Edgar would marry.

"You could write to her," their mother interjected. "It would be the perfect way in which to learn more about her."

"Perhaps," Edgar hedged but it was clear that their mother liked this idea.

"It would be an excellent way to get to know her. There is no need to trouble yourself over how little you know when there is a simple solution. Hazel would welcome your letters, I am sure. And until she is able to return and meet you in person it would be an excellent way in which to learn to be comfortable with each other."

"Aye, I am sure that is true," Edgar acknowledged, but Kendrick wondered whether he would actually be inclined to write even a single letter. It was difficult enough getting Edgar to promise to write to them while he was away. He usually wrote once a week only because their mother made him feel guilty if he didn't. But his letters were quite short, especially in comparison to the volumes that their mother wrote to him.

"She is a lovely girl," Fiona repeated, "and you will be most pleased as you get to know her." Edgar inclined his head in agreement, promising to write a letter to Hazel as soon as possible so that the two could begin a correspondence and get to know one another better. Kendrick wondered just when 'as soon as possible' might actually be.

# CHAPTER 4

THE ABRUPT SHAKE woke him quite sharply and he very nearly sat up straight in bed. It had been quite some time since he had been shaken so roughly awake and he was not nearly used to it anymore. Though once he had quelled his racing heart and shook the sleep from his eyes, he was not surprised to see Edgar standing at the side of his bed, already dressed for the day.

"What are you doing about so early? And in my room too?" Kendrick grumbled, attempting to roll back over in bed.

"It is not early," Edgar replied, staring at him in confusion. In fact, Edgar was looking at him as though he had lost his mind, glancing toward the window and striding over to it in order to draw the curtains. "Look, the sun has been shining for hours already." Kendrick quickly turned back the other way again as the bright sun shone in his eyes.

"Aye, perhaps that is so but it is a time when even the chickens have not left the roost," Kendrick replied. Edgar laughed at that.

"Perhaps not. But then I suppose it is a good thing you are not a chicken. Come now. Let us get on with the day. Since you are up, let us go for a ride," Edgar urged.

"Since I am up? I was not up. I was asleep in my bed. Enjoying my day," Kendrick protested, attempting to pull his pillow over his head to block out the brightness, and Edgar's energy.

"You were not enjoying the day if you were asleep. You must be awake for that. Now come, there are only so many hours of sunlight and we are wasting them with quibbling here. Let's go." With that, Edgar strode out of the room, simply expecting that his wishes would be followed. And they would be, Kendrick grumbled good-naturedly to himself as he climbed out of bed.

The slight chill of the morning air nearly sent him back under the covers, but it would be warmer once he was dressed. And warmer still once they were outside and riding through the fields. With a sigh for the lost sleep, Kendrick began to dress for a ride. It would be nice to catch up with his brother, though he did wish that perhaps it could be done at a later time of the day.

Still, Edgar had always been athletic and had always been the type to get up and out of bed quite early in the morning to do...well, any activity that he could. He took early morning rides and even swam in the creek at this early hour. He was always doing something energetic, which was also why he couldn't stand to wait around in a carriage after being cooped up at sea for so long. It was a wonder he traveled at all with how often he was confined because of it.

The six years between the brothers was not enough to put a wedge between them and Edgar always made sure to spend plenty of time with Kendrick whenever he was home. In fact, these early morning rides were only a part of the way that they would often spend time together during the brief interludes between Edgar's trips. Often there was not a great deal of time between when Edgar returned home and when he left again so they made the most of it. Though perhaps this time he would stay closer to home for a while as he was to be wed.

"There you are. I was about to come back in again to see if you had gone back to bed," Edgar teased when he finally left the room.

"I did consider it," Kendrick admitted. "If only you would not wake me at such an unholy hour, perhaps I could be better prepared."

"It is late, Brother. I have already been up and about the grounds twice this morning. And you have been lying in bed."

"Cook is not even up yet," Kendrick argued. "There is no coffee and no breakfast."

"Ah, we don't need anything warm just yet. There is bread in the kitchen if you need something to eat before we go. Otherwise let's be off." Kendrick grumbled a bit more but took a loaf of bread from the kitchen and followed his brother to the stables.

At least the grooms were about, though they did seem surprised to see anyone in the stables this early. No one said a word though, quickly saddling the horses that Kendrick and Edgar always rode and helping them into their saddles.

They set off at a brisk run across the open field until they reached the trails. Talk impossible while they raced along. It was only when they had both pulled up their horses to travel more calmly through the rough terrain.

"Now, tell me all about what I have missed being gone," Edgar instructed.

"It has been quite a long while since we have seen you," Kendrick agreed. "Though not much has happened here. There are new horses in the stables. We purchased two new ones from town for breeding purposes. And mother has had a time of redecorating in the manor."

"You know those are not the things of which I am concerned," Edgar told him with a shake of his head.

"It is your estate," Kendrick replied and Edgar scoffed.

"Aye, in name alone. And I know that you and mother will ensure that it is cared for in the best way possible. I trust that the decisions you both make while I am gone are the best ones and that is why I do not concern myself with such things. What has happened with you since I have been gone?"

"There has not been much change in the past year in that regard," Kendrick told him. In fact, Kendrick had not ventured off the estate much, save for rides through the grounds and a trip into town every once in a while.

"There is no young woman who has captured your fancy?"

"Not in the slightest," Kendrick replied as they rode companionably, side-by-side. Sometimes the two would race, but for now they simply rode alongside one another, more relaxed than anything.

"And nothing to occupy your time?"

"I have been writing poetry."

"Aye, you were writing poetry when I left, as well. Are you finally happy with the quality of your work?" Edgar was always very supportive of Kendrick's dreams and had been one of the first to tell him that he should continue to write. It had happened when they were both quite young, while Kendrick was still writing poems that spoke of cat's whiskers and horses tails. When he was only a child.

Even today Kendrick remembered how Edgar had discovered one of his journals and read through the pages. Kendrick had been embarrassed and had thought that his older brother, who had been 12 at the time, would make fun of him for his poems.

But Edgar had told him that they were good and had encouraged him to continue working at it. In fact, Edgar had bought him his very first poetry book that was just for him, rather than the ones in the library.

"I do not know if I will ever be truly happy with it," Kendrick replied, pulling himself out of the memory. "There is always more to do and improvements to make."

"And yet you have always been an excellent writer." Kendrick laughed at the praise but he did appreciate it, coming from his brother. "The writing then, it has continued to improve, and it has occupied your time well."

"Aye, I suppose it has," Kendrick agreed and Edgar smiled, though there was something a little distant in that smile. "What is troubling you, Brother?"

"Oh, it is nothing of any matter," Edgar replied, but then he fell silent for a long moment. "Have you ever fallen in love, Brother?"

"No. I can't say that I have. I can't say that I would even know the feeling if it were to crop up." Edgar nodded sagely but did not speak and Kendrick felt obliged to ask, though he felt concern at the thought of what the answer might be. "Have you?"

"No," but Edgar answered quite quickly. "At least, I do not believe that I have. I have met women who were certainly deserving of love. Women who I could perhaps have learned to love. But none that I found myself truly in love with." Kendrick was the one to fall silent a moment now, weighing his words before he spoke again.

"Are you happy?" he asked.

"Generally? Yes, yes I am quite happy." Edgar agreed and Kendrick could tell that he was. But it was Edgar's style of life that made him happy. And that style of life was certainly set to change very soon.

"About your match? The betrothal?" Edgar thought for a long moment and Kendrick thought perhaps he would not answer.

"I am happy," he replied finally, and Kendrick could tell that he had given it a great deal of thought in those few moments of silence. "I have long known that I would need to step up soon. To take on the responsibilities of the earldom and my place. I have abandoned you and mother and the estate as well for a long time since Father died."

"Neither of us wanted you to stop your travels," Kendrick told him. And they had never resented the fact that he continued on with those travels either. Their mother had never been upset to continue to run the estate as she had since their father fell ill. And Kendrick had never felt deprived in having to care for some of the other decisions that needed to be made that she could not handle.

"And I appreciate that a great deal more than you know," Edgar told him with a smile. "But it is time I step into my role. And marriage is the first step in that process. Settling down and putting down roots here is important now."

"You are staying then?" Kendrick asked, cautiously.

"Aye. I will have to return to London to give a report of things in Johannesburg, and to settle the remainder of the trade agreements. But then I will return. And I will not travel further than London again until the wedding." He paused a moment, "I presume Mother wishes it to be soon."

"The duchess wishes it to be done before winter," Kendrick agreed. Edgar nodded his head at that.

"It will be good to have it done quickly."

"And Hazel? Are you content with marrying a girl you do not know?"

"I trust you and Mother. If you both believe that Hazel is the perfect wife for me then I am certain that she is." It pleased Kendrick that Edgar was so firm in his resolution and that he was so confident that things would be just fine. He truly believed that if their mother and himself approved of the match it had to be a good one.

"You will not dispute the match then," Kendrick stated, and Edgar looked to him as though the thought had never entered his mind.

"Why would I?" Edgar seemed truly confused at the idea of it and Kendrick was even more assured that Edgar would do every-thing he could to make the match a success. Silence fell between the two for several long moments as they led the horses around to head back. "Enough of this plodding along. Let us race now, shall we?" Without waiting for an answer Edgar urged his horse to a gallop and Kendrick laughed before urging his to do the same.

The fast speeds were definitely what he needed to wake up the rest of the way. The cool breeze whipping across his face as they ran across fields that had long been familiar haunts for them. They had ridden these fields from the time they were small. Had played in the knolls and grasses. Had climbed the trees on the outskirts of the area. They had practically lived in these fields. And Kendrick knew exactly where this race was heading.

The two pulled up, breathless, at the edge of the clearing, their horses panting heavily and both of them doing the same. Yes, this race was one that they had had many times. And it was one that Edgar nearly always won. No matter how much Kendrick practiced with his horse he could not beat the camaraderie that existed between Edgar and his own, no matter how much time Edgar spent away.

"I must ask a favor of you," Edgar stated, growing serious and Kendrick turned toward him.

"Anything," Kendrick agreed immediately.

"These letters to Hazel that Mother wishes me to write ... I am no writer. The letters I send to you and Mother are the extent of what I can hope to achieve. To write letters to another with the hope of getting to know her...I am not up to the challenge," Edgar admitted.

"I could help you with what you could say. We can work on them together," Kendrick offered.

"Perhaps," Edgar began, but then continued, "but it would be best if you would write the letters yourself."

"Me?" Kendrick was startled at the prospect. How could he write letters for Edgar that would be to learn more about his future wife?

"I am no good at writing letters. I would likely scare the poor girl off and I know that is not what anyone wants. But you have a way with words, and a way of making people feel at ease."

"It is not proper for me to write to her," Kendrick protested, wondering just how Edgar could think that it was right for him to even try.

"You would be writing as me. In place of myself. There would be no impropriety in it." Kendrick gave him a wry look. "There would be no appearance of impropriety then. No one but you and I would know that it was not me writing the letters."

"It would be deceiving Hazel," Kendrick replied, and Edgar inclined his head in agreement.

"It would be only a few letters. Just to appease Mother and to learn a little of the woman that I shall marry. There is no harm in that, is there? It shall be a brother helping another in matters of love," Kendrick still wasn't sure but Edgar always did have a way of convincing him of things and so he reluctantly agreed. "Thank you. And when I am finally wed, I will find you a wife as well," Edgar promised with a smile and a laugh. Kendrick shook his head.

"It shall be a long while before I shall be ready to wed. I shall wait until I am an old man, like you," he teased, and Edgar reached to cuff him with mock outrage, but Kendrick was already on the move, his horse bolting back toward the manor.

Edgar was racing after him in a moment, the horses running as fast as they could as the two boys tried to best one another. In the end, it was too close of a race to call, though Kendrick insisted that he had gotten back to the stables first, and Edgar said the same for himself.

"You are certainly blind! I was clearly here a full stride ahead of you," Edgar cried.

"Ha! You were most definitely blinded yourself by the dust from

my horses hooves or you would have seen that I was practically in
the barn before you reached the edge of the barnyard," Kendrick
retorted.

"You were not even close, little brother," Edgar shoved him
good-naturedly, though very nearly into a stall full of hay, and
strode toward the end of the stable.

The grooms were ready as the two boys swung themselves down
from the horses and handed over the reins, still bickering in a
friendly fashion as they made their way back toward the manor.

When they arrived in the breakfast hall it was to find their
mother anxiously seated at the table, though she visibly relaxed as
soon as she saw them.

"Where have you been? Oh, goodness, I was so worried."

"Whyever would you be?" Edgar asked, his tone surprised and
more than a little confused.

"All that time on your own may have made you forget that a
mother worries," she replied and both boys looked slightly abashed.

"We were up early and decided to go for a ride."

"*You* were up early," Kendrick replied, "and decided to coerce
me into a ride." The teasing began again in earnest and Kendrick
could tell it had at least slightly appeased their mother. Though she
still looked somewhat concerned.

"I woke and neither of you were here. I did not know what could
have become of you," she added.

"We are sorry. We thought it would be a good morning for a
ride. It was so clear and warm out," Edgar told her.

"Don't leave without telling me again. Not knowing where you
are worries me greatly." Edgar gave her a hug and Kendrick
followed suit.

"We are grown men, Mother. It is not as though we are little
boys anymore," Edgar's tone was gentle but firm, and their mother
gave a sad smile as they sat and filled their own plates for breakfast.

"Aye, that you are. Yet it is difficult for a mother to think of her
children as such. No matter how many years it has been."

"We shall be your children always," Kendrick added, taking a
bite of his eggs. "But not little boys. We can take care of ourselves."
He gave a gentle smile and she returned it with one of her own.

"Perhaps inform a servant at least that you are going out. I
should hate to be expecting you for breakfast or for tea only to find
that you have left already." They both acknowledged that not letting
her know about their plans could be an inconvenience in such a
case.

"We will make sure to keep you informed," Kendrick promised, though he knew it would be difficult to get Edgar to follow through with that. After all, he was so used to being on his own he likely never even thought of telling someone else where he was going or what he was doing.

Still, he nodded his head and the three of them continued with their breakfast. It was like old times again, before Edgar had left on this last trip. And they were all enjoying the long moment.

# CHAPTER 5

KENDRICK STOOD NEAR THE WINDOW; his gaze directed toward the fields but he didn't see them. In fact, he didn't see anything in particular. Instead, he was thinking of his next poem. Something about the blue skies perhaps. Or the birds flying by. Maybe even the horses galloping through the meadows, as he and Edgar had done earlier that day.

"Ah, Edgar, you will simply adore Hazel. She is a lovely girl. Absolutely beautiful and so smart," their mother gushed.

"I am sure she is a wonderful girl," Edgar agreed, though of course he knew nothing about Hazel himself. Or at least, he had admitted he remembered very little about her from when they were younger.

"Kendrick? Oh, Kendrick, tell your brother more about Hazel. You certainly know more than I do." Kendrick paused a moment, collecting the thoughts and memories he had of Hazel. It had been a while since he had seen her, after all.

"She is quite pretty," he agreed with their mother, "but there's much more to her than that. She's...soft, very gentle, and very shy. She does not take to many people. It takes her a bit to be comfortable around them."

"A quiet girl may not be a bad thing. Some of the ones I have met on my travels are quite outspoken...and not in a manner for productive conversation," Edgar replied.

"Have you met many women on your travels?" Kendrick was momentarily distracted and Edgar nodded.

"Aye, I have. All different sorts. Some who are very much like the proper ladies you would expect in London. Others who are...very learned women. More learned than many men I have met. And of course, women that fall into all types in between. As well as some who are...a lower class altogether." Kendrick had an idea of what his brother was talking about, but of course Edgar would not say more in the presence of a lady, even if that lady were their mother.

"Well, Hazel is a proper lady, and one of the learned sort as well. She is also very kind and has a very good heart. I have watched her care for baby birds that have gotten lost in the gardens. And she is kind and caring to the servants in their household. She likes to help people wherever she can."

"That is certainly a good trait in a lady, and a wife," Edgar agreed, pleased. "Would she like to travel?"

"I am sure there are some places that she would very much like to go," Kendrick acknowledged.

"You cannot possibly expect to take a wife on the sort of travels you have done thus far," their mother protested and Edgar paused a moment then acknowledged that it was highly impractical.

"I should like to travel to London regularly. I will need to on matters of the estate. And perhaps to the Continent," he replied and his mother gave a satisfied nod.

"She should be able to accompany you on such trips. But to lands such as those you have just returned from there is no chance for it. Such places are not for a lady."

"Of course," he acknowledged but Kendrick could tell that he was somewhat disappointed at the idea of not returning to those places he most enjoyed visiting.

"Hazel will make an excellent wife," Kendrick jumped in. "Of that I am certain."

"That is good. She sounds like she shall be. And I thank you, Mother, for making such a match." Edgar seemed somewhat distracted himself, looking away from them as if he was thinking hard on something.

"We are honored to have such a match. To have my son marry the daughter of a duke is more than I would have hoped for."

"It is not a surprise, Mother," Kendrick replied. "Given how close you are with the Duchess." Their mother simply laughed.

"I can only hope that Hazel will like me as well, for a husband."

"Of course she shall. There is no reason that she would not," their mother seemed offended at the very idea that Hazel would not approve of him. "You are, after all, quite handsome. And so worldly. And you are very mature. And such a kind young man."

"I thank you for your high praise, Mother, but you must

acknowledge that you are somewhat biased in my favor," Edgar's eyes sparkled with the words and his mother's softened as she smiled at him.

"Tell your brother what a wonderful man he is, and how wonderful he shall be for Hazel," their mother instructed Kendrick.

"I suppose you shall do," Kendrick replied, teasingly and they all laughed.

"It would be best if you wrote to her as soon as possible," their mother reminded Edgar. "That way the two of you could get to know one another a little better before she returns home."

"Certainly," Edgar agreed, but he glanced at Kendrick with a slightly wary look. "I will write to her tonight." Their mother was certainly pleased and returned to her embroidery, but Edgar still looked a little uncertain as he strode toward the window. His gaze out onto the fields was a little less blissful than Kendrick's had been.

In fact, Kendrick himself felt slightly tormented as well. He just knew that Edgar would come to him for help with his letter. After all, Edgar did not like to write letters and Kendrick did know Hazel. At least he knew her much better than Edgar did. But was it right for him to write to her as Edgar?

He had known it was best not to write to her himself once she had gone away. It would be considered most improper, after all. So Kendrick knew little of what had happened in her life since she had left. Only what the Duchess had told his mother while he had been around.

But this was different, right? It was him writing but he was writing on behalf of Edgar. And Edgar had every reason to write to Hazel. And it could not be considered inappropriate because the two were betrothed. It felt wrong though. To be almost lying to her in such a way. Still, Kendrick knew that if his brother asked again he would not refuse. He never did, after all.

"My Lord, My Lady," they all looked up as the door opened and Margaret entered with a low curtsey toward Edgar first and then their mother. "Dinner is ready."

"Ah, thank you..." Edgar trailed off and their mother jumped in.

"Margaret. Thank you. We will be along shortly."

"I do not remember Margaret," Edgar told them as the girl left. His brow furrowed in confusion as he glanced toward them.

"Beth was wed since you were last home. And so, she has left to be with her husband. We hired Margaret to replace her." The explanation certainly satisfied Edgar and Kendrick realized he had mostly been concerned that he did not recall members of the staff by name, not that they had hired someone new without telling him.

Another dinner of all of Edgar's favorite foods made him laugh.

"You are all planning to turn me into a fat earl who does nothing but sit about in the drawing room all day," he teased.

"If it will keep you at home where you belong then so be it," their mother retorted playfully and they all began to laugh.

"I must not gain too much or my betrothed shall decide she does not care for me after all," was Edgar's comment and they all brushed it off.

"Nay, she shall adore you," their mother replied.

"Hazel is not so superficial as that," Kendrick added.

"Well, that is good for me as Mother continues to ply me with more and more food."

"You came back too skinny after your voyage," their mother reached out to pat his face and his stomach. "Did they feed you at all on that ship?"

"Yes, Mother. We all ate just fine on the ship," Edgar assured her

"Then Africa. I knew you shouldn't go."

"I am fine, Mother. I was ill from the lack of water at one point but I have certainly gotten over that. And now there is always quite enough food."

"Well, you can rest assured that there shall always be quite enough food in our home. In your home," she added.

He smiled and did not say anything more. Instead, they fell into a comfortable silence as they finished their dinner. The roast deer tasted quite good, and the vegetables along with it were some of his favorites as well. Cook had even prepared mince pies and apple crumble for the occasion.

By the time the meal was over they were all ready for some rest and each retired to their own rooms for a time.

At least, they began by retiring to their own rooms and Kendrick was just settling in to try his hand at another poem when there was a knock at his door and Edgar entered.

"I need your assistance." He did not waste any time with pleasantries before he began, but then that was always Edgar's way so Kendrick did not mind.

"I am not comfortable writing your letter for Hazel," he protested. "You are the one who should write to her."

"You write so much better than I," Edgar protested in return, shaking his head.

"All you need to do is determine what you wish to say to her and you will be fine."

"I do not know what to say to her at all."

"I can help you with the writing, but you are the one who

should come up with what you would like to say," Edgar shook his head.

"I trust you. You say whatever you would want to say if you were in my place. And I am sure that it will be just fine."

"It is supposed to be a letter from you. A letter for you to learn what you want to know of her." But Edgar simply gestured back to Kendrick, seemingly certain that his request would be honored.

"It is fine. I am sure you know best what it should say. I have no time now. I must be going to the club where I have friends waiting. I had informed a few of them of my return and must go to see them now."

"But-" Kendrick began but Edgar had already rushed back out the door and he was left practically speaking to himself, nervously looking at the still blank page before him.

He did not know what to do now. Perhaps it was best if he wrote the letter for Edgar. Edgar would expect him to. And Edgar would not write his own letter. And if there was no letter to Hazel then their mother would be most unhappy. He sighed. And Hazel would prefer a poetic letter to whatever Edgar might have been able to come up with anyway. So perhaps it was best if he did write. But what to write?

*Dear Hazel,*

Was it appropriate to begin the letter in so informal a way? Should he use her title instead in writing?

*Dear Lady Tumbler,*

That seemed too formal. Perhaps something in the middle, between the two.

*Dear Lady Hazel,*

Yes, that seemed better. He glanced at it again and then set to work.

*Dear Lady Hazel,*

*I am Edgar, Earl of Aethelred. I have only recently returned from a trip and learned of our betrothal and wished to write to you right away so that we might become better acquainted prior to the occasion of our wedding.*

No, that was too formal again.

*Dear Lady Hazel,*

*I am Edgar, Earl of Aethelred. I have only recently returned from abroad and learned of our betrothal. I wished to write to you right away as I would like to get to know you better before we are wed. Especially as I have been told that the wedding shall take place with some haste, in order to take advantage of the beauty of the summer.*

*It has been quite some time since I have had the honor of seeing you, though I do remember our childhood being spent together much of the time. I must confess to spending a great deal of that time engaged in other things, however, and not in getting to know you.*

*For myself, I have been traveling quite a bit, which has led to spending very little time around those whom were quite important to my family during my childhood and yours.*

*My travels have taken me around the world and allowed me to experience a great many things, though I am eager to take on this new adventure of being a husband. Unfortunately, these travels have taken me away from home for quite some time but I am eager to begin taking on the responsibilities there. I have left this much in the hands of my dear mother to this point and she has done wonderfully, however it is my place to step forward now. This will allow me to be much more at home than I have been in the past, when we were not able to meet as much as perhaps we would have liked.*

*Still, my mother and brother have certainly spent time with you in the years since and have remembered you very fondly. In fact, they have been telling me of all of your virtues since I have returned. And I am certain that they must be right. If even half of what they have spoken of your goodness and your virtues is true then I cannot have done better in a future wife.*

*I am sure that they are quite correct in their esteem of you and as I put a great deal of value in the opinions of both my brother and my mother, I feel confident that we shall suit one another as well. I flatter myself that you shall find me an acceptable husband as well, and hope that this correspondence will allow us to determine this for certain.*

*I very much look forward to the opportunity to meet and to sit alongside you in conversation, however I am given to understand you are completing your own education and have no wish to interfere with this. I believe a learned woman is a great asset to a household and shall be most proud to have a wife who has been well educated as you no doubt have been.*

*As such, however, I have no choice but to learn what I can of you through these means. Through the placing of pen to paper, of imparting ink to parchment, on the hope that you shall be inclined to reply and share what is in your own heart.*

*I hope that you shall be honored to hear some of what is in my own heart, as I know no distance is too great when someone lives in your heart.*

*Sincerely,*

*Edgar*

Yes, that would do. At least it sounded nice and hopefully Hazel would appreciate it. But then, after Kendrick had sent the letter with a servant with directions to post it immediately, he wondered if he might be doing more harm than good. After all, once she received a few such missives from Edgar — or who she assumed to be Edgar — would Hazel be upset when she met the real Edgar who was nothing like those letters?

To be sure Edgar would be a kind and caring husband. He would be glad to have a wife who was educated, and he was looking forward to meeting Hazel. But he was not a poetic person and he would hardly be considered the sort to write the letter Kendrick had written. He could only hope that this information would not upset Hazel too much when she found out about it.

For now, he was helping his brother. And perhaps he could convince his brother to respond when Hazel sent her own letter back.

# CHAPTER 6

"OH, THE DAY IS SO FINE," Louise sighed with pleasure, spinning in a circle like a young girl, arms spread out wide. Hazel laughed and followed her own inclination to do the same, though they were both much too old for such things now. It did feel so nice to be outside in the warm sun after so long indoors over the cold months. Even recently there had still been cooler days that kept them indoors or forced them to bundle against the chill before they could venture outside.

"It is wonderful, isn't it? Even still, we haven't much time before classes this morning. We should likely be studying."

"Ah, how can you speak of studying when there is such a beautiful day to be enjoyed?"

"When the teacher is Madame Brooker, I certainly can," Hazel retorted and Louisa sighed.

"Yes, perhaps." The two girls settled under a tree for a few moments so they could study and still enjoy the warmth of the day. "Have you thought more on your betrothal?"

"I have," Hazel replied, pausing a moment to think before she spoke again. "I have thought about it quite a bit and I am certain that my mother would not make a match that was not advantageous for me. That was not to a man I could be proud to marry."

"And yet?" Louise prodded and Hazel sighed. Louise did know her so well.

"I wish that I had a chance to know a bit more about him for myself. I am sure my mother knows enough to make this decision. And I know that she knows the Countess, Edgar's mother, quite well. However, I do not know him at all. If I could but learn a bit

more about him before we are to be wed it would be much better."
Hazel sighed, gazing off into the distance.

"I am sure Edgar will be an excellent match for you and that he
will make you very happy. Your mother would not choose someone
for you that would do anything else," Louise assured her.

"You are right..." Hazel did feel a bit better to have someone else
reinforce her belief, but it was still difficult to think that she might
never learn anything of the man she was supposed to marry until it
was time for them to marry. And he could send for her any time,
could he not? To hasten the marriage? As her betrothed it was his
right to bring her home from school whenever he wished.

She worried that he might not want her to finish out the term.
And then she would not be officially graduated. It was only a few
weeks, but she had been looking forward to it. And there had been
many girls during their time that had left school early to be wed.

Hazel sighed and tried to push the concerns from her mind. She
would take things one day at a time and each day that she was not
sent for would be all the better. There was no use in feeling anxious
about it when she did not even know if it would happen.

History was first, and just as the girls had suspected Madame
Brooker had a hard lesson prepared. And a test at the very end that
neither of them felt truly prepared for. Though it was nearly impossible to be fully prepared for anything when it came to Madame
Brooker. Even if you had read and studied the entire lesson you
could rarely feel confident of a good day.

"Miss. Tumbler, have you something to say on the matter of the
Continent?" She had not realized she was daydreaming again, but
of course Madame Brooker always knew when someone was not
paying attention. Now Hazel blushed slightly and shook her head,
looking down to her textbook quickly. "That is what I thought.
Please ensure that you pay attention for the rest of the lesson or I
shall be forced to report this to the headmistress." A report to the
headmistress would mean being forced to write lines or some other
sort of penance for her distraction and that she certainly did not
want. Especially when the day was so fine and all she wanted was to
finish her lessons and get back out of doors.

"Are you all right Hazel?" Louise asked with concern when they
left class.

"Yes, only distracted."

"With thoughts of your betrothal, no doubt," Hazel nodded and
glanced away from her friend.

"What if he is not what I had hoped for? What if he is not the
sort of husband that will make me happy?" It was the fear that had

weighed on her most and the one that she had been most reluctant to voice.

"You mother would not match you with someone who would not make you happy," her friend replied firmly. "I have only met your mother a few times, Hazel, but she is not the sort to make you a match that would upset you. She cares for you far too much for that."

"You are right," Hazel said slowly. Her mother did love her a great deal. And she was not the sort to make a match for Hazel only for a title. The fact that the match was with an Earl said as much. While an earl was a good match it was likely not the best title that her mother could get for a husband for her. And that meant she had to have made the decision for another reason. She had to know more of Edgar and that he would be good for Hazel.

"Come now, do not worry where there is no reason for it. Let us go back to our rooms for a moment at least," Hazel followed Louise to their bedchamber to drop off their books. "Ah, singing. Perhaps I shall stay here instead," Louise sighed.

"Come now, singing class is one of the best of the day."

"Perhaps for you. For me it is another chance to embarrass myself. Oh, to sing in front of the rest of the class..." Louise shuddered in mock horror. "It is the worst part of my day."

"It will not be as bad as that," Hazel replied with a laugh.

"That's easy enough for you to say. But not all of us sound like an angel when we sing. For myself I sound like a dog. Or a wolf," Hazel laughed outright this time and even Louise gave a small smile. "All right, perhaps not quite that bad. But it is quite bad."

"It will be fine. Don't leave me to go alone. Besides, if you do not show up for class, they will send someone looking for you." Louise flopped down onto her bed and attempted to look ill.

"I shall tell them I feel terribly."

"You looked pained perhaps, but it will not fool the nurse. And you know she is the one they shall send for you. And if you cannot fool her, she will give you castor oil. You can be sure of it." Louise made a disgusted face and shook her head.

"It is almost worth it to be able to avoid singing class."

"Come, do not make me go myself and attempt to lie to Madame Lowton that you are ill. You know I cannot do it," Hazel pleaded.

"No, if there is one thing you cannot do it is lie convincingly," Louise admitted. "All right. Let us go then."

They were just about to leave the room when a maid knocked at the door, presenting Hazel with a letter when she had opened it.

"Thank you," Hazel glanced down at the letter and Louise continued to gather her things.

"Has your mother written again?"

"No," Hazel replied, surprised. "It is from Edgar."

"Edgar? Your betrothed? Well? Open it, go on." Louise was at least as excited about the letter as she was, or perhaps even more so, but she shook her head reluctantly.

"I cannot. There is no time. We shall very nearly be late as it is." She slowly set the letter down on her bed and turned away from it.

"Oh, but don't you want to see what it says?"

"Of course, but we don't have the time. Come, let's go and we'll be able to return soon and see." Louise grumbled slightly but followed Hazel out of the room.

Of course, walking away from the letter was the easy part. Hazel struggled through the entire singing class trying not to think about just what might be written there. What could Edgar have written her? Was he sending for her to come home? But wouldn't her mother have written her that? Or wouldn't one of the two have written to the school?

"Miss. Tumbler?" She walked as serenely as she could — Madame Lowton would penalize her for not walking in a ladylike manner — to the front of the class for her performance. At least singing was something that came relatively easily to her and she did not need to think too hard about the performance she gave, because she did not think she would have been able to.

When it was finished she returned to her desk, barely noticing the performance that Louise gave, or the ones given by the other girls in their class. All she could think about was what the letter might say, and what Edgar might have to tell her. Nearly before the bell rang for the class to be finished, she rushed out of the room. The other girls moved out of her way quickly, though with a few exclamations of surprise. But she did not pay them much mind. Louise, reluctantly, hurried off in the opposite direction where she had been called upon to help with the younger girls. But she made Hazel promise to tell her more about the contents of the letter as soon as possible.

For now, Hazel was happy to have a moment to herself to look at the letter before she had to share it with anyone else. Perhaps there would be something in the letter that would be difficult for her. Or difficult to share with Louise. She wanted time to prepare for that.

She was so nervous that the first time through she simply skimmed over the letter, looking for words that would signify she was being sent for. Or anything that could be upsetting. But there did not seem to be anything of the sort so she took a deep breath and began again. This time she read it slowly, taking in every word. And then she read it a third time.

It was lovely. Actually, she was quite surprised at how lovely it sounded and at the fact that Edgar wished to get to know her better before they were wed. He wanted her to stay in school. He wanted her to be educated. He was also a well-traveled man. That meant he was no doubt very well educated himself. And he was pleased with what he already knew of her. All things that she was so pleased with herself.

"What does it say?" Louise did not even pause as she rushed into the room, sinking onto Hazel's bed beside her as she tried to look at the letter.

"Oh, it is wonderful, Louise. It is simply wonderful." She could hardly stop smiling at the thought of it and looked down at the words again as she told Louise everything. "He has traveled around the world, and he is only just returned from a trip now. And he is eager to meet me and learn more about me. That is why he has written."

"Is he coming to visit?" Louise asked in surprise and Hazel shook her head.

"No, he is not coming to visit. But he has also not sent for me. Oh, Louise, I worried that he would want to wed quickly or that he would not want a wife that was too educated. But he seems pleased that I am such. And he has no desire to bring me home early. At least nothing in his letter."

"Oh good. I could not bear to lose you," Louise exclaimed, grabbing her hand. "What else does he say?"

"He has heard a great deal about me from his mother and brother but he still wishes to learn more from me. Oh, he writes beautifully, Louise. And he sounds just wonderful."

"And he is an Earl."

"Yes, but the title means little to me," Hazel brushed it off.

"Of course, you are set to be Duchess, after all. He shall actually gain a better title in marriage to you."

"Aye, I suppose that is true," Hazel acknowledged, though she was not interested in discussing titles. She glanced down at the letter again. "He writes so nicely, Louise."

"Oh, I am so glad. And to appreciate an educated young lady is even better." Hazel had to agree. She was more pleased than she had thought even that she would not be called away from her education too soon. There was not much more to the term but she very much wanted to finish it.

"I will have to write to him. Right away. I shall do it now," Hazel stated, pulling out a piece of paper and her pen to begin. Louise sat silently on the bed, but Hazel hardly noticed her anyway, absorbed as she was in just what she was going to write.

*Dear Lord Edgar,*

She took her cue from his manner of addressing the letter to herself in beginning her own letter.

*I am most pleased that you have taken the step to write to me.*

Was that too formal? Did it sound a little forced?

*Dear Lord Edgar,*

*I am very happy that you have written to me as I too am very interested to learn more about the person I am to marry. Just as you trust your mother and brother's judgement, I trust my own mother to make a match that will be excellent for me, but I still would like to know more about you.*

*I am very honored that the Countess and Lord Kendrick...*

It felt strange addressing him that way...

*I am very honored that the Countess and Lord Kendrick have such good things to say about me and I have many fond memories of them as well. I hope that when we do meet I can do justice to what you have heard.*

*Your travels sound wonderful, and I am sure that you have learned many secrets of the world in this way. I have only had the opportunity to travel as far as Bath and London myself but what I have learned through my history classes has been exciting about other areas of the world. I am sure you have wonderful stories to tell.*

*I do not remember much of our childhood together as you have stated. I do recall spending many happy hours with Lord Kendrick; however, I do believe you spent a great deal of that time at reading, being much older than us both. I am most eager to reacquaint myself with you as well.*

*Your letter pleased me greatly and I appreciate the beautiful prose of it. You are an excellent writer and certainly have a way with words.*

*My classes here are quite thorough, and we learn history, French, singing, literature, and a small amount of math and science. It is the literature and French that I enjoy the most, though I have been told that I have a knack for some of the others.*

*I do appreciate that you find a learned lady to be an asset to you and am pleased to continue my education here as long as it pleases you. The term will commence in just a few weeks' time and I will return home then. This will give us a chance to meet again and I greatly look forward to it.*

*Please do not wait until then to write to me but instead write as soon as you receive this letter and whenever else you like. I shall be most happy to receive your letters.*

*Sincerely,*

*Hazel*

She read it through carefully once, then twice before she folded it and sealed it, sending it off with the servant before she could second-guess herself or anything she had written. It sounded nice enough to her ear, though after she had sent it she wondered if she should have written more. Or perhaps less. Or perhaps let Louise read it before she sent it away.

"Well, there's no need to worry about it now," Louise replied when she voiced her concerns. "You've sent it off and now you can only wait until he responds. And I am certain that he will," Louise was firm in her response and Hazel tried to feel just as confident.

It would be fine. The letter was well written and it did honor to her education and her station. She had nothing to be concerned about. And besides, it was going to her betrothed. With a deep breath she sank down beside Louise again. There was nothing to do now but wait, as Louise had said. Though she found herself already impatient for a response.

His words had certainly had an effect on her and she found herself overwhelmed with just what he might write in his response. He already sounded exactly like she would have hoped and she could not wait to learn even more.

# CHAPTER 7

"HER GRACE, the Duchess Tumbler has arrived, My Lady." Fiona smiled excitedly and told Margaret to let the duchess in. Of course, she hardly needed to be invited, being such a close friend, and of course being the duchess as well. But Rose always waited anyway, for proprieties sake.

As she swept into the room and took a seat, Kendrick also entered the room, pleased to see her too.

"Ah, Your Grace, it is lovely to see you again."

"He has taken my words, Dear," Fiona laughed, greeting her old friend.

"It is wonderful to see you both. Though of course it has been only a few days."

"What is the purpose of your calling, Your Grace?" Kendrick asked.

"As if I need an excuse to visit an old friend. And one who last time kept me waiting so long before calling on me," there was that twinkle in her eye again and the three of them all laughed. "Ah, but this time I have come to meet my future son-in-law. I have been informed that he has returned from his travels."

"He has, Your Grace, only a few days past. And he is already at work."

"He is in, then?"

"Aye, he is in. He is currently in the study going over business matters but I shall call him for you," Rose inclined her head in acknowledgement and Kendrick excused himself from them to hurry upstairs. As soon as he had walked out the door, and before it had even closed all the way behind him, he could hear the two begin talking of their children and the wedding they were set to plan.

Kendrick couldn't help but laugh as he went to his brother, taking his time to give the two ladies a few moments alone to set their plans.

Edgar looked up as soon as the door opened, his finger still on the ledger before him as he copied numbers into a book. He gave Kendrick a smile when he saw him but then returned to his work for a moment before he closed it and set it to the side.

"What can I do for you?"

"The duchess is here to meet with you."

"Ah, Lady Hazel's mother." He leaned forward slightly, his gaze intrigued as though he were waiting for more information.

"Yes, she's downstairs with Mother now."

"We should go down immediately," In fact, Edgar had already risen from his seat, a determined look on his face as though he were about to attempt negotiations on a trade. Not that any negotiations were needed here. The match had already been made.

"There is no need to rush," Kendrick laughed. "The two are very good friends so I am sure they have a great deal to talk about." At that Edgar sank back into his seat with a smile.

"That is good then. We can certainly give them some time. Have you had a chance to write the letter for Hazel?"

"I have," Kendrick replied, though slightly uneasily. He still wasn't sure how he felt about writing a letter on Edgar's behalf, pretending to be him. "I wrote to her that you travel a great deal and that you have only just returned. And I asked her about herself."

"I am sure that you did well," Edgar replied. "I trust that you did us both justice in your letter and that you will make me sound like a good future husband."

"Yes, but-"

"It is best if you do the writing, Kendrick. I trust that you will do a good job at it and I do not need to know the specifics of what you write." Kendrick felt even less pleased about this but Edgar was under a great deal of pressure. After all, it had been a long time since he had been back and there was a great deal to catch up on with the estate.

Mother had been handling things in his absence, at least as much as she could. But there were things that a lady could not handle, even one as educated as their mother.

"Let us go and meet with the duchess. What can you tell me about her?"

"She is a wonderful lady. And a very dear friend of Mother. She laughs a great deal and likes to joke and tease."

"That is good. I should definitely not be happy with a stoic or rude mother-in-law," Edgar replied, and Kendrick had to laugh.

"She is certainly not that. And she does not stand on ceremony about her title either. She is friendlier than that."

"Good. Good." By now the two had reached the doorway and Edgar strode in ahead of Kendrick. "Your Grace," he approached the duchess immediately, bowing over her hand formally but with a warm smile. "It is a pleasure to meet you."

"Ah, and this must be Edgar, your eldest son," she added with a quick glance toward Fiona. "it is a pleasure to be reacquainted with you. It has been a very long time."

"That it has, Your Grace. I have been traveling for quite some time."

"Well, you shall have to tell us all about it sometime. For now I am most excited to hear about your plan to wed my daughter."

"I had been told that the plan is yours, Your Grace," Edgar teased and the duchess laughed.

"Well, perhaps that is true. But you shall be the lucky groom who shall have her."

"I am honored that you would entrust me with your daughter."

"See to it that you do justice to that honor," Rose replied, with a more serious tone. It was clear that she thought very highly of her daughter and was very protective of her.

"I certainly will, Your Grace." There was a smile at that and Rose gestured for Edgar and Kendrick both to be seated again.

"I am most anxious to have Hazel back so that she can meet you. She is set to return at the end of the term in only a few weeks."

"I am anxious to meet her as well," Edgar replied with another smile and at that moment the door opened and the butler entered.

"For you, My Lord," he informed them after a deep bow to the duchess. He handed the letter to Edgar who gave an absentminded nod in response. As the butler showed himself out Edgar glanced at the address.

"It is from Hazel Tumbler."

"Oh! I did not know that my letter had even reached her yet. Or that she would write," Rose exclaimed excitedly.

"I had asked Edgar to write to her so that the two can become better acquainted before they are able to meet in person," Fiona replied and the duchess seemed pleased.

"That is excellent I cannot wait for the two of you to get to know one another better. I am sure that you shall be very happy when you do."

"I am sure that we shall learn a great deal to like about one another," Edgar agreed and tucked the letter into his pocket. "This I will hold to read later."

"Ah, yes, that is probably best. I am sure that it is a letter to be read in private. It is never for prying eyes when young people are writing love to one another," Rose agreed with a twinkle in her eye. Kendrick wondered what might be in the letter, but he could tell that Edgar was not concerned. In fact, Edgar did not even seem interested and he was sure that if the letter had come when it was only the two of them Edgar would have directed it immediately to Kendrick.

As it was, both ladies were watching Edgar, but he did not betray any thoughts about the letter as he continued to converse with them. He did seem to be pleased with what he was learning about the duchess, which was certainly good. Though Kendrick did not know how anyone could dislike the duchess. She was a very friendly and pleasant person. Not at all what one would expect from someone of her station.

"Well, I must take my leave before I overstay my welcome," the duchess said finally, rising from her seat.

"Oh, not at all. Do not ever feel that you are a bother to us. You are always welcome in our household, as I am certain my mother has told you before," Edgar assured her.

"She may have said that once or twice," Rose laughed and Fiona joined in. "Just as you are all always welcome in my own home. I do hope that you shall call soon."

"Aye, that I will do, Your Grace. And I hope you will do me the honor of letting me know when your daughter returns at the end of her term," Edgar continued.

"That I will do. Though I am sure she will inform you of it as well," the duchess laughed again and Edgar held out his arm to accompany her out of the room.

"Your brother has made quite an impression," their mother replied once they had left. "And to have Hazel write him back so soon is an excellent sign."

"Yes, it is," Kendrick agreed, though he felt uneasy lying to his mother about the letter as well. Once she had excused herself as well Kendrick headed upstairs to the study where he was sure Edgar would be waiting. He was not disappointed as his brother was sitting back in his chair, the ledger before him again, though he was only glancing over it when Kendrick walked in.

"Ah, there you are. I hoped you would come up here." He pulled the letter from his pocket and finally opened it. Kendrick had been wondering what it might say this entire time but Edgar did not seem as interested. At least he had not opened it before Kendrick arrived.

As he read the letter aloud Kendrick could not help but smile. The words and the style of writing certainly reminded him of everything he knew of Hazel. And showed a great deal more in terms of her education. She was pleased with the letter, happy to get to know him better — Edgar — Kendrick had to remind himself, and was certainly a smart young lady.

"It was an excellent letter then. She was most pleased to receive it. And she shares a great deal about herself as well. I thank you for your assistance with this. I don't know what I would do without you," Edgar praised and Kendrick felt good about what he had done to help his brother. "Here." He accepted the letter from Edgar without thinking but when Edgar then turned back to his ledger he was confused.

"What would you have me do with this?"

"I need you to write her back. And you will need the letter for that, won't you?"

"I wrote the first letter so that it would pave the way for the two of you to converse. I cannot continue to write to her pretending to be you," Kendrick protested.

"It is better if you do the writing. You are much better at it than me. And besides, she would recognize the difference now." Kendrick had to admit that Edgar was right. The difference in their penmanship alone would raise questions. And the difference in their writing style would raise even more.

"It is you who needs to get to know her better," he insisted anyway.

"And I can do that through you. I have already learned a great deal and I am sure that your writing will please her far more than my own."

"And what will happen when the two of you are wed?" Kendrick protested.

"I hardly think I should have to write her letters once we are wed. She will never know who wrote these early letters. In fact, once she returns from school she will never know anything of the subject."

"Perhaps, but it is dishonest," Kendrick informed him.

"The purpose of the letters is for us to get to know one another, correct?" Edgar said patiently.

"Yes," Kendrick agreed.

"And that is what is happening. I am getting to know her this way."

"But you do not even know what I am telling her about you."

"Whatever it is she seems to be happy about. And I trust that you will do me justice," was Edgar's flippant reply.

"You do not know that. I could tell her that you have lived with barbarians on the seas for the past seven years and are a scoundrel yourself." Edgar laughed at that.

"I have indeed lived with some barbarians. And there are some that might call me a scoundrel, but you would never write such a thing," he replied. Kendrick knew it as well. No matter what he may have ever known about his brother he would always say the best things he could. And if Edgar had lived with barbarians it certainly didn't show in his mannerisms anyway.

"I do not like doing this. It feels dishonest to fool her in this way." Kendrick announced.

"The letters are doing what they are meant to do. They are allowing me to get to know Hazel and allowing Hazel to get to know me. That is the most important part. It is the only thing that matters."

"You truly do not think you should write your own letters?"

"I do not have the ability to write the way you do. And I do not have the time even if I did want to. There is a great deal to do here to get everything in order. Our dear mother has tried her best but she has not been able to handle everything in the manner it should be. I do believe Father left her a terrible mess of things when he passed."

"He struggled to keep up with things at the end," Kendrick agreed and Edgar looked morose for a moment. Perhaps thinking of the fact that he had been too far away to return when their father passed, and had not even heard of his illness until likely after he was already gone.

"Well, that means there is a great deal for me to do," Edgar resolved, "And I know that you can take care of things with Hazel. She will much more appreciate your writing than my own."

"It is not right," he insisted again and Edgar glanced down at the ground, as though somewhat embarrassed by what he was about to say.

"You are a much better writer than I," he repeated. "I am afraid that I might say something to embarrass myself, or her, if I were to write." With another weak protest Kendrick finally agreed to write another letter in response to Hazel's. Though it still made him feel uncomfortable and he worried that he should refuse.

As he took the letter back to his own rooms he sighed. He never had been able to say no to his brother. Even as children Edgar had always been able to talk him into things and he had always followed along behind him wherever he went.

# CHAPTER 8

HE STRODE from one end of the room to the other. Across in front of the bed and then to the window. Then back toward the bed and over toward the dressing area. And back to the window, where he paused to stare outside for several minutes.

With a sigh, Kendrick returned to the table where his pen and paper sat, ready to begin the next letter. The one Edgar had received from Hazel lay beside it, unopened. As soon as he had arrived back at his room he had taken everything out and set the letter on the table and then began to pace.

Was it right what they were doing? Was it right for him to pretend to be Edgar and to write letters to Hazel that she would never know actually came from him? Would she be angry if she knew? If she were angry she would have every right to be. They were deceiving her and Kendrick felt badly about it even if Edgar didn't.

But what choice did he have? He could refuse. But then Edgar would not write to her at all and their mother would be upset. Or he could tell Hazel the truth, that he was writing on behalf of his brother, which would be the more honest option. But it would be inappropriate for him to write to her. And she might think poorly of his brother to find that he had not written in the first place.

*Dear Lady Hazel,*

He stopped, not sure what to write next. The letter Hazel had written still lay there and he hesitated a moment before opening it. It was not an invasion of privacy if Edgar had showed him the letter, was it? Or perhaps it was since Hazel had intended the letter only for Edgar's eyes. Or had she meant it for the eyes of the person who had written the previous letter? She thought those two people were one and the same, but they were not...

Kendrick sighed again and settled more comfortably into the chair. He might as well get this over with and write the new letter. It was the best thing to do in the situation. At least he hoped it was.

*Your mother came to visit today to meet with me* — writing that word gave him pause again but then he continued. *It was very nice to see her again as it has been a very long time. In fact, I must admit I did not remember much about your mother before seeing her again today. I quite enjoyed speaking with her and I feel quite certain that if you are anything like your mother I shall be more than pleased to have you as my wife.*

*Your letter arrived while she was here and while we were all meeting together in the drawing room. My mother and brother were also present and all teased me quite a bit upon seeing it. I am not ashamed of the fact that I somewhat enjoyed it, as I was extremely pleased at receiving your response so quickly. It tells me that you were eager to respond as it has been only a short while since you must have received my own letter.*

*I feel as though I am already developing feelings for you, with the account I have received from my own mother and brother and of course from your mother. And the letter I have received from you has also led me to like you even more. I can tell already that you are quite intelligent and kind and most certainly gracious and lovely. In fact, I am even more anxious to meet you every time I hear more about you.*

*You are right that my travels have been quite exciting and I have had the opportunity to meet wonderful people and see exotic lands. I have traveled as far as the West Indies and even beyond. I have even had the opportunity to travel to colonies and lands that are not yet colonized in search of goods for trade and to establish lines of trade. But I confess that those travels have been quite lonely at times.*

*While I have met many people during those experiences, the fact that I am often gone means that I have none that I would consider a close friend. It leads to quite a life of solitude. But it certainly does make you appreciate your loved ones even more as well. It is why I appreciate my mother and brother so much, and it is why I am anxious to begin our life together. I know that having a wife such as you will bring stability to my life in entirely new ways.*

*Having a partner at my side through everything and anything that life may throw our way is a wonderful feeling. The idea that I shall never have to be alone again makes me happier than I would have thought possible. And I relish the thought of being everything to you that I hope you shall be to me. I shall be your rock and your support, come what may. And I can only hope to have you at my side in everything that I do.*

*Though it has been some time since my father passed and the earldom became mine I must admit that I have not taken on the full responsibilities as I should. Some of this has been due to a lacking on my own part. Unfortunately, I find myself often feeling tied down when I am forced to stay in one place for extended periods, but I know that with your love and your guidance I shall be once more happy to remain at home.*

*You will be the friend I have often sought, as well as the partner I desire most. And I am finally now certain that everything in my life will work out for the best. With you by my side there could be nothing else.*

*Sincerely yours,*

Kendrick set the pen down, reading through the letter one more time. It was truly open, vulnerable, honest. It was everything that he would want to say to the woman he was betrothed to. If, in fact, he was betrothed. And if he were Edgar.

One more skim through the letter and he carefully penned Edgar's signature at the bottom. Yes, the letter was perfect. Though he was not certain that it was what Edgar would want to write he knew it was the truth and that was what mattered. The fact that Edgar himself would never write a letter so boldly honest was beside the point. That was why he had asked Kendrick to do it for him, after all.

With that he handed off the letter to the butler to send out with that day's post. Hazel should have it in her hand in no time.

⁓

"Miss. Tumbler?" Hazel looked up from the sketch she was working at. It was free period and she would much rather be spending this time with a book, but the drawing was not quite right and she knew Madame Kelser would not be pleased.

"Yes?" The girl before her held out an envelope and Hazel felt her heart leap with joy, though she tried to quell the feeling at least until she could see who it was from. Just because a letter had arrived for her did not mean it was from him. It could just as easily be from her mother.

But as she accepted the letter with thanks and a barely concealed smile she could easily make out the name delicately written across the front. It was him! Edgar had written to her yet again and she could not wait to see what he had to say. Would he have liked the letter she sent? Was he interested in what she had to say?

She almost tore the letter open right then, but then she registered the many other girls all around her. Many were already looking her way because they had seen that she received a letter. They were already scouring her face for a telltale sign that the letter was from a beau or that there was something, anything, to gossip about.

It was best to hide her feelings and hide the letter until she could be alone. But with free period almost over there would be little chance of that until long past dinner. Tonight was choral practice, after all. But it would be worth the wait to have the letter all to herself. And more importantly to have her reaction to the letter all to herself.

Of course, it seemed as though her classes took forever and she barely remembered anything about any of them. At some point she remembered Louise asking her what it was that had her so distracted but she did not respond.

"Miss. Tumbler, your answer?" Hazel looked up, startled. She flipped haphazardly through her book but she wasn't even sure what page she was supposed to be on let alone what the question had been.

"Um...I –" she trailed off and Madame Brooker pursed her lips and shook her head.

"Page 253, Miss. Tumbler. Please pay attention. Miss. Elton, your answer?"

"1843." Even looking down at the correct page she wasn't sure she knew what the question was. But she tried to focus on the rest of class. Luckily Madame Brooker did not call on her again because she still wasn't so sure she knew anything that was going on.

"If you told the teachers that you were recently betrothed they might go easier on you," Louise said, catching up to her after class.

"They didn't go any easier on Mary last year. They told her that she needed to pay attention in class or she might as well leave early and go get married."

"Well, you've got to finish out the term. It's so close now. But what has gotten you so distracted?"

"I've got another letter," Hazel replied quietly, barely able to hide her excitement.

"What does it say?" Louise asked, nearly as interested as she was.

"I haven't read it yet. I wanted to wait until I had some time. But with classes and then choral practice it's going to be so long." Hazel sighed.

"I wouldn't be able to wait that long. We've got a few minutes now. What if we went now?"

"No. I want to be able to read it carefully and to respond right away. And I can't be late to class. You know Madame would be most disappointed."

"You can disappoint the teachers once in a while, you know. You don't have to be perfect all the time." Louise very nearly sounded disapproving that she wanted to be a good student but she shook her head.

"I'll wait until I can really enjoy it. It will take longer, but it's something to look forward to this evening." Once again, Louise looked disappointed but finally agreed.

"You'll tell me as soon as possible, right?"

"Of course." She would definitely be sharing the contents with Louise. Of that she was certain. She would need someone to celebrate the news with, after all.

It seemed like a lifetime before the final bell of the day rang. And even that wasn't the end of it. Instead, Hazel raced back to her room, or as close to racing as a proper young lady was allowed, and dropped her books on the desk, slipping into her gown for choral practice.

She took one last look at the letter sitting on the desk, even picked it up so she could look more closely at the name written out across the front, and then sighed, setting it back down.

There was no time now. Choral practice would begin in only a few minutes and she could not be late. She had a solo, after all, and they were set to work on that first. Her letter would have to wait.

"Ah, Miss. Tumbler. There you are. Step over here, if you would, and we will begin from the fifth measure." The words had always been beautiful but now she felt the emotion hidden within them even more strongly. The love and the deep yearning seemed even more telling as she sang the words this time, and everyone seemed to notice.

"That was lovely, Hazel." One of the other girls told her.

"You sang it so well," another gushed and she could only smile, thinking of the reason she did so well at the words. She had thought she could feel them before, but it was nothing compared to the feelings she had now.

With a soft sigh she sat back with the rest of the girls and joined in the second song. Normally choral practice was one of her favorite parts to the day, but today she was simply glad when it was finished so she could hurry back to her room for the letter. The letter she had been waiting all day for. And now, as she tore it open, she hoped that it would be everything she had been wishing for.

It was.

In fact, the letter was more than what she had wished for. It was absolutely perfect. The honesty and the openness in those words caused her eyes to tear and she had to go back and read them again.

Could a man be more perfect than Edgar was? And so perfect for her especially. He was exactly what she could have wanted in a husband and she could not help but smile, reading the letter for a third time before she sank into a chair and immediately pulled out her own stationary to reply.

*Dear Lord Edgar,*

*I have truly never felt so at home and so understood reading some-one's words as I did just now reading yours. It was as if someone had plucked my own thoughts and feelings from my mind and put them onto paper for me. And yet, it is your thoughts and feelings on the page.*

*I am certain that things will begin to be better for you very soon, and that your concerns shall soon be at an end. I know that I will be more than pleased to be at your side to assist in all of these endeavors you seek to undertake. And I know that I shall be ready to be your pillar of strength whenever you need me.*

*Your words were very touching and so beautiful. In fact, I could not imagine anything better. I want nothing more than to meet and to begin our lives together so that we may truly come to cherish our feelings for one another. Everything I know of you thus far makes it quite simple for me to feel as though I have known you forever and that you are perfect for me in every way.*

*I am certain that we shall be a perfect match and that nothing shall ever endeavor to tear us apart.*

*Ever yours,*

*Hazel*

As she read through the letter from Edgar again she felt a fluttering in her stomach, and her own response gave voice to everything that she was thinking and feeling. It told him how she felt in a way that left her feeling vulnerable, but ever so pleased at the same time.

Sending off her response was a little frightening, but at the same time she knew that it was exactly what she wanted.

# CHAPTER 9

"KENDRICK!" He looked up from the poem he was struggling with — did nothing of consequence rhyme with forest? — and to his brother. "This has only just arrived."

"What is it?" For a moment he fancied that the letter in his brother's hand might actually be for him, though he had no idea who it might be from, but a quick glance at the penmanship on the front and the name that it spelled said otherwise. "You have received another letter?"

"Aye. Could you take care of this for me?" His brother's voice was not wholly rude, but certainly distracted and Kendrick flipped the letter over to see that the seal had not even been broken.

"Have you not at least read it?"

"I haven't the time now. And besides, it's not truly anything I know about. It's you who needs to read the letters."

"It's you that she is writing to," Kendrick replied, attempting to wave away the letter, nervously.

"I am busy, Kendrick. I have a meeting that I must go to. I am already late. Besides, you have been writing such nice letters. She is pleased with those. To have me write a letter at this stage would be most jarring for her. I thank you." And with that Edgar was gone, before Kendrick could say anything else.

With a sigh he broke the seal on the letter, hesitating before he pulled the pages out. After all, she really did not mean for him to read her letter. But there was nothing for it. Edgar was not about to read it and certainly not about to reply to it. So it was best if he did so. At least, that was what he continued to tell himself as he gently removed the crisp parchment from the envelope, the soft scent of roses wafting from it as he did.

He paused a moment at that, before he began to read the letter, quickly at first and then slowly.

It was clear from the words on the page that Hazel was certainly becoming attached to the author of the letters. For a moment he felt himself inordinately pleased, and then remembered that she was falling in love with his words, believing them to be from the man she was betrothed to. That was certainly not a pleasant thought.

The fact that he was the one sending and receiving letters with her was a sobering one. He felt awful to be deceiving her like this, but even as he thought that this was a terrible idea and he, or Edgar, should come clean, he took out another piece of stationary to begin his next letter.

*Dear Lady Hazel,*

*I find myself anxious for the post each day because each day brings a new letter from you. I am that anxious to receive each one to learn more about you and to feel as though I am just a little closer to you with every word. Your letters bring joy and happiness to my days and I enjoy reading them over and over, imagining that it is the two of us sharing a true conversation. But that will be possible soon enough.*

*I could not bear the thought of stopping these letters. I do so want to get to know you even better and appreciate that you seem inclined the same as well. I only hope that you are as pleased to receive my letters as I am to receive yours and I flatter myself, by the words that you write, that you are.*

*You are the light of my days even now, before I have seen you. And I know that you shall only become dearer to me as time goes on.*

*I would very much like to learn more about you. Please tell me everything. What was your childhood like? I know that our mothers are quite close and I have heard some things but I wish to hear the stories from you, to know what your life was like and what was most important to you.*

*Tell me also about Bath. What is your school like there? Who are you close to? What do you like best? In short, tell me anything and everything that you can because I feel as though I could never know enough about you.*

*You could fill pages and pages with information and I would still yearn to know even more because even that would not be sufficient. Tell me anything and tell me everything. I can only be happy if I know that none shall ever know you as well as I do.*

*Sincerely yours,*

*Edgar*

He hesitated only a moment before he pulled out a second sheet of paper. Writing out a small postscript to go along with the letter.

*I've included a poem here, that makes me think of you. It is one that I am quite proud of, though I am certain that there is more that could be done with it.*

This time he didn't hesitate to send the letter off and instead he did so with a smile, anxiously awaiting the time when the letter could reasonably be considered delivered.

Kendrick did wonder idly whether the letter he had just sent was too bold and too honest, but then that was what she seemed to appreciate most. And it was best that he be honest, wasn't it? At least as honest as he could be?

⌇

"Ah to be that young again," Louise sighed with a contented smile as they watched the first-year girls running and skipping through the courtyard.

"It is not that long ago that it was us doing the same, excited about going home for the long break. Anxious to talk to someone, anyone, else after being cooped up here for so many months." Hazel laughed and Louise gave a slight shrug.

"Perhaps. But it seems ever so long ago. And now we are set to leave here for the last time. To travel on home again to stay."

"It will be quite nice," Hazel replied and there was silence a moment as Louise fell into her own thoughts.

"It shall. But I do believe I shall miss being here. And I shall certainly miss you."

"I shall miss you as well. But it is not as though we shall never see each other again."

"What if we don't? You are returning to the city while I return to the countryside. We are quite a fair distance apart."

"But you must come to my wedding," Hazel insisted. "After all this time spent in each other's company you are certainly my best friend, and I could not have the ceremony without you there." It was an exaggeration and they both knew it, but Hazel truly couldn't imagine not having Louise with her. And Louise was flattered to think it all depended upon her.

"Ah yes, your wedding. Perhaps you shall barely return before you are married off," Louise teased but Hazel only smiled serenely.

"Perhaps I shall be. Oh, Louise, before I used to wonder at my future wedding. I wondered who I might be chosen to marry and what my life would be like. Now it is all directly before me. The husband I am destined for. The life I am set to live. And I find myself even more anxious than I ever was before."

"Are you not happy to be betrothed?"

"Oh, Louise! I am so happy. So pleased to have such a future husband." Her eyes were bright with her happiness and Louise smiled in response.

"I am glad that you are happy. And that you shall have a husband that makes you that way. You deserve every happiness, Hazel."

"I always knew that my mother would try to choose a good match for me. Someone that I could care for and that was also a respectable match for the daughter of a duchess. But I could not have imagined that the match she would choose for me would be such a perfect one as this."

"What else do you know of him?" Louise asked, reclining slightly as she settled in.

"Not much, I'm afraid. It's been quite a while since I saw him. Edgar was a bit older than myself, and he was often away. What I remember about him is very general," she tried to think hard about any details she could. "I remember he was somewhat scrawny as a boy, but then he would have been quite young at the time. And I believe I recall blonde hair.

"He was always very absorbed in his books, even more so than Kendrick and I. And smart, very smart."

"What do you think he will be like now?" Louise asked. "Will he be handsome?"

"Oh, I have no way of knowing. His brother had begun to be handsome the last time I saw him. I am sure that Edgar likely is as well," but Hazel's eyes furrowed as she tried to think of any little details she could remember. But it had been so many years and the little she remembered seemed to be the top of his head as he was bent over a book and she and Kendrick were playing in the garden.

"Well, he shall be quite smart then, with all that reading," Louise hedged.

"Oh certainly. And I am sure he will have wonderful stories to tell of his adventures," Hazel agreed.

"Miss. Tumbler?" The two girls both looked up at the voice, but it was Hazel who received the letter with a gleeful look.

"Oh! Thank you!" The maid curtsied and left the room while Hazel practically tore open the letter and Louise crowded in close, though she let Hazel read the letter privately before she reached for it herself.

As Louise read over the letter Hazel began to write her response.

He wanted to know about her childhood and about her life here. Well, she could tell him a great deal. She found herself extremely pleased that he wanted to know so much and that he was so excited at the prospect of learning about her from her younger years all the way up.

*Dear Lord Edgar,*

*I was so pleased to receive your letter and began immediately to form my response to it, anxious as I was to have it sent out so that you could again be reading my words.*

*I can never learn enough about you, or read enough of your words. I am grateful for each and every letter and have read each multiple times. In fact, I looked at this one multiple times before I began to write to you again. I am most pleased that you wish to know about my life though I'm not sure where to begin.*

*My childhood was most happy. My father is the Duke of Deighton, as you well know, and was busy much of the time, however my mother and I spent a great deal of time together. I had a governess until I came here to school, however Mother still enjoyed us being together as much as possible.*

*She and I would take long strolls through the garden. It was perhaps one of my favorite things and a memory I hold dear with her.*

*Of course, your brother and I were close friends as children as well. Your mother and mine have remained close ever since their own childhoods and it brought Kendrick and I closer together.*

*Perhaps you do not remember much of that time, as you were older and already in your studies, but, as young children, he and I used to play together. Often we would run through the fields near your home or we would sneak into the kitchens in mine to get little cakes and cookies, as many as possible.*

*I am not sure at what point Kendrick and I began to drift further apart. I only know that there was a time when he stopped coming around and I stopped asking after him. And soon thereafter I was sent here to Bath anyway. It had long been talked of, but I was old enough that it was certainly time.*

*Since coming to Bath I must say I have greatly enjoyed my studies. We learn a great deal here and I have studied French, singing, literature, and sewing. But we also have classes on history and sciences here that are not common in many girls' schools. I do hear that they are not as thorough as those at the boys' schools, and I wouldn't wonder that they are, but it is interesting to learn anyway.*

*Louise is my closest friend since coming here and I do not know what I would do without her. In fact, I am not sure what I shall do without her when we both leave school at the end of the term. She lives a distance from myself and while visits are possible it will be quite different to not see her every day as I have grown accustomed to.*

*She is very friendly and outgoing where I can sometimes be reserved. And she is exceedingly loyal and honest, sometimes even to a fault. There was a time she very nearly spoiled the surprise we had planned for another girl's birthday because she had to tell a fib to get her to the right place.*

*We have been close since my coming here several years past and even share a room here. She is also most excited about my betrothal and has been nearly as happy as I to see your letters arrive each day.*

*Our studies are coming to an end here and we are all considered proper young ladies who are prepared to enter society. I know that I am most anxious to return home and see my dear mother again. And of course to finally have the opportunity of meeting you as well.*

*I would love to know more about you. Tell me about your childhood as well, your travels, anything that comes to mind. I feel as though I am already getting to know your heart, but I would like to know more of your mind as well.*

*It will not be long before we are wed and you shall be everything to me even more than you are now.*

*Sincerely yours,*

*Hazel*

As she sent the letter off, she began immediately to count down the hours until she could reasonably, or perhaps even unreasonably, expect a letter in response.

≈

**Three Weeks Later**

Putting everything into her trunks felt a bit bittersweet. On the one hand she was glad to be going home, but packing everything away felt strange. Even when she used to go home for a while at the end of the term there were things she left in her room. This had been her room for nearly ten years, after all.

But today she was packing up everything. All of the little things that had made this space uniquely hers over the years. All the things that she saved and enjoyed returning to after her breaks.

The sketchbook she had brought along after her first art classes. The handkerchiefs she had been so proud of when she'd embroidered that difficult rose pattern. A pretty drawing one of the other girls had done for her several years ago. An old diary she had kept only sporadically since she first came here.

Under the bed was a small suitcase where she stored some of her favorite books so she could always go back to them. On a shelf in the closet were are few letters from her mother. Tucked in the back of the desk was...what was that? She felt around and pulled out a small book.

Her brow furrowed in confusion at the sight of it as she could not place just what it was. In fact, she was just about to set it aside to ask Louise if it was hers when she opened the front cover. Inside was an inscription. To her. From Kendrick.

Suddenly she remembered the book of poems he had sent to her when she first went away to school. They had not talked in quite some time by then, but he had heard she left and had sent this book to her. It was the only thing he ever sent to her. He never even responded to the thank you note she sent upon receiving it.

Now she took a moment to flip through the familiar poems. She had read them over many times during her first year here. And had even returned to it a few times after, but along the way she had forgotten about it. A smile lit her face as she looked at it now. It would be nice to see Kendrick again too, she thought to herself.

It was odd to even think about the fact that she was never going to come back here. Never going to sit on this bed and contemplate her life. Never going to sit at that dressing table and comb out her hair. Never going to run down the halls to get to class on time.

There were so many 'nevers' that it was almost impossible to put items into her trunk for tearing up. Ah, to be as young as the girls on the lawn, she thought, casting a glance out the window to where a group of girls played under the trees. Blissfully unaware of how much they would miss this place when they left it for good.

Back then she had thought that she would be here forever. That her education would never end and each year she would be dutifully returning for the new term. But now...now she wished that was the case.

At least, partially.

But, on the other hand, she thought of what she was going back to. Her dear mother, who she missed so much when she was away. And of course Edgar. And her pending marriage.

She took a small box from the drawer of her desk and set it ever so carefully on the bed, moving to empty the small hanging space that was hers as Louise entered the room with an armful of her own things from the laundry.

"Oh, it's going to take me forever to pack all of these things," she grumbled good-naturedly. "How did I ever end up with so many things?"

"You bring a whole new wardrobe each term. And then you leave the old one behind at the end of the next one," Hazel replied with a laugh.

"Perhaps you're right. But these clothes are never going to all fit into my trunk. I'm going to have to send for another one," Louise laughed as well, dropping the things onto her own bed. "How is it that you have so few things to take?"

"My trunk will be full as well," Hazel told her. "But I take most of my things home with me at the end of each term. There are only a few things I've left every year."

"Ah, that is true. I never traveled home with more than a carpet-bag. You took your trunk with you each time." Louise sank down onto Hazel's bed and her eye caught on the box there. "What is this?"

"Oh, that is nothing," Hazel attempted to pluck the box back from her hand but Louise leaned out of her reach and opened it. Letters tumbled from inside of it and Louise squealed with pleasure.

"There are so many more letters here than I have seen. Have you and Edgar been writing every day?"

"Very nearly," Hazel admitted and Louise's eyes sparkled as she shook out a few of the letters.

"*I have been spending a great deal of time riding with Kendrick. When I am not working on business. It is nice to be home and see my brother. It has been far too long since I have had the chance.*" Louise read from one of the letters before flipping it over and looking at another.

"Oh, don't," Hazel began.

"*Mother is most pleased that I am home again and that I intend to stay. I think perhaps she would have jumped at any chance to have me married off so that I would not travel again. I am only fortunate that your mother proposed a match before one was offered that would not have been as pleasant for me.*" Louise spoke in a tone of longing and fluttered her eyelashes in a silly gesture of love. Hazel, on the other hand, look flustered and reached out for the letters again.

"Louise-"

"Oh, do not worry. Here is your box. And your letters." Louise handed them over and Hazel gave a relieved sigh, folding the letters and placing them carefully back in the box. Then she tucked the box itself down into the trunk, carefully cushioning it into her gowns.

"It is special to me."

"The box or the letters?" Louise teased.

"Both," Hazel admitted. "The box belonged to my mother. And her mother before her. It has been passed down several generations. And the letters are important as well."

"With so many letters between you I am sure that you must know everything about him by now."

"I believe that I do," Hazel replied with a contented smile. "We have written as often as the post will allow for and I feel quite confident that I know the man I am about to marry better than anything."

"It is lovely that you do," Louise admitted. "It is doubtful that I shall have that chance before I am married."

"Are you betrothed too?" Hazel asked, excited for her friend.

"Not just yet but I am sure it shall not be long before I am. My father will wish to have me married off now that my schooling is complete." Louise's voice was difficult to decipher, her eyes uncertain and her lips pressed together.

"You seem unhappy about it," Hazel replied with concern.

"I am not entirely unhappy," Louise corrected. "I am only...uncertain. I wish for a happy match more than an advantageous one. But my father shall seek one that is more advantageous. He would never wish me to be miserable," she added quickly, "but he may not understand what would make me truly happy."

There was silence between the two girls for a long moment and Hazel thought about how happy she was to have a good match before her that was both advantageous and pleasant. She wished with all her heart that the same would be true for Louise.

"I am sure he will find you a good match. And you shall be just as happy as I am," Hazel promised, clutching her friends' hands close. She was relieved when Louise smiled. Her morose feelings overcome as she laughed.

"I will wish it as well," but this time she spoke with more happiness and Hazel felt much better as well.

"You must write to me immediately once it happens," Hazel instructed and Louise smiled.

"Of course I shall. And you must write to me about your wedding."

"Of course. I shall need you to attend. You are my dearest friend, after all." Louise teared up then.

"Oh, you are my dearest friend as well. I shall miss you ever so much. And knowing that there is no next term for us to see one another is even more difficult." The two girls hugged each other close, tearing up even more at the thought. It had been so long that they had been together, after all.

"It shall not be so bad. We will find chances to meet up. And perhaps I shall find you a husband close to my home. And then you and I can be as close as my mother and Edgar's mother."

"That would be perfect. You have said that your Edgar has a younger brother. If Edgar is to take on the duchy from your family and his brother is to become an earl it may be a perfect match," Louise jested but Hazel wondered if it might be a good match after all. And then the two of them would be sisters and living so near to one another. She smiled and promised herself that she would look into it.

"Oh Louise, what shall we do in the meantime?" she exclaimed.

"You shall be so focused on your wedding you will forget about me," Louise predicted.

"I could never forget about you. But I will certainly be focused on my wedding." Hazel gazed off, thinking of what was to come. "I cannot wait for the wedding to take place," she added. "I just know that I am about to marry my soulmate. That he is perfect for me."

"And you know so much about the man already."

"Aye, I feel as though I have known him forever. And I am certain that I am already falling in love with him. It is not difficult to do. Especially when you know him as I do. He is perfect for me." She sighed with happiness at the thought of what was to come and placed another folded gown into her trunk.

"He certainly seems to be," Louise agreed. "I wish you all the best. You deserve it. After all, you are the best friend and simply a wonderful person." Hazel blushed slightly and smiled.

"You are too kind to me. You always have been. I cannot wait to return home to see my mother and meet Edgar, but I will certainly be sad to leave you."

"And I you," Louise agreed, giving her another hug as the two thought about just what it was going to mean to leave this place for the final time.

# CHAPTER 10

WITH ALL THE time she had spent preparing for her final tests and packing her things to return home, Hazel had very nearly forgotten about the graduation ball. All of the senior girls would get to attend and there were gentlemen coming from one of the boys' schools down the way, as it would be their graduation ball as well.

Luckily, the duchess had not forgotten and when Hazel returned from her final class, somewhat late in the day owing to the large outpouring of tears from all of the senior girls and even some of the teachers, her dress was waiting.

"Oh, goodness." She stopped short on seeing it there, spread out beautifully to showcase the gorgeous hue to the green, and certainly the beading throughout the bodice. It was the most beautiful dress she had ever seen. Of that she was certain. And she wondered just how she could bring herself to touch it, let alone put it on.

As she was running the smooth silk over her fingers Louise finally made it back.

"That Mary Hadler is certainly a crier, isn't she? Oh, I did not know if I should ever get away from her but I-Oh! Look at that. That is beautiful, Hazel." Louise hurried over to the dress, delicately touching the beads at the bodice. "For the ball? It is perfect. You shall be the most beautiful one there." Hazel laughed, but she was certain that anyone who wore such a beautiful dress would likely be considered the loveliest one there.

"Mother must have had it made for me for the occasion. I forgot entirely about the ball."

"It is lovely. You must try it on."

"I think I want to wait," Hazel replied. "I'll put it on for the ball." Louise was not so happy with that idea, but Hazel liked the idea of putting the gown on for the first time that day. It would make the experience that much more special.

After a few more minutes of both of them admiring the dress Hazel put it away, waiting excitedly until the day she would get to wear it. Not that it was going to be long. The ball would be held in just a few days' time and that time passed quickly.

With no classes the girls spent the next few days enjoying the nice weather and finishing up any packing they needed to do. And of course everyone spent time preparing for the ball.

Each day Hazel would walk to the closet and look at the dress again, running her fingers over the silk or touching a bit of beading or lace. She could not believe that such a beautiful thing was hers, after all. But she was excited about being able to wear it.

The day of the ball, however, there was utter silence from the older girls as they spent the entire morning in their rooms preparing their dresses and their hair. Making sure they looked their best for the special occasion.

Louise and Hazel were no exception.

While the younger girls gossiped and scurried about the campus wondering just what was going on behind all of those closed doors Hazel was trying to determine just how she would style her hair for the special occasion.

This was their graduation ball, after all. It was meant to be the most spectacular occasion possible, and to mark their progress throughout the years. It needed to be treated as such.

"Oh, it never will stay the way I want it to," Hazel burst out with a glance into the looking glass.

"Why don't you style it the same way you always do for a ball? It looks lovely as it is."

"I thought I would try something different for once. Oh, but it just refuses to do what I want it to."

"Here, let me try." Louise stepped in behind her, twisting her hair carefully onto the top of her head and securing it with pins. In fact, the way Louise did it looked even better than what Hazel had been trying to do and she beamed at her reflection in the mirror.

"It's perfect. Now you."

"There's not much to be done with mine. It never holds a curl. I can tuck it up, I suppose." Louise frowned at her own reflection, patting her hair as she did.

"I am sure we can do something with it," Hazel insisted, taking a closer look and beginning to pin it here and there. "There, what about that?"

"Oh! How did you do that? I shall need to be able to tell the maids back at home so they can do it as well." Louise stared into the mirror, turning her head one direction then another to see her hair more clearly. "It looks lovely."

Now was the time they had both been waiting for. Louise had sent for a new dress for the ball as well, and both girls were excited to try on the gowns they had received. For Louise, the pale pink color of her gown was a perfect complement to her blue eyes and the rosy color that always came to her cheeks. Her soft brown hair complimented it all perfectly.

Both girls took a few moments to fawn over the gown, admiring the way that it draped about her waist and how it fell in elegant waves all the way down. The bodice fit perfectly, a slim style with just a little beadwork to complement the neckline. She looked stylish and exactly right for the ball. But they were both excited to see what Hazel looked like in her own gown.

For herself, Hazel was nervous. Certainly the gown would fit perfect and look lovely, but that did not reassure her much more. Instead, she held her breath as she took the dress out and then very carefully slipped it on. Louise helped her to button the back before either of them took in the look of the dress, but when she did turn to see the looking glass her mouth dropped open.

"Oh! Hazel!" Louise even seemed to be at a loss for words, staring at the beautiful gown. The green of the gown complimented her perfectly. The fitted bodice and the modest neckline were perfect for the occasion. The waistline sat right at her natural waist, making her look even more slender while the full skirts were just right to draw attention but not be too cumbersome for dancing.

"It's lovely." It was the only thing that Hazel could think of to say but it did not seem to do the dress justice. How could the seamstress have created such a lovely gown? She had never seen anything like it.

"You shall certainly be the most beautiful one there," Louise promised, her eyes still wide at the beauty of the gown. But Hazel immediately felt more nervous, glancing down at the dress with a more critical eye. "Whatever is the matter?" Louise asked in surprise, looking at her more closely.

"Do you think...will Edgar find me to be beautiful?" Louise laughed aloud and then rushed to comfort her.

"He should have to be blind not to find you beautiful. Oh, Hazel.

You are the most beautiful I've ever seen. And that has nothing at all to do with the dress even."

"I wonder though. He has been around the world and surely he has seen beautiful ladies there."

"I am sure he has," Louise agreed. "And that is why it is even more telling that I know he shall find you the most beautiful of them all. Have you written to him again recently?"

"No, not recently. We had decided to stop for a bit as we shall see each other in only a few days' time. I will be home then and he is coming to dinner at the manor for my welcome."

"That shall be exciting. To see him so quickly. And to begin planning your wedding of course," Louise teased.

"Oh, I am sure our mothers have already begun the planning. But I shall certainly like to have a part in it as well." Hazel replied with a dreamy sigh. Yes, she was most excited about planning the wedding and finally having the chance to join her life with the man she was now certain was just right for her.

With another last look in the mirror for both of them Hazel pronounced that it was time to go. The ball would begin in just a moment and it was time to take their place in the hall.

Of course, walking down the hallway was its own pleasure, with all of the younger girls standing there watching enviously. Every one of them could not wait to be walking those halls themselves with their beautiful gowns, graduating seniors from the school.

It seemed like only days before that Hazel herself was one of those girls. One of the youngest groups who were huddled in a corner together with the widest of eyes. Many of them never having even been to a ball before as they were not yet 'out' themselves.

"Are you ready?" Louise asked, as they reached the end of the line of their peers. Each of the girls was wearing a beautiful gown and each smiled as the two joined them. Though it was clear that several were staring with no little envy at Hazel's beautiful gown.

"I am," Hazel replied and they waited as each girl was announced and allowed to enter the ballroom alone, so that those in attendance could admire them one at a time. Finally it was their turn and Hazel squeezed Louise's hand once before the girl stepped forward and presented her card to the servant at the door.

"Lady Louise Van Dorn." Her name was announced and Louise stood tall with a broad smile as she made a customary pause at the top of the stairs and then descended.

That meant it was Hazel's turn and she took a deep breath before she stepped forward and held out her card with a hand that still would shake even though she tried to quell it.

"Lady Hazel Tumbler." Her name was announced and Hazel stepped forward to the top of the stairs. All eyes were on her now and she struggled to keep the smile on her face from slipping with anxiety. But she was determined to look her best as she stepped out into the ballroom. Especially with all those people, teachers and seniors, watching her and so she glided carefully down the stairs and into the room.

The music was set to begin in an hour, with small plates being served immediately. And of course the opportunity to showcase members of the graduating classes of the girls' school, beginning with a presentation of singing and piano. The graduating class of the boys' school would listen to them along with their teachers. It was this part that Hazel had forgotten entirely when she was preparing for the evening.

Though of course she had been warned that she would be called upon to present, she had not thought of it again in the ensuing days. But then, a lady must always be prepared to be called upon to play or sing — or sometimes both — and as such she had a couple of songs prepared when her name was read.

"Go on," Louise murmured in her ear with a gentle shove that was hidden enough no one else saw anything but a friendly hand on her arm. And so Hazel put on a smile over her nervousness again and approached the piano for her second presentation of the evening.

The music swept her away, as it always did. And the beautiful song once more made her think of where she was about to go and what she was about to do. A wedding to a lovely young man, and the beautiful future that was promised by that beginning.

At the end of the song there was a flurry of applause and Hazel stood to curtsey and smile yet again before fading back into the crowd. Her presentation was, once again, the last, and then it was time for the band to take over and the dancing to begin.

Nearly immediately there was a gentleman there to ask her to dance and another for Louise. In fact, the two did not lack for part-ners for the whole of the evening, barely having enough time to share a few words in between sets before they were again swept onto the dance floor.

Though each of the gentlemen she danced with was pleasant and friendly, and some were even downright handsome, Hazel could only think of Edgar.

When one gentleman gave the most gracious bow she wondered if Edgar would be as elegant. When one gentleman was a superb dancer she wondered if Edgar would be able to glide across the floor in such a way. When one gentleman was a delight to talk to she wondered if Edgar would be so eloquent.

Every moment, and every gentleman before her was another chance to wonder what Edgar would be like once she had the opportunity to meet him. Would he be everything she had hoped he would be? Would he be the perfect husband that she thought he was from his letters?

With a sigh she begged off the next gentleman that approached her, saying she needed a moments' rest and a little water, which he happily fetched for her. He even stayed with her to converse and made her smile even as she felt herself distracted by thoughts of another.

When the evening had ended she was more than pleased with how it had gone. Her official presentation into society as a graduate had been wonderful and she now could not wait until her mother came to fetch her the next day. Hazel was more than ready to return home and meet her future husband.

"Oh, Hazel, it was a wonderful evening," Louise gushed. "I am so happy for all of it." And now I cannot wait to return home and see everyone again."

"I agree," Hazel replied. "It shall be nice to see my family." With that the two girls slipped into their nightclothes and fell into an easy slumber. Their families would be there before they knew it to bring them home, after all.

Despite the late night all of the girls were up early the next morning making sure they had everything they needed in their trunks and saying last minute goodbyes to all of their friends.

For the younger girls it was only a temporary goodbye. But the older ones knew that they might never actually see one another again. For them this parting was bittersweet.

"Miss. Tumbler, your carriage has arrived," a servant informed her and she hugged Louise one last time.

"Promise me that you shall come to visit soon."

"Of course," Louise agreed and both girls tried not to cry as Louise walked her outside where her trunk was being loaded onto the back of a carriage. It was then that the door opened and she was surprised to see her father alight the carriage, turning back to assist her mother out of it.

"Papa!" She hurried to him and was greeted with a warm hug.

"Ah, there you are. It has been too long since I have seen you. You have grown into quite the young woman." Hazel beamed with the praise and then turned to greet her mother with another hug.

"It is good to see you, Hazel," her mother added and both

assisted her back into the carriage. It was quite a surprise to see them both here. She had thought her mother might come, though she had often returned home from school alone in the past. But she had certainly not expected her father to come to see her return home.

As they left the school she reached out the window to wave one last time at Louise and the other girls in the courtyard and then settled in for the ride home.

"How was your term?" her father asked, and Hazel eagerly recounted everything she could.

"It has been a wonderful last year," she began, "I've learned ever so much and I finished at the top of the class in French and music."

"That is wonderful, Hazel," her mother replied proudly.

"And what do you think of your betrothal?" her father asked next and Hazel smiled again.

"I am excited for it, Father. Edgar and I have been exchanging letters and I feel that I know him very well."

"Have you now? Well, that is a good thing as well. I am glad that you feel happy about the coming marriage," he smiled at her and she could not help but smile brighter in response.

"I am certain that he shall be a perfect match for me. And I just know that everything will be all right." Her voice was resolute, as was her conviction on the subject.

"I am glad you feel that way," her mother added. "I had worried that perhaps you would feel a little slighted that you were not at least consulted on the matter. Or that perhaps you may have met someone in Bath," her mother smiled.

"Oh no, Mother. I always expected that you would choose my future husband and I am very grateful that it is someone I am so pleased to know as Edgar. I am certain he shall be an excellent husband."

"I believe so as well," her mother replied with a smile. "I had not seen Edgar in some time, but I do know that he is a very respectable young man and of course I know his mother well."

"And an earl is an excellent match for my daughter," was her father's addition. "He shall be well disposed to become the duke when I am ready to step away."

"Oh, that won't be for a long time, Father," Hazel insisted.

"Perhaps. Perhaps not. I may wish to spend time on other things once there is someone to take my place." They all knew it would still be quite some time before the duke would choose to leave his position but each laughed and relaxed back into the carriage. They would be home soon enough and Hazel was more than happy to just enjoy the moment with both of her parents.

Before long she would be leaving their household yet again, but this time it would be so that she could be wed. And that time, she would not be returning.

# CHAPTER 11

Fiona was pacing from one end of the drawing room to the other, deep in thought. It was in this manner that her boys found her upon return from their morning ride. In fact, she seemed so caught up in her own thoughts that she did not even notice them at first.

"Mother?"

"Oh, there you are. Back already?" she asked.

"It's been over an hour," Kendrick replied with a confused glance to her.

"Well, I have been deep in thought."

"About what?" Edgar asked her.

"The Duke and Duchess picked up Hazel from Bath just yesterday and we have been invited for dinner. They would like Edgar and Hazel to meet and to get to know one another in person." She was clearly excited about the prospect, but also somewhat nervous.

Kendrick too felt nervous. And perhaps something else. There was something about the news of Hazel and Edgar meeting that made him feel sad. Maybe even a little sick to his stomach. His heart felt heavy. But all of these things he felt in a fleeting moment before he quickly pushed them down. There was no time for this kind of thing, after all. He had more important things to think about when it came to Hazel and Edgar meeting at last.

"There is a great deal to prepare before dinner," their mother added.

"Prepare? We shall be going to their manor, won't we?" Edgar asked.

"Yes, but that does not mean that we should not prepare ourselves. We must look our best, after all," Fiona replied.

"It is a simple family dinner, Mother," Edgar said. "I am sure they do not expect us to stand on too much ceremony."

"We may not need too much ceremony but we should still take care. You shall be meeting your future wife and her family, after all."

"I have met Hazel and her family before," Edgar answered back somewhat flippantly.

"It has been a long time. And you have not met her as her future husband. It is important that you make a good impression on her family." This time their mother sounded quite firm on the issue.

"They are not likely to change their mind about the betrothal, Mother. And I hardly think that any minor mistake I may make in dress would be sufficient to make them doubt our match anyway." Edgar was quite unimpressed with the entire affair and seemed not to have a care for going out of his way.

"It is still important," Fiona insisted and the two boys finally accepted it. A few extra moments in their dress would not be a terrible thing, after all. "Now, it is important that you are polite to Hazel but do not act too familiar unless she does so. I do not want the Duke to think anything inappropriate of your conduct."

"Of course, Mother," Edgar agreed easily.

"And Kendrick, I know that you remember Hazel from when you were both younger but it is important that you are also not too familiar with her."

"Of course," he repeated, though the words were a little more difficult for him to say than Edgar.

"Things have changed since you and Hazel were children and you must not be inappropriate regarding your relationship." He nodded in response and sank into a chair by the window. It was difficult to think about meeting with Hazel and not being able to immediately tell her all that he knew. They had been friends as children, but it was different now and he was not sure how she would feel about his knowing so much about her this way.

"I must get to work now. There is much to catch up," Edgar finally said, rising from his own chair. Their mother sent him off with a few last minute comments and recommendations and Kendrick rose quickly.

"I have a few things to take care of as well," he managed quickly before following Edgar to the hallway. "There are things we must discuss," was his response to the questioning look from Edgar.

"What is it you would like to talk about?" Edgar asked as they walked toward the study.

"The letters that I have been writing to Hazel. It is important that we discuss them before dinner tonight," Kendrick urged.

"Whatever for?" Edgar looked confused at the very idea.

"You and she will need to talk at the dinner. And there are things that both of you have discussed in the letters that she will expect you to know." Kendrick felt incredulous that Edgar did not see this himself.

"I am sure it shall be fine," Edgar replied, his tone still flippant and unconcerned.

"You really should take a look at the letters," Kendrick tried to insist but Edgar shook his head again. They had stopped in the hallway at the top of the stairs but it was clear that Edgar was only barely listening.

"I have other things I need to take care of. Things that are more pressing." Kendrick knew that his brother was a kind man and would take care of Hazel well, but he still wished that Edgar would take all of this more seriously. It was important that he at least know what Hazel had talked about in her letters.

"I am concerned that she will want to talk about something and you will not know anything about it."

"Breakfast is ready, my Lord," they both started at the servant who had approached nearly silently and then gave a nod.

"Go on and tell Mother and I will be down directly for breakfast," Edgar instructed hurrying down the hall before Kendrick could say another word. He sighed and returned to the drawing room again, escorting their mother to the dining room instead.

Perhaps he would still be able to convince Edgar before they were set to go to see Hazel. He was doubtful, but at least he would try. For now, all he could do was try not to let on his feelings in front of their mother. It would not do for her to find out that Kendrick was the one who had been writing to Hazel. Certainly she would not be pleased with it.

Once Edgar had rejoined them they began to eat, and their mother turned immediately to her new favorite subject, Hazel.

"I am so pleased that my son shall marry the daughter of a duke! Ah, Hazel shall be an excellent wife for you. And she is well educated in everything important."

"The school she has been to, it is a comprehensive school?" Edgar inquired.

"The young ladies are taught the usual subjects with some light introduction into other areas such as mathematics and sciences," their mother replied and Kendrick tried not to frown at the fact that

Edgar should know that. Hazel had spoken of it in her letters, after all. She would expect him to know.

"It is a good school then. I will be most pleased that my wife is educated and in things more important than language and singing." Another inward cringe when Kendrick thought of the fact that singing was one of the things that Hazel was most proud of herself for.

"It is indeed an excellent school. And she has been there for several years. But do not discount the more feminine studies, Edgar. She is no doubt proud of all of her accomplishments, including music," their mother admonished.

"Yes, I am sure," Edgar replied, "but I would much rather a wife with more thought than one who simply knows how to play the piano all day." Their mother smiled indulgently and didn't say anything further. Kendrick simply stared down at his food and tried to force himself to eat it.

The thought that Edgar knew so little about Hazel and may well embarrass himself and her in their first meeting caused his stomach to hurt yet again. What would happen if he said something to offend her at that first meeting? Or said something that he should have already known? Would all of it end up coming out?

He worried that Hazel might find out and that she would be angry. After all, it was wrong what they were doing and he knew it, even if Edgar didn't. Still, he tried to push the thoughts away. Edgar obviously wasn't concerned. He didn't seem to care at all, in fact.

"Now, remember, a young lady likes to have attention bestowed on her. Be polite and be sure to be very attentive, their mother added."

"Of course," Edgar sounded distracted to Kendrick but their mother was so absorbed in her own thoughts she did not even notice.

"And be your sweet self. She will certainly be impressed by you and she shall be most happy to get to know you in person. Letters certainly cannot do you justice."

"I think it may rain today," Edgar interjected, glancing out the window, and their mother turned toward it.

"Oh, I hope not. Not for such an important dinner." She seemed very concerned; her brow furrowed as she contemplated the skies.

"We will not be having dinner outside," Kendrick teased. "Tea perhaps, but not dinner, surely." Their mother laughed but he could tell that she was still somewhat concerned.

"Rain is a bad omen."

"Oh, Mother. Don't tell me that you believe in such things. Rain is nothing at all about the occasion. It only means that the fields shall get what they need," Edgar replied.

"Oh, but I do wish the skies would be bright for your first meeting with Hazel," she replied with another frown.

"We cannot control the weather," was the only reply she received and Edgar returned to eating, without a care for it.

Kendrick too looked outside with a little dismay. Traveling in the rain by carriage would not be overly pleasant. And it truly would be unfortunate to have to see Hazel again for the first time under a cloud of storms. But perhaps it was all for the best. After all, it seemed fitting with how they had been deceiving her all this long.

"Oh, Martha, please prepare some of your scones for us to take along this evening." Kendrick looked up in surprise at his mother's voice. He had been so preoccupied with trying to eat that he had not even noticed Martha return to the room with a new platter of fruits. But now the older woman smiled and nodded.

"Of course, My Lady."

"Rose has always loved the scones that Martha prepares. And last time we visited I forgot to take them to her. Oh, did she give me trouble for that," she laughed and Martha returned to the kitchen, no doubt to get started on the preparations.

"We shall go for dinner then?" Edgar asked, finally turning back to the conversation.

"Yes, do not be late for us to leave," their mother warned and Edgar nodded his head.

"I will be ready. For now I must retire to the study. I have things that must be taken care of before we go."

Kendrick again followed after him. This time meeting him in the study and taking a seat before his desk.

"I do believe we need to talk about Hazel's letters." Edgar shook his head, looking exasperated.

"There is no need for that," he insisted again.

"What if Hazel wishes to speak to you about something she has written? Or something that you have written? You could very well end up with trouble."

"I am a good conversationalist. I shall be fine." Edgar sounded quite confident, and in fact he was still staring down at his ledgers and mostly ignoring Kendrick.

"But there have been a number of letters and I do not wish for you or her to be embarrassed," Kendrick protested.

"I can hold a conversation well. And I will be able to maneuver the conversation into a direction of my choosing with ease." Edgar simply waved off his concerns.

"Edgar-"

"You would not lie to her about me. Of that I am certain. And that means that I already know all of the things you could say about me. So there is nothing to learn." Edgar's tone was rather flippant at this and Kendrick started to speak but had no chance. "And anything I may have learned about her in a letter would still need to be discussed anyway. You cannot possibly learn enough about someone from a letter. Things need to be discussed in person." Edgar stated with a quick glance upward at him.

"She will expect you to know the things you have discussed however. Even if they would need to be talked of again," Kendrick insisted.

"It will be fine. I have a great deal of work to complete before we leave and I need to get to it."

With that Edgar put his head back down and began flipping through the ledger before him. There was no doubt about it. Kendrick had been dismissed and there was nothing more to say. He knew it was a lost cause and sighed as he rose.

"I do hope that it will be fine," Kendrick replied, though he did not feel nearly as certain of it as Edgar. Still, he left the room and went on to his own.

Tonight was going to be an extremely important night for all of them, and he could only hope that Edgar would be able to hold his own the way that he said he would. Otherwise everything could fall apart in only a matter of a few hours.

# CHAPTER 12

"THERE YOU ARE, MISS," Trina informed her, finishing the last of the buttons on the back of her dress. It really was a pretty gown. One that would look perfect for this very important dinner.

Hazel was still nervous that Edgar would not like her or that he would see something amiss about her appearance. But there was nothing she could really do about it now. They were set to arrive in just a half hours' time and she was all but ready.

A knock at the door announced her mother's arrival just before she walked into the room. Her face immediately said that she was pleased with Hazel's appearance and as she dismissed Trina from the room she approached her daughter.

"You look lovely, Dear. Edgar will be most pleased." As always, her mother seemed to know exactly what she needed to hear and it helped her feel much better.

"What does he look like?" she asked, voicing something she had wanted to ask in her letters but hadn't known quite how to say. Her mother smiled, looking at their reflections in the mirror.

"He is quite handsome. I remembered he was from before he left this last time and when I saw him just a few weeks ago he was certainly as handsome, likely more so, than he was then. He is tall and very athletic. His mother says that he enjoys being active and spending time out of doors. He enjoys riding."

"Oh good. I enjoy going for a ride as well. But I have hardly had the chance to do so while away at school," Hazel replied.

"He has green eyes and blonde hair, just like his brother. But perhaps a little slimmer than his brother," she added delicately.

"Kendrick," the name was right at the front of her mind, the same as it had been ever since her mother first mentioned her marrying Fiona's son. She could very much remember Kendrick and all the fun they had together when they were young. "It has been so long since I have seen him."

"He is much as you probably remember him, except grown a little older. He is quite handsome as well, and a sweet, dear boy. And he is so attentive to his mother." Hazel smiled, thinking that Kendrick had certainly grown into a fine man as well. It was definitely nice to know.

"I am excited to see him as well," she added. Her mother returned her smile.

"I am sure that you will be pleased with your former playmate."

"I do hope so. I have missed my friend. It would be nice to know that he has grown into a good man."

"And he is very happy with the match between you and his brother. He has expressed such several times. As well as his love for the both of you."

"It is good that he is happy about it as well," Hazel acknowledged and her mother agreed.

"Aye, that it is." The two fell silent for several moments, looking into the mirror. Hazel absently fussed with a few strands of hair that seemed to be placed just a little bit off from what she wanted. Or maybe it was just that she was so nervous she had to do something. "Are you certain you feel ready to meet Edgar?" her mother asked gently.

"Of course, why would I not be?" Hazel turned to her mother in surprise.

"You seem distracted, Dear. And perhaps a little tired. Are you tired from the journey back from Bath?"

"No, Mother. I feel well enough for this. I am excited to meet my future husband." Her mother brushed her hand over Hazel's forehead. It was a gesture that she had done many times while Hazel was young, but not in a very long time. Still, the familiar gesture and the soft look made Hazel feel calmer.

"It seems so strange that you are old enough for a husband. It was not so long ago you were only a little girl. And now you are all grown up." She sounded almost melancholy at the thought, her smile slightly sad now.

"I am not too grown for you, Mother," Hazel replied, leaning against her mother's shoulder.

"I want you to be happy, Dear. You would tell me if you were not, wouldn't you?" she asked with a concerned expression on her face.

"I would," Hazel agreed, though she wasn't entirely sure that she would if she felt it would make her mother unhappy.

"My Lady? The Earl and his family have arrived," Trina informed them, returning to the room with a curtsey.

"Ah, thank you." Rose turned toward Hazel and carefully helped her to smooth her dress before setting a hand on her shoulder. "You look lovely, Dear. You shall certainly make an excellent impression on Edgar and his family."

"Thank you, Mother."

"Where are they?" Rose asked Trina.

"They are in the drawing room with the Duke, My Lady," Trina replied and the two followed her out of the room. Hazel could feel her heart racing as she did and she worried that everyone would be able to hear it. She was nervous, exceedingly so, but she tried not to let on, following her mother into the drawing room with her head high, as she had been taught.

The men stood immediately as they entered and Hazel's eye immediately caught on Kendrick. It had been a long time since they had seen each other, but she would recognize him anywhere. He certainly had turned into a handsome young man and she could not help but smile at him.

His smile in response made her feel much better, though she was not sure why it had such an effect on her. But then she turned her gaze to the other man in the room, well, the other man besides her father. This had to be Edgar.

There was something vaguely familiar about him, though she likely would not have recognized him if they had met in town. Still, there were things he had in common with his mother and Kendrick, and a certain air about him that seemed to call to mind the boy who always loved to read.

He was certainly handsome, and as he extended his hand toward her she could not help but smile at his manners. She placed her own hand in his and curtsied as he bowed over her.

"My Lady," he said softly as he did.

"My Lord," she replied, with a gentle smile, feeling as though this was the culmination of everything they had been writing to each other.

"Hazel, it is so good to see you again," she turned from Edgar to his mother. It was quite nice to see Fiona as well. After all, it had been quite some time.

"I am glad to see you again as well," Hazel replied. "It has been so long."

"You were a young girl when last we met, and now you have

certainly grown into a lady. Oh and such a lovely one at that." Hazel laughed and Fiona gave her a warm hug. Yes, it was nice to be back among family, Hazel thought.

"If you should like to come with me, dinner shall be served in the dining room," her mother informed them all and Hazel smiled when Edgar stepped forward to take her arm. Butterflies filled her stomach as they walked arm-in-arm down the hall. This would be exactly what her life would be like from now on, side-by-side with Edgar.

As he settled her into her seat and took the one beside her she waited anxiously for him to begin the conversation. It was his place to do so, after all. And he did not make her wait even a moment.

"How was your time at school in Bath?"

"Oh it was quite wonderful. But of course you know all about that," she replied with a laugh. The slightly uncertain look on his face made her wonder for a moment but then he changed the subject again.

"I am sure you are glad to be home, however."

"Oh yes. I have missed my family a great deal," she admitted with a smile to both of them. "And I am certainly glad to be able to meet you."

"I am glad to finally meet you as well," Edgar agreed.

"I am sad to leave Louise however. It shall be strange not having her near me at all times." There was another confused look on Edgar's face at the mention of Louise and Hazel wondered what it could mean. She had often spoken of Louise and how close they were. Yet Edgar looked like he wanted to ask who she was but then changed his mind. Instead he fell silent a moment as though trying to find a different topic of conversation.

There was certainly something strange about the way Edgar was acting, and the fact that he did not seem to remember anything from her letters, even though he had written back with exacting detail. He had certainly read them in order to reply the way he had. But then why did he not know them now?

She waited, anxiously, while dinner was served to each of them and then picked up her fork as a way to distract herself. She was not feeling quite hungry, but Cook had prepared the dinner especially for her and she wanted to enjoy it.

"You have been away for quite some time, have you not?" he managed finally, looking slightly wary for her answer.

"Indeed. It has been several years I have been at Bath," she agreed, though she wondered at this question that he already knew the answer to. "Of course, I have been able to come home several times during that. At the end of each term and for holidays. But it is not the same as being home all the time."

"I am sure it is not. I understand what it is to miss home from my travels." Edgar replied, taking a few moments to begin eating.

"Yes, from your letters I gather your travels have been most exciting, but I know it has been difficult being away from your family," her tone was eager, glad to find a subject that they could easily converse on. She could see her mother and father out of the corner of her eye exchanging glances. There was a small smile on her father's face but her mother seemed less impressed.

Fiona seemed rather oblivious to anything being wrong, smiling broadly as she continued to eat. Kendrick on the other hand, seemed to recognize that there was something amiss as he stared down at his plate and almost nervously picked at his food.

"Yes," Edgar agreed, but there was a level of hesitation in the way that he said it, and the way that he looked away from her slightly. "My travels have taken me away quite a bit." This, at least, was a safer topic as he seemed comfortable talking about the places he had visited.

"I would love the opportunity to travel. It would be quite wonderful to see other parts of the world," Hazel ventured.

"You have been to the continent, have you not?" Edgar asked with a slight smile, though it faded quickly as Hazel's brow furrowed at the question. They had spoken about her lack of travel. That she had only ever been to Bath and to London. How could he not remember?

"I have not," she replied, her tone slightly stiffer than she intended. It was becoming clear that he did not remember the letters that they had shared. Or that something else was very wrong. Their conversation had been strange from the start and she wondered just what it could mean.

She took a bite of something from her plate, though she was not sure even what it was because she could not taste it. All she knew was that it was something to do while she struggled with what to say next.

All of her hopes were starting to falter as she looked at him. Edgar looked somewhat uncomfortable, though he was struggling to hide it. The tension in the room was palpable to everyone, though they all looked down at their plates and made small talk while Hazel struggled to make sense of it all.

The end of the meal came quickly, with everyone rushing to finish their food. Or at least rushing as much as propriety allowed for. And Countess Anderton rose immediately following the meal.

"It is time that we take our leave," she announced and her two boys rose with her.

"Oh, why don't we take some tea in the drawing room," Rose asked, though it was clear that she was not sure that was the best course of action. Propriety, however, dictated that she offer tea following the meal.

"I think it best that we leave your family to rest. It has been a long journey from Bath, and I am sure Hazel is looking forward to a little more time enjoying her family."

"It is lovely of you to think of such a thing," Hazel replied, grateful for an easy way out of this awkward situation.

"It was quite nice to see you again, Hazel. And I look forward to us seeing one another again soon," Fiona pressed her hand to Hazel's with a soft smile that the girl easily returned. It was difficult to be upset with Fiona, after all.

Kendrick approached as well, bowing over her hand and offering a small but slightly awkward smile. No doubt he was uncomfortable about the conversation that had taken place and the feeling of the room, but tried to hide it with that familiar smile. It soothed her slightly, though she was not quite sure why.

Edgar had the grace to look slightly abashed as he bowed over her hand and took his leave in a very polite but slightly stiff manner. Hazel could only wonder just what had happened and why things had gone so very wrong.

She had been certain that tonight would show her exactly why Edgar was the perfect man for her, and now she was left feeling lost. What had happened to the man from her letters? Why did this man before her seem so very different and so very foreign to her?

# CHAPTER 13

ONCE THE EARL and his family had left, Hazel went with her own family to the drawing room, but the conversation there was stilted as well. She could tell that her parents also were confused about what had just happened. They did not know the contents of her letters to Edgar. But their troubled expressions mimicked her own.

Her own level of frustration made it clear just how she felt about the conversation that had taken place, or lack thereof.

"It has been a long day. I believe I shall retire early," she finally said, rising from her seat. It was the best thing she could do since she was too stuck in her own head to be of any good as a conversationalist.

It was a testament to how poorly things had gone that neither of her parents attempted to convince her to stay. They both seemed to believe it best for her to go to bed as well. Perhaps things would look better in the morning.

Dinner had not been what she expected. She had thought that everything would be perfect between herself and Edgar. Had assumed that they would pick up in person the way they had left off in their letters.

But it had not happened.

Everything that Edgar said made it seem as though he had never read her letters at all. But how could that be? He had written back to her and shared such beautiful things. Yet he did not seem to remember any of it.

Her mind raced as she walked from one end of the room to the other. Her room had never seemed so small before as it did now. As she searched for some explanation, any explanation, for what had happened at dinner.

"Would you like to get ready for bed, Miss?" she stopped suddenly, startled by the sudden voice and turned to find Trina standing in the doorway, a confused expression on her face.

"Perhaps that would be best," Hazel agreed, though she wasn't sure that going to sleep was going to make her feel any better. Or even that she would be able to sleep with everything that was running through her head right now.

Still, she waited as Trina gathered her nightclothes and began the process of getting out of her day clothes. She had put on this dress with so much hope. So much anticipation for what this evening would bring. And now, as she changed into her nightgown, she found herself wondering just what was in store for her future after all.

"I noticed the earl and his family when they arrived. The two boys certainly are quite handsome, are they not?" Trina didn't wait for an answer before continuing on. "So tall, and broad-shouldered as well. Either of them would certainly make a fine husband, I am sure." Trina sounded quite resolute, with a smile on her face as she spoke. In fact, she sounded as though she quite approved of the pair, with no real preference between them.

Hazel did not speak, simply following through the motions needed to get ready for bed. But Trina was not about to be deterred.

"They did seem to leave in a bit of a hurry though. And I am sure I'm not supposed to say but the two boys did not seem to be pleased when they left. Something must have happened between the two because they certainly seemed gruff in the way they looked at each other."

Hazel wondered what that might mean but still did not speak, trying to puzzle out anything she could from Edgar's behavior tonight.

"Why, is there something the matter, Miss?" Trina finally asked and Hazel hesitated a moment before speaking.

"Dinner did not go as planned tonight," she finally admitted. "The earl and I are betrothed; I am sure you know."

"Aye, Miss," Trina acknowledged.

"We have been conversing through letters for over a month and yet...it was as if he did not even know me. It was as if...as if we had never written at all," Hazel sank onto her bed, frustrated.

"Ah well," Trina continued to bustle about, turning down the bedsheets — more difficult with Hazel already sitting on the bed — and blowing out a few of the candles throughout the room. "It is entirely different to meet someone in person than it is to speak to them through letters. I know my Thomas was always so eloquent in his letters but when you spoke to him face-to-face," she made a sound in her throat that seemed to convey her displeasure, "it was awful."

"I did not know you had been married, Trina," Hazel replied in surprise. It would be strange for her not to know. Trina had been with the family since long before she would have married. But she simply waved off the comment.

"I never was. Thomas and I were set to marry, but he was lost at sea before it could come about."

"Oh," now Hazel felt a little badly about her own melancholy state but Trina did not allow that either.

"I was quite young at the time. Who knows if it all would have worked out for us to be wed anyway. Lord knows we had barely more than two shillings between us to pay the pastor. And my father never did approve of the match. It's likely all for the best. And you'll see. Things will work out better for you as well."

"Do you think so?" Hazel asked hopefully and Trina gave her a smile.

"Aye, certainly. You just need a little time to yourself to think it over. And you'll see, things will be better between the two of you in no time." Trina seemed so sure that for the moment Hazel felt much better, sending her off with a smile and promising that she would get some sleep.

But as soon as Trina had left the room the certainty that she had instilled in Hazel seemed to flee as well. Was it really just that he was more comfortable writing to her than speaking to her in person? Certainly that couldn't account for everything, could it?

Hazel pulled the box of letters from under her bed and began to flip through them again. As she read each of them she smiled, thinking of just what they had meant to her and the things that she had learned about the man she was going to marry. Or at least, she had thought so.

With a sigh she set the last letter down in her lap and looked toward the window, lost in thought. The man she had met tonight was not at all the same as the man in the letters. There was nothing about him that seemed to say he had ever spoken to her and yet...they had spoken nearly every day in these letters.

He had seemed so attentive in his writing. Had seemed like he really cared what she had to say and really paid attention to everything she told him. But then tonight...tonight the man before her had been completely different. He had acted as though he barely knew her and like he was only just meeting her for the first time. It did not make any sense.

As she poured over the letters yet again there was a knock at the door. For a moment she wondered if Trina had returned for some reason, but it was her mother who entered the room, smiling when she saw the letters in Hazel's hand.

"Ah, my dear, tell me, what is the trouble?" She brought the chair from the dressing table and sank into it.

"Oh Mother, he did not seem anything like the man I have been writing to. There is certainly something wrong. Why, it was as if he knew nothing about me," she practically wailed.

"Hazel, you have been writing to this man for some time now, but it is quite different to write to someone and to speak to them face-to-face. Many a young man is very nervous when it comes to meeting his betrothed for the first time. Even if they have been writing for some time," her mother assured her.

"Do you think so?" It was much the same as what Trina had said, but was that really the case? Was it really just that Edgar was shy when they met in person? She herself had been a little nervous about the experience.

Her mother gave an indulgent smile and pulled Hazel close to her for a hug and Hazel felt slightly better already.

"I am sure that there is something very simple the matter. Perhaps he was very shy tonight. Perhaps he simply felt uncomfortable being around all of us and discussing things he had discussed with you in a more personal way. Perhaps he was out of sorts tonight. There are a number of perfectly reasonable explanations for what you see as strange behavior," her mother insisted.

"Yes, I am sure it must be something simple," Hazel brightened at the thought. Things did not have to be so bad as she had thought. It could all be a simple misunderstanding. And everything would be better once she and Edgar had spoken again and cleared it all up. Surely it would all be better then.

"Oh, Hazel, I am sure that he will prove to be everything you believed him to be. Just give him a little time."

"Thank you, Mother. You have made me feel much better already." She smiled, already feeling calmer.

"I am glad. Now, get some rest and you will feel better still in the morning. And I have no doubt you and Edgar will both ready to speak again then."

"Yes, it shall be just fine then," Hazel agreed. Her mother stayed only a few more minutes, helping her gather together the letters she had spread across the bed, and then rose.

"There is always an explanation for things. Certainly this is much simpler than you may fear." Hazel agreed again and her mother kissed her forehead like when she was a little girl. "Get some rest."

"Yes, Mother," Once her mother had left Hazel glanced down at the box in her hand once more and then tucked it back under the bed. Surely her mother was right. Surely there was a very simple explanation for what was going on and she and Edgar would be able to work it out in no time.

All of the nervous thoughts and fears that had been going through her head were slightly abated and she tried to push away the last vestiges of her concerns. For now, she would sleep and tomorrow she would decide what she was going to do next. It was no use worrying about it anymore, she told herself firmly.

Edgar would be able to clear it all up in no time.

# CHAPTER 14

KENDRICK PACED WORRIEDLY from one end of his room to the next. At this rate he was going to wear a path through the floor with how often he spent in this exact pattern, yet he could not help but worry.

Things had gone exactly as he had feared. He had worried that by not discussing things with Edgar before the dinner there would be a problem. He had told Edgar that they needed to talk it all over so that he knew more about Hazel. This was exactly what he had been trying to prevent by insisting that his brother read the letters.

But, if he was honest with himself, reading the letters would have only helped part of it. The true problem was that he was not his brother. And he had not written the letters the way that he should have.

He groaned and sank down into a chair, pulling out the letters that he had received from Hazel. Sure, he had pretended to be Edgar when he wrote. He had used Edgar's name and he had mentioned Edgar's travels and being away from the family. But he had not truly represented Edgar's heart when he wrote. Rather, he had written these letters as himself.

The man that Hazel was expecting to meet not only knew more about her than Edgar did, but had an entirely different personality. It was not fair to Hazel, or to Edgar. And there was a great deal he would need to do in order to remedy this situation. After all, it was his own doing.

Remembering the confusion and the lost expressions on Hazel's face when she was attempting to converse with Edgar caused a pang in his chest. Yes, Hazel had been hurt and it was his own fault. *He* had caused her that concern. *He* had caused her to question whether something was seriously wrong.

There had to be something that he could do and he told himself that he was going to figure out exactly what it was and fix things. Edgar and Hazel were betrothed, and he was going to make sure that they would come together the way that they should. He was going to make sure that his mistake in writing the letters was remedied in a way that made both of them happy.

Hazel and Edgar would do well together. Of that he was sure. But he needed to do his part first. He should have been doing that from the start. But from that first letter he had attempted to make Edgar someone he was not. Or perhaps he had simply gotten caught up in the writing himself and his own personality had shown through entirely by accident.

Whatever the case, it was beyond time that he turned it all around and began writing as Edgar would instead of as himself. But how to change his methods in a way that would do honor to Hazel and everything she thought she knew of Edgar and Edgar himself? How to change everything that he had written in a way that would not let on what had truly happened?

Kendrick dropped his head into his hands and groaned to himself. Certainly there was some way to make it all right. Some way to ensure that Hazel never found out the truth but that she also came to know Edgar better instead of Kendrick. And most definitely some way in which she would give Edgar another chance. But it would take a great deal of work. If Kendrick could even figure out what it was.

For now, he changed into his nightclothes and retired to his bed. There was nothing that could be done tonight, after all. It would be best to get some rest and look at things again in the morning. Surely it would all seem better then, wouldn't it? And perhaps after a good nights' rest he would be able to come up with a plan. It was the only thing he could think of. He did not want to be the reason that everything fell to ruin for his brother and Hazel.

In fact, in the morning he did not feel any better. He did not necessarily feel worse either, but there was certainly no improvement. Things still looked just as uncertain as they had the previous night. He wasn't quite sure what to do about the situation with Edgar and Hazel, but he knew he needed to do something.

Still, as he entered the hall for breakfast nothing had come to him yet. Hazel had looked hurt and confused, and Edgar had looked uncomfortable and nervous. How could he possibly fix that?

"Kendrick?" he glanced up in surprise, pulled from his musing by his mother's concerned voice. "Are you all right?"

"Yes, yes, I'm fine," he assured her but it was clear she didn't believe him. Luckily for him the situation with Edgar was more important to her and so she turned toward Edgar instead.

"And you? Are you all right?"

"Yes, Mother," Edgar replied, though it was clear he was also lost in thought, concern still etched on his face.

"I had thought you and Hazel were writing to each other. And that you had come to like her," their mother said.

"We were, and I did," Edgar answered, though he gazed down at the sausages on his plate.

"But it seemed as though you two hardly knew one another when you met at dinner. And you both seemed quite out of sorts about it," she hedged.

"I was nervous and I behaved improperly," was the response, though Kendrick and Edgar both knew that was not the truth. Kendrick looked up sharply toward his brother at the lie and he found that Edgar was looking right back at him. The confidence on Edgar's face was certainly not mirrored in Kendrick's as he quickly glanced back down to his plate.

"It seemed as though you were confused by the things that she said." Their mother added.

"Perhaps a bit," he admitted and Kendrick kept his gaze on his food.

"Did she not talk about those things in her letters?" Their mother was clearly trying to get to the bottom of things and both Kendrick and Edgar were hoping that she would not.

"As I said, I was quite nervous and I believe that I may have forgotten a great many things. Perhaps she did mention those things to me in her letters, but I was...not able to recall."

"It does not appear that you have made the best first impression," their mother acknowledged and Edgar simply inclined his head in response. "Your next meeting will certainly need to go better than dinner or you may find yourself with a rather unhappy future wife," she admonished gently.

"Aye, that I am sure of," Edgar agreed, continuing to pick at his own food.

"Perhaps it would be best if you were to look at your letters again so that next time you feel more comfortable, and you don't forget the things you've already been told," Fiona instructed.

"Yes, it would likely be best," he agreed, still looking down at the food on his plate.

The entire room fell silent for several long moments and then Edgar rose from the table, his plate still full with barely a bite taken from it.

"I will take my leave now. Kendrick, when you have finished perhaps you would come speak with me in the study?"

"Of course," he agreed, certain that his brother would want to talk more about the dinner the night before.

Once Edgar had left their mother turned to him, her face reflecting her concern over the issue.

"Do you know what happened? He seemed so happy about meeting her and then for the meeting to go so poorly..." she trailed off and Kendrick attempted to put on a brave face.

"Did it go so poorly as all that? There was some confusion, and perhaps it was not as spectacular as we had all thought, but it was not so terrible as you might imagine," he insisted.

"Wasn't it?" his mother seemed to latch onto the hope that perhaps she was overthinking things a little.

"It was just that you expected it to be so perfect that it seemed worse. Perhaps if we had started with more reasonable expectations it would not have seemed so," Kendrick attempted to ease her concerns, though he did not feel she was overreacting in the slightest.

"Yes, perhaps you are right." His mother seemed mollified with the explanation and Kendrick was glad. Because he himself actually did think that it had gone quite badly and was concerned about what would happen at a second meeting. If things went in a similar way there would be no way to pretend that all was well.

"Now then, I shall excuse myself and see what it is that Edgar needs," Kendrick added, though he was sure he already knew. Their mother did not, however, and she smiled at him, feeling better already.

"Perhaps you can ease his mind as you have done mine."

"I hope that I can," Kendrick told her before leaving the room. But he did not know what he could do to make Edgar feel better as he knocked at the door and was bade to enter.

It was clear that Edgar was worried. He was sitting at the desk with the ledger before him but he was not doing anything. He was not doing figures or reviewing the numbers. He was simply sitting, very still, with a stern look on his face.

"Ah, Kendrick. It is good you are here. And good it did not take you any longer or who knows where my thoughts would have taken me."

"What did you wish to talk to me about?" Kendrick asked and Edgar gave him an incredulous look.

"Surely you do not need to ask."

"I did not wish to assume," Kendrick replied, his tone still slightly formal as he struggled not to express his displeasure with his brother. Also he did not want to find himself saying anything that implied the fact that he had warned his brother of this and been proven right.

"Things at dinner went terribly. I had assumed that I knew enough to get by and that we would be able to have a good conversation without my knowing what was in the letters the two of you have written. Certainly I was wrong in that belief. I should have listened to you Kendrick. You do always have good ideas." Kendrick felt slightly better that Edgar at least realized he had made a mistake and he sank into the chair before his brother.

"What are we going to do about it now?" he asked and Edgar looked relieved that Kendrick wanted to help.

"I could tell that Hazel was very upset, and that she felt confused and that there was something very wrong. I certainly did not feel very good after seeing her in such a way. And now I feel most guilty. I am hoping that I can make it all up to her by being more knowledgeable and attentive the next time that we meet."

"I am sure that would go a long way toward making amends. I have already convinced our mother that it was nerves that caused much of the miscommunication. And that it was the fact of our expectations being too high that caused it to appear worse than it was."

"It is good you have managed to convince her of that. It is too bad that I cannot also be made to believe it," Edgar sighed. "It is my own fault for not doing what needed to be done before. So now I am going to make it right." He looked determined and Kendrick wondered just what his plan would entail.

"Did you like Hazel?" Kendrick asked him.

"Certainly. She is a lovely girl from what I noticed at dinner. She is quite beautiful and also very sophisticated and cheerful. She shall most definitely be an excellent duchess." Edgar sounded so certain as he spoke, and Kendrick knew that every bit of it was true but still...there was something off about the way it sounded. Something that felt a little bit cold and empty.

There was nothing of true affection or feeling for her. Nothing of love certainly but perhaps it was too early to expect that Edgar would say that he loved her or was falling in love with her. Still, there could have been a little interest shown. Instead, it was...rather dull. Still, what could he really expect from Edgar?

"I need to know more about her. Everything you can tell me will help me to have a better meeting with her the next time."

"Of course," Kendrick agreed, though he felt a little strange telling Edgar everything he knew about Hazel. He comforted himself by saying that everything in the letters had been meant for Edgar anyway. In fact, he should feel worse about reading the letters himself than he did about telling Edgar what they had to say. But it still did not feel that way. It felt as though he were betraying her confidence to share the personal things she had written.

He paused a moment, wrestling with his feelings and his thoughts on the matter. Was it wrong to feel this way? The confidentiality that was being breached...whose was it? Was it wrong for him to read the letters? Or was it wrong for him to share them? It seemed as though each time he thought he knew how he felt on the issue he was torn yet again.

But for now there was nothing more to think about. Even if he did not want to share, Edgar needed to know as much as possible from those letters. If he did not...things would not go well with the betrothal.

It did not matter that it felt as though Hazel was writing directly to him, looking into his very soul as he was looking into hers. The information contained in those letters had been intended for Edgar, and it was Edgar who must know what they said.

"What did the two of you talk about in your letters?" Edgar asked, finally paying attention to him.

"Hazel has been at Bath for several years now. In fact, she went when she was just past ten and has been there ever since. She does come home for all of the holidays and breaks, however and she loves spending time with her family. It's just her and her parents, the Duke and Duchess.

"The girls do have some outings while at school and she says that Bath is a lovely place. She has met several friends through her school, but Louise is her best friend. The two have been in school together all this time and have shared a room at the school. She's excited about leaving school and starting her life but she is upset about Louise and the fact that she will be so far away."

"Louise is the one she mentioned last night," Edgar interrupted.

"Yes, the two have been nearly inseparable since starting school together. They are always looking out for one another, and Louise is the first person she told about the betrothal," Kendrick continued.

"Hazel is quite smart. She doesn't say so herself but it comes through in her letters anyway. She does very well in singing and art but she loves all of her subjects and her school actually gives girls a little bit of education in all subjects, including math and sciences."

"That is good," Edgar said happily. "It is not simply a finishing school designed to produce a wife who does nothing but paint all day. It gives them more sense and a strong mind," Kendrick was glad that Edgar approved of Hazel having a mind of her own and certainly of her having a solid education.

"Aye, the school teaches them a number of things and I believe she will certainly be a source of good conversation for you as well."

"That is good. I would not want a wife who cannot at least speak a little on the subjects that are of importance to me," Edgar added.

"She is excited to be married and was quite excited to meet you as well. In her letters she talks of her happy childhood and how her parents have always seemed happy together. She wishes for a relationship that can be as happy for herself."

"I do hope to make her happy," was Edgar's promise and Kendrick nodded. Yes, he did believe that Edgar would do what he could to make Hazel happy and to be a good husband to her. But was that enough? He shook the thought from his head and continued on.

"I told her a little about your travels. That you have been gone away for a long time but you are glad to be back home among your family, though perhaps that is not as true as I claimed to be," Kendrick teased and Edgar laughed.

"I am certainly happy to be here with our Mother," he replied and Kendrick could not help but laugh.

"We had talked some about the two of us spending time together, and riding, and how you enjoy being out of doors as much as possible. I also told her about that time you spilled ink all over Father's ledger and it took him weeks to get everything sorted out," Kendrick added and Edgar looked at him in mock anger.

"*You* were the one who spilled that ink!" he replied with another laugh.

"Well, you have admitted to Hazel that it was all your fault," Kendrick retorted, though he could not help but break into a laugh that Edgar echoed.

"Ah, well, I suppose I can take the blame for it. The ledgers are all clean now, see?" he gestured toward the book in front of him and Kendrick reached toward it with an exaggerated movement toward the ink well. "Ah, on second thought do not look. I will take care of the ledgers," they both laughed again as Edgar quickly stoppered the ink and put it into the drawer, moving the ledger further away as well.

"She is very interested in hearing more of your travels," Kendrick said finally. "As she has never traveled herself. She has only read of a small number of the places that you have visited." Edgar nodded his head, listening intently, and glanced out the window.

"Perhaps telling her of some of those travels would help to appease some of what I have ruined."

"It may go a long way," Kendrick replied. "I believe that is most of what we had discussed, and any details you would be able to pick up in a conversation. I can bring you her letters as well if you would like to read them directly."

"Perhaps it would be best. I am sure you have given a good summary, but I do not wish to be caught unawares again." Kendrick agreed that it was a good idea and rose to leave the room. "What should I tell her about dinner yesterday?" Edgar asked, his nervousness finally showing through.

"Tell her you were nervous. That when you sat down to dinner with her you were so nervous that all thoughts fled your mind and you could not remember a thing. Apologize and ask her if you can begin anew. She is a sweet person. She will grant you another chance." Edgar looked relieved at that and nodded his head.

"You are an excellent brother. Despite that business with the ink well," he smiled but then his face turned serious again. "I do owe you a great deal for all of this." Kendrick simply smiled in return and shook his head.

"We are brothers. It is what we do for one another. I wish you and Hazel all the happiness." As Kendrick left the room he wondered just how things were going to go for Hazel and Edgar. Surely Hazel would give him another chance. And Edgar seemed very dedicated to doing things right this time around. He certainly wanted to make sure that he fixed his mistakes.

But if things were going to go better the next time that they met why did Kendrick feel so empty inside? Instead of feeling lighter and happy that his brother was finally going to make things right with his future wife he felt...worse. His heart felt heavy and he wondered just what all of this was going to mean for him as well.

# CHAPTER 15

WHEN TRINA KNOCKED at her door the next morning it seemed as though everything about the night before was but a bad dream. In fact, it took a moment for Hazel to even remember it. And when she did the dreadful feelings that she had experienced immediately after were gone.

She did feel somewhat disappointed, but talking with Trina as well as her mother had helped her to stave off some of those feelings. Things were not as bad as she had thought. Surely Edgar was just nervous and showed it in a way that was different from her own.

"I should like to go to town, Trina. I shall ask Mother and Father after I am ready for the day but I wish to be dressed for it."

"Of course, Miss," Trina replied, helping her to find a pretty blue dress that would do quite well for strolling through town. "How are you feeling this morning?"

"Quite a bit better. Talking with you and with Mother certainly did make me feel much more at ease. And a good night of sleep surely did a good job as well."

"That is good. I am glad you are quite all right," Trina replied.

"I am," Hazel agreed with a smile, "I am certain that you and Mother are correct and he was simply nervous about our first meeting. It is the only thing that makes sense." Her voice was firm and she found that she actually did believe it. Though maybe there was a small amount of doubt in her mind that she pushed away.

Trina gave her a smile and continued with helping her to dress. Once she had been fully buttoned into it and her hair pinned up Hazel thanked her and hurried off down the stairs. She had a plan for how she would like to spend the day and she was hopeful that her parents would approve.

"Ah, Hazel, there you are. I was just about to send Martha for you. Breakfast is ready."

"Good, I am quite hungry," It was no surprise, given that she had not eaten well at dinner the night before. Her mother gave her a smile but did not say anything about their conversation the night before. Her father likely knew nothing about it and they would both keep it that way.

"Well, we shall go in for breakfast now," her father stated, leading both of the ladies into the next room.

"I should like to go into town today to do some shopping," Hazel informed them as they sat down. Both of her parents nodded their agreement.

"Of course, be sure to take Trina along with you," her mother told her and it was Hazel's turn to nod.

"Of course,"

"Is there something special you are in need of?" Rose asked as they each began to enjoy their meals.

"I am in need of a few things. Some new drawing pencils and a new journal. And I should like to pick up a new book to read,"

"You may wish to speak with the seamstress as well," her father added. "We are expecting to host a ball to welcome you home, and of course to announce your betrothal."

"I will certainly speak with the seamstress then, Father," she smiled and he gave her an indulgent one in return.

"And before long we will need to begin the preparations for the wedding," her mother announced and Hazel found herself immediately thinking of all of the lovely things she would need for the wedding and for her married life after. She would be moving into Edgar's home, after all. Surely they had all of the necessities, but she would need a new wardrobe of her own as a married woman, and it would be expected that she bring some of her own things to the home.

Perhaps a trip into town would be good so that she could think on any of the other things she may need in her married life rather than just the things that she would like to replace now.

"I shall go immediately after breakfast if you do not mind," they both agreed that it was best to go early and so as soon as they had finished eating she went to gather her things and get Trina.

With the sun shining, it was a lovely day and Trina was just as glad to get out of the house as she was. Even better, Trina was willing to walk the short distance into town with Hazel and so she was able to truly enjoy the weather. If they purchased many things they would need to have them sent for but that was a minor inconvenience when they could enjoy the sun and the slight breeze as they strolled.

"Are you in search of anything in particular, Miss?" Hazel was just about to relay her list, and her interest in strolling through some of the shops as well, when she spotted Kendrick across the way.

"Oh! We must go and say hello," she insisted and before Trina had even realized it Hazel was moving across the street to meet with him.

Kendrick standing at a stall pouring over the many options for quills was certainly not a surprise. In fact, it was exactly what she would have expected from him and she could not help but smile before he even saw her.

A part of her recognized that it was inappropriate for her to approach him rather than waiting for him to approach her, but it was Kendrick, after all. They had been childhood friends and surely there was no need to stand on propriety when it came to childhood friends.

"My Lord," she curtsied low as he turned in surprise that quickly turned to pleasure.

"My Lady," he returned with a bow and then they both began to laugh. The overly formal greeting was certainly not usual for them and they both found it amusing. She was pleased that the smile he gave her seemed genuine, and friendly rather than stiff or polite.

"It has been too long, Kendrick. Before dinner last night I do not think I had seen you in years."

"It has definitely been a long time," he agreed. "And I was very glad to see you. I have heard bits and pieces about you and your education since you left but it is not the same as actually seeing you."

"I cannot say I have heard enough about you to satisfy my curiosity," Hazel admitted and Kendrick agreed yet again.

"Neither have I. Even with what I have been told it has not been enough. Would you care to walk with me?" Kendrick held out his arm and Hazel took it eagerly. She certainly was glad to have the opportunity to speak with her old friend again.

"What have you been doing since I have been gone?" Hazel asked finally as they began to stroll down the street with Trina falling in behind them.

"I have been doing much the same as you, I suppose," he replied and Hazel turned to him with a sparkle in her eye.

"You have also been learning to paint and stitch?"

"Ah, perhaps not exactly what you have been doing," Kendrick laughed and she found herself falling into easy banter with him. It had been years since they had spent time together but it was as if no time had passed at all. "I have been finishing my own schooling and I have been taking care of Mother. Edgar has been gone for quite a while this last time and so there was a bit of the work about the estate to handle."

"Ah, I am sure that it is nice to have him returned," There was a strange look on Kendrick's face when she mentioned Edgar and it took a moment for her to even remember that Edgar was to be her husband. How strange that only last night she had been distraught at the thought of her and Edgar not getting on perfectly and this morning she had very nearly forgotten all about him.

"It is nice. But there are some things that fall into a routine when he is not here and those have all changed again now. Mother and I tend to eat breakfast slightly earlier most mornings when it is the two of us however Edgar is generally still at his morning ride during that time so we must wait. And we have also fallen into the habit of reading together in the evenings, after tea. Often Edgar is not as keen on our readings, though he would not say anything," Kendrick admitted.

"Have you told him that he is spoiling your fun?" she teased and Kendrick laughed.

"We have not. He would probably up and leave us to travel back to Asia or some part of the world that we have not yet heard of."

"Do you miss him when he is away?" her voice was gentle and he was quiet a moment.

"I do," Kendrick replied more seriously. "My brother and I were not as close as perhaps you and I once were, but we were certainly friends, and I would like to think we still are. Much as I would like to think about yourself and me."

"I would certainly like to consider us still friends, as well," Hazel agreed and the reply seemed to please him. His smile certainly made her feel better as well.

"Ah, remember all of the times we used to get into trouble as children? Running through the manor and upsetting the staff," Kendrick smiled at the memories.

"Oh, and that time you fell down the stairs. It was just after we had been told to be careful and you had hurt yourself dreadfully, but you tried to be brave because you did not want to get in trouble again," she laughed, her entire body shaking with it.

"I did not want you to get in trouble after you pushed me down the stairs," Kendrick told her, raising an eyebrow in a faux expression of seriousness.

"I certainly did not," she retorted with mock outrage and they both began to laugh again. "It was not like the time you pushed me too hard on the swing and I fell into that mud puddle. My new dress was ruined. Mother was furious."

"You told her that you had tripped and fell outside the barn," he remembered

"I did not want you to get into trouble then," she replied, as though it were the most natural thing in the world. "Though I had to tell her that I was running because she was certain that I had tripped over tools or something that the gardener had left, and I was afraid I was going to get him in trouble instead."

"We had some wonderful times together," Kendrick looked as though he were lost in the memories and Hazel could not help but smile at them as well.

"I am sorry that I did not write to you while I was at Bath. I certainly intended to when I first left. And I must have composed the start of a dozen letters. But I could never find the right things to say, or the time to say them," she admitted.

"I should apologize at least as much. I was here all this time and yet I never wrote to you as well." The conversation between the two of them flowed easily and it was like they had never parted at all.

There was something so comfortable about being here with him. And something so sweet about the way he held her arm gently and guided her around obstacles. Also the way that he stopped so patiently when something caught her eye, and listened to everything she had to say.

"Can I ask you something?" she asked.

"Of course," he agreed instantly, but she still hesitated.

"About your brother." There was something in his eyes at that but he did not falter as he looked at her.

"There are a great many things I can tell you about Edgar," he teased but still that...something, lingered in his eyes.

"Edgar and I have been writing for some time. Ever since our mothers set the betrothal," she added.

"I had heard that," he told her.

"The letters we have shared were detailed and talked a great deal about our lives and our hopes and dreams. We talked about a great many things and it felt as though we got to know each other so well. But then at dinner it was like speaking to an entirely different person. He did not even seem to remember any of the things that we had spoken of." She looked up at Kendrick with a worried expression and saw that there was something guarded about his own.

"Edgar is generally a very quiet person," he told her. "Being open and communicating with someone new is difficult for him in person. Perhaps when he is writing it is easier for him to be that way."

"Is that all it is?" she pressed and he gave her a small smile.

"I am sure he was simply nervous at meeting you for the first time. He knew that it was an important occasion and I am sure he felt that there were a lot of expectations for the evening. It may have been more than he could handle at the time."

"That is much the same as my mother said," Hazel replied, feeling even more at ease now.

"I am sure that a next meeting between the two of you will go much better."

"I certainly hope so. I want him to be comfortable around me. And I certainly wish to converse with him the way we had before, in our letters. He is a wonderful letter writer, after all."

"Is he? He rarely wrote to Mother and I while he was away," Kendrick informed her.

"Well, he has written wonderful letters to me and I must say that I have quite fallen in love with what I have found there. Everything he has said is so beautifully written and so poetic," she trailed off with a distant smile and barely noticed that Kendrick was quiet for a long moment.

"I am sure that things will be fine the next time that you meet," he repeated. There was a bit of hesitation to his tone and Hazel wondered briefly what it could be. But there was also something about his eyes and the way that he looked away from her that said he would rather not talk about it and so she allowed it to pass.

Perhaps they would have another opportunity to speak and maybe that time he would feel more inclined to share what was troubling him.

They had stopped in front of a shop now while she looked at the brooches on display. There were several lovely ones that she knew would look great on one of her gowns.

"You have been to visit my mother recently?" she asked, as she gazed over one in particular with beautiful green stones.

"Aye, my mother and your mother visit quite frequently. At times I accompany them."

"Then you have likely been keeping an eye on our favorite spot much better than I have," she laughed.

"I have not had a chance to visit our favorite tree, however," he smiled.

"I have not either since I have been home. Will I find our box of treasures still there?" she asked.

"I am sure that you would," he replied and they both smiled brighter at the memory of the box they had buried under the tree when they were little. It had held a few things that each found special, including a hair ribbon she had loved and a book of his favorite poems. "Remember how you put that brooch in and then told your mother that you had lost it?"

"Oh, she was so mad at me. But I told her I had no idea where it was. Perhaps we should dig that box back up and I can show it to her again," Hazel laughed.

"She may well have forgotten about it by now," Kendrick told her but she shook her head.

"Oh no, she mentioned it again when I was preparing for one of the dances at school, that it would be nice if I had it."

"And you didn't tell even then?" he seemed surprised.

"We promised we'd never tell," she told him with a smile. She would not break their secret pact.

"Miss, it is getting quite late," Trina said finally and Hazel and Kendrick looked around, startled by how the sun had started to venture past midday. In fact, Hazel was also startled as she finally remembered Trina was even there. The girl had been so quiet the entire time that she had not even noticed her.

"Oh, goodness. Time has gone so quickly." Hazel glanced around her and realized that many of the shops had closed up already, and others were preparing to do so. Kendrick looked just as surprised at the revelation.

"The Duke and Duchess will be getting worried, I am sure," Trina added gently and Hazel had to agree. They would wonder where she was and it was best that she be on her way.

"It was nice to see you again, Kendrick. It was just like old times."

"But with less dirt on our clothes," Kendrick laughed and she agreed.

"I would love to catch up some more. Perhaps you could come and visit at the manor sometime soon."

"I would like that very much," Kendrick replied and bowed over her again.

"It will take us some time to walk back, Miss," Trina added and Kendrick looked surprised again.

"Did you walk all the way here?"

"We did. It is such a nice day and it seemed silly to take a carriage when we could go on foot."

"It is getting late. Please, let me escort you back home."

"That would be lovely," Hazel agreed, allowing Kendrick to take her arm and lead her back down the path. It gave them a little more time to talk as they wandered their way back, and really there could be nothing improper about it. He was the brother of the man she was betrothed to, and there was Trina after all.

It seemed like the walk home was even shorter than the walk into town, despite her being somewhat tired from all the walking that day. Talking with Kendrick made the time go quickly and she found she was still smiling when he left them at the front door of the manor, he refused to come in for tea before continuing on to his own home.

"Hazel? Is that you? Oh, goodness, I was just about to send Andrew looking for you," her mother told her. "You have been out quite a while."

"We ran into Kendrick in town and he escorted us to the shops," she replied, though they had not really walked into any of the shops after meeting up with him.

"Well, that is nice. It has been some time since the two of you have spoken, has it not?" Her mother seemed pleased that she had a chance to meet with a friend.

"It has," Hazel agreed. "It was wonderful to see him and to have an opportunity to talk again."

"I am glad you had a good time." Her mother smiled and let her know that dinner would be served soon. Hazel and Trina hurried upstairs so she could freshen up before she was called back down but all she could think about was Kendrick and the afternoon they had had.

# CHAPTER 16

"How was your trip into town?" her mother asked as Hazel sat down to dinner with the family.

"It was very nice," Hazel replied, taking a look at the roast chicken and vegetables before her. "I mentioned that I saw Kendrick there. We had a chance to talk as we walked through town."

"Did you see Edgar there?" her father asked and Hazel shook her head.

"No, Kendrick was alone." She turned back toward her mother. "We were able to talk about a number of things."

"Oh? Like what?" her mother seemed genuinely interested so Hazel told her about their conversation and how they talked about their memories from childhood.

"I was happy to have a chance to speak with him. It has been so long since we talked last."

"You have not spoken since you started at school, have you?" her mother asked.

"I believe I saw him in passing once, but not long enough to actually speak to one another."

"When you and Edgar are married you will see Kendrick quite often," her mother observed and Hazel was startled slightly by the thought of it. Something about it just seemed strange but she smiled and nodded anyway.

"We spoke about Edgar," she admitted.

"Did you? And what did he have to say?"

"I asked about his strange behavior. He said that Edgar was

simply nervous and that there was a lot of pressure about us meeting."

"It is just as I said," her mother replied, obviously relieved. "The poor boy has only just returned from another country and to find out that he is set to be married is likely quite a bit for him. And then to meet you for the first time...I am sure he was quite nervous."

"I am glad that is all that it was," Hazel agreed. "I was very nervous myself that there was something more to it." As the conversation turned to other things Hazel found herself still thinking about meeting Kendrick and everything that they had talked about. It was a truly wonderful time and she could not help but smile thinking of it.

Later, when she was back in her own room trying to fall asleep she continued to think of it. Kendrick had been so kind and attentive the entire time they were together. He seemed to remember everything about their childhood and he certainly still knew how to make her laugh.

In fact, there had been no tension and no awkwardness. They had simply picked up where they had left off all those years ago. At least, that's the way it had seemed. It had always been like that between them. From the time they were young they had always gotten along so well.

But of course, now was the time she should be thinking about Edgar. She should be making plans for their future, or at least daydreaming about what it would entail. But instead she barely even thought about Edgar. Her mind was completely filled with Kendrick.

As she drifted off, she wondered if Kendrick really would come over so they could dig up their treasure from the front yard.

As soon as Kendrick left Hazel and her maid at the door to the manor he began to wonder about their conversation and their time together. Was it strange that they had remained together, talking, for so long?

"Kendrick, you have made it home in time for dinner. We weren't sure," Edgar teased leading him toward the dining hall. "It was just announced that the meal is ready for us. Come then. You can tell us where you have been all day."

"Oh, Kendrick, you have made it home. I was starting to worry," their mother added as she saw the two boys enter the room. "You have been gone so long."

"I am sorry to worry you. I was only in town."

"All day?" she seemed surprised and he had to acknowledge it was odd for him to stay away all day. Usually he spent as little time in town as he could, simply fetching what he needed and heading back home again.

"I met with Hazel while in town."

"Oh? And how was it meeting with her?" she asked.

"She is the same Hazel as always," he laughed.

"What did you speak of?"

"A number of things," he replied. "Of our memories mostly. A little of our lives since."

"I am sure it was nice to have a chance to converse," his mother smiled.

"It was. I certainly have missed the opportunity to speak with her," Kendrick admitted. "I told her also that Edgar was certainly interested in meeting with her again and that he had been nervous at dinner."

"I thank you for that," Edgar interjected and Kendrick gave him a smile.

"She is anxious to see you again and remedy that previous experience."

"Good, that is good. I will call on her soon," Edgar promised and their mother gave him an approving smile.

"Certainly you did not speak about that all day. What else did the two of you talk about?" his mother asked and he could not help but smile.

"A great many things. As I said, Hazel is the same girl she always was, only older. It was the same talking to her today as it was talking to her so many years ago when we were young children." He could not help but smile at the thought, his voice soft as he remembered the encounter.

"It is wonderful that you were able to have such a nice talk," his mother added and Kendrick smiled in response, but in actuality he felt a bit guilty and uncertain. Was it really so wonderful? Was it even appropriate for them to speak in such a way? Even more, was it appropriate for him to feel the way that he did about her company and being around her at all?

Hazel was soon to become his sister-in-law. She was currently betrothed to his brother. Could he, in good conscience, continue to have conversations with her the way that he had? He wasn't sure and the wondering was certainly weighing on him.

As he spoke to his mother and brother about his day with Hazel, however, he realized that Edgar did not seem to mind in the least.

This, at least, appeased him slightly. If Edgar was not upset then surely it could not have been too bad of a situation, right? Surely there could be nothing inappropriate if Edgar was all right with it?

Kendrick was not so sure. Especially when he truly began to examine his feelings about the day and realized that his feelings for Hazel just might not be the sisterly ones that they should be. The way he felt about her and the day they had shared...it felt like something different. In fact, he worried that he was attracted to her in a way that he wanted her for himself.

"Did you only just part from Hazel before dinner?" their mother asked.

"Yes, she and her maid had walked into town and I walked them back to the manor before coming here," he acknowledged.

"That is good. It is getting quite late," Edgar replied and it made Kendrick feel even worse that his brother was unconcerned about his walking Hazel home.

"I believe I shall retire early," Kendrick said rather suddenly and they both looked startled.

"Are you all right?"

"I feel a bit weary. Perhaps it is too much walking today," he replied, not looking at either of them. Both expressed concern but then allowed him to leave the table and hurry back to his own rooms where he readied for bed.

Yes, something was certainly off about all of this. He wasn't sure how he felt about Hazel and about Edgar, and most definitely he wasn't sure how he felt about the two of them together. The feelings that were starting to come up were certainly strong and he worried that it could mean problems ahead.

As he tried to settle into bed he found his mind racing, pulling his thoughts in a million different directions. And as much as he tried to quiet it and fall asleep there was just nothing he could do.

With a sigh, Kendrick rose from bed again, sitting at his desk to write. Thoughts and words began to spill out of his mind and onto the paper before him, which at least allowed him to get them out. And maybe just getting them out would be enough to make them go away, but he was not sure.

The words flowed from his pen as though they had a mind of their own. Detailing the beauty of the young woman that she had become and the intelligence that shone behind her eyes and in her smile. The poem was one of the best he had written, and for that he was proud. But the fact that it was about Hazel certainly did not help matters. He was certain that this was not appropriate with the woman who was to marry his brother. But there was nothing to be done about it. The words would come out entirely unbidden.

And, finally he felt that he might be able to sleep. As he read over the words one last time and set the diary away he took a deep breath and returned to his bed. Yes, now he might be able to sleep, though it was a guilty feeling that came over him even now, as he struggled to forget the words he had just written.

Hazel was the only thing on his mind as he finally managed to drift off.

# CHAPTER 17

*THE SEAMSTRESS BUSTLED about her with a mouthful of pins, tucking one here and another there. Lifting the skirts on the beautiful gown to just the right length and slipping yet another pin in. Then a slight tuck at her waist and another pin.*

*By the time she was done the dress looked perfect. Of course, the pins sticking around were still apparent, but it was clear what the dress would look like when it was done. And each tuck and line was simply gorgeous.*

*Hazel sighed happily and her mother smiled in response. The gown would be everything she had ever dreamed of and so much more.*

Sunlight streaming through the window woke Hazel from pleasant dreams of dress fittings for her wedding, and selecting the perfect flowers to adorn the staircase.

But of course, she needed to ensure that her future husband was actually interested in the wedding before she started planning, she reminded herself as she woke. She sighed slightly and forced herself to climb out from under the warm covers.

As she paced back and forth across the room she wondered just what she should do. Kendrick, her mother, and Trina had all said that Edgar was likely just nervous. They had convinced her thoroughly the day before, but was that really it? Even if that was the case should she not say something?

There was a light knock at the door and Trina entered, seemingly surprised to see her up and walking about the room.

"Are you in need of anything, Miss?"

"No, not right now, Trina. I think I should like to be left alone."

Trina hesitated and then spoke up again from the doorway.

"Are you quite all right? You look very worried, Miss," Hazel sighed and acknowledged that she was. In fact, her image in the mirror seemed to also reflect that fact. The furrowed brow and the grim line of her lips making her appear quite worn out.

Even the brightness of her eyes and the soft wave of her hair, which had decided to lay properly for once, could not bring a smile to her face. Rather, she felt out of sorts.

"I should like to speak with Edgar, but there is no way to do so. I cannot simply visit him out of the blue. We may be betrothed but what would people say about such a thing?"

"Perhaps you could write to him," Trina replied instead and Hazel brightened immediately. Of course. Why had she not thought of writing him? Writing was how they had gotten to know one another in the first place, after all. Why should she not write to him now to find out more about just what was going on?

"That is excellent, Trina, thank you. I shall get to it immediately."

"Would you like assistance in getting dressed, Miss?"

"Oh-" she started to wave Trina off when another maid entered the room, curtseying low.

"Miss, the Countess is here to see you." Hazel's eyes widened and she rose quickly, Trina hurrying to select a gown from her wardrobe and get her into it.

"If the Countess is here, perhaps Edgar is with her. Then I would not need to write a letter,"

"Perhaps, Miss, but either way we had better get you prepared as quickly as possible." Hazel definitely agreed, though she found it difficult to concentrate on getting dressed when she was worried about whether or not Edgar was there to see her. Maybe they could clear everything up now.

"Not that dress, Trina," she called out as Trina took a light pink one from the wardrobe. "The blue will do nicely."

"The blue is at the seamstress, Miss. Remember, it needed to be let down."

"Ah, well then, the green," she replied and Trina brought the dress to her quickly. So quickly, in fact, that she very nearly knocked a bottle of ink from the table right onto it. Instead, the ink splattered behind, causing a large stain to spread across the hem of Trina's skirt. "Oh, no!"

"It is no matter, Miss. This gown has washed up well with far worse." Trina brushed off her concern and simply set to work tugging the nightclothes over Hazel's head. "Oh, goodness, this is stuck today."

It was stuck. And the reason seemed to be that the buttons had captured a large portion of Hazel's hair as each tug felt like it was pulling her hair out. She gave a somewhat muffled shriek as Trina finally succeeded in tugging the dress over her head, pulling her hair quite soundly in the process.

"I am sorry, Miss," she replied, though she very quickly returned to all business, tucking the nightclothes away and pulling the new gown over Hazel's head. She had her buttoned into it in no time, though buttoning up her shoes proved to be another matter entirely, and set to work on her hair.

"It's all over tangles today," Hazel groaned as the brush tugged its way through yet another knot in her hair.

"Perhaps you have been tossing and turning quite a bit," Trina replied and Hazel had to agree if her hair was any indication.

"Oh, do not worry so much about it. Just hurry. The countess is waiting."

"I do not wish to take it all from your head," Trina replied and Hazel huffed out a sigh as the girl increased her speed incrementally.

"Are you finished yet?"

"I suppose I can tuck it up now. But it does need some more brushing, Miss."

"We have to hurry," Hazel replied immediately and Trina carefully began to tuck the curls up with pins.

"There. It shall do. But only do not move too much, Miss. It is rather precarious."

"It shall be fine," was Hazel's response as she glanced in the mirror. The updo was not as good as Trina would normally do, but it was acceptable. Especially for such late notice.

Once she was ready, she hurried out of the room and down the hall. The maid had said that the Countess was in the gardens and so she rushed out of the house, slowing as she reached the gardens so she would not appear out of breath before the Countess.

It was a good thing too, because her mother was sitting there beside the Countess, but Edgar was not. Luckily for Hazel she walked up at a time when both were absorbed in their own conversation and she had time to school her features out of their disappointment.

"Ah, Hazel, there you are," her mother interjected suddenly, looking up at her. "I wondered when you would arrive."

"I had a late start this morning," Hazel admitted, though she did not say that she had still been in her nightclothes when the maid arrived for her.

"After all that time at school I am sure you are enjoying a little time to rest," Fiona replied with a smile and a twinkle in her eye that said she was not upset to be kept waiting. Hazel was relieved though not surprised, since the two older women had clearly been enjoying their conversation before she arrived.

For now she took a seat at their table and returned the smile.

"Aye, perhaps I am enjoying it a little too much," she agreed. There was a laugh from both the women and Hazel smiled at them both again. They always did look lovely and today was no exception.

Her mother always had her hair pulled back into a beautiful knot on the back of her head, with a simple diadem around her forehead. When Hazel was young she had always asked her hand-maiden to tie a ribbon around her own head to look like her mother.

The beautiful diadem was the same one she had always worn, and Hazel knew it meant a lot to her because it had belonged to Rose's own mother many years before. Not that Hazel could remember her grandmother who had died when she was quite young.

Fiona coughing slightly as her laughter continued pulled Hazel from her memories and she looked over at the other women.

Fiona always looked very nice as well, though her style was somewhat different from Rose. Instead of a diadem she often wore her hair unadorned, opting instead for a few curls to accent her face and fit in with the style of the ton. She said she did not want to appear too matronly, especially since she said she was not that old yet anyway, always with a laugh.

Today both wore soft pink dresses. It happened quite often that they selected the same color of dress without realizing it and they had come to consider it quite a lark. But of course, the styles were slightly different as Rose opted for brighter accents in the form of lace and baubles.

Fiona, on the other hand, opted for ribbons and bows scattered across the bodice and the full skirt of her gown. But Hazel had always loved the style of both women and had modeled her own style after a combination of the two.

"Kendrick tells me that he ran into you in town yesterday. Did you enjoy your talk?" It took Hazel a moment to realize that Fiona was talking to her and she tried to quickly join back in the conversation.

"I did indeed," Hazel replied. "It was just like old times talking with Kendrick again. I felt quite at ease with him."

"Oh, I remember how well you two got on when you were

younger. Always running about the gardens and getting into mischief." This time it was Rose's eyes that sparkled as she laughed at the memory.

"I certainly remember that as well. All the times they would come back to the house with torn clothes or dirty, oh so dirty. Talking about fairies in the glen and crocodiles in the pond."

"The first time they came running back to tell me about crocodiles in the pond I very nearly fainted!" Rose laughed. "I sent poor Robert, our groom at the time, to go and take care of it. He stalked out that pond for hours before I got the whole bit out of them that it was a story they'd made up for their games." Hazel remembered it as well, and how they had never realized that saying there was a crocodile in the pond would cause an uproar.

"Ah, you two were the best of friends. Thick as thieves, you were," Fiona agreed. "It was so nice seeing the two of you together, getting along so well. If only you could have helped each other to behave a little better though," there was a gentle admonishment there, though she did not seem too grieved by it. "But my! Did you have fun."

"It was fun. And I certainly missed that as we grew older and drifted apart," Hazel acknowledged.

"Yes, it was sad to see the way the two of you stopped spending so much time together. But seeing you as a young lady is certainly wonderful on its own," Fiona stated, giving her an approving glance. Rose looked proud, a pleasant smile on her own face. Hazel blushed slightly and managed to articulate her thanks only because of the training she had received.

As the two older women fell to discussing some of their other memories from so long ago Hazel found herself caught up in her own. But hers were memories of herself and Kendrick as they played together. Those were some of the best memories of her childhood. When they would run and play in ways that she had long been unable to do.

But also the times when she had been sick and Kendrick had come to keep her company. For every time they had raced from the gardens to the pond there were also memories of times that she had sat wrapped in blankets by the fire while Kendrick sat in a nearby chair and read to her.

The large tomes he selected from the library were never ones she would have chosen, but he always made them come alive and would often have her feeling better in no time. In fact, his reading often made her feel better than anything that Cook would make or the warm fire that the servants made for her.

"Hazel?" It took a moment for her to realize that anyone was talking to her and then she blushed a little more furiously when she noticed that she had been asked a question that she did not hear.

"Off in your own head, are you Dear?" her mother asked and she managed a nod. "Well, it is nice to see you so happy anyway."

"Oh to be so young again," Fiona replied. "To have such happy thoughts just sweep you away like that."

The conversation quickly turned back away from her and for that Hazel was glad, though she paid much closer attention to it going forward so she would not miss anything more.

When Fiona left Hazel finished her tea with her mother and then excused herself back to her own rooms. It had been two days since she had seen Edgar and there had been nothing from him in the way of communication. So it would fall to her to write and she was determined to do it directly.

*Edgar,*

*It has been two days since our dinner and I feel the need to write to you today to express the thoughts I was not able to express that evening.*

*I must say that I was quite disappointed in our interactions that night. However, I have had some time to think on it and I wanted to speak with you before I put too much stock into anything.*

*I very much enjoyed our letters and getting to know you. And I felt that you were getting to know me as well. The letters and communication we shared that way were very important to me while I was in Bath.*

*I wish to understand better what happened between those last letters and our dinner the night before last. Was it perhaps me that was not to your liking? Or was there some other reason for your behavior that evening?*

*I do hope that we can meet again soon and work things out. I am sure there must have been some sort of misunderstanding to cause such trouble. At least, I hope that it was only a misunderstanding.*

*Please do reply soon and help clear up this situation. I shall be awaiting your letter, or better yet waiting to see you in person,*

*Sincerely,*

*Hazel.*

With that she sealed the letter and delivered it to the butler to post immediately. There was nothing more that she could do now. She had put it all into Edgar's hands.

# CHAPTER 18

He glanced up at the window and sighed. The sun was shining in and he tried to feel happy and excited about it, but he was drawn back to the page before him. It had started out easy, but now he was struggling with the next words.

Kendrick also found himself struggling with the fact that the words already on the page were about *her*. Hazel. Yet again he found that the poems that filled the pages of his book were all about her sweet smile, her long red hair, her smart mind...it was all he could seem to think about lately.

Of course, each time a thought of her entered his head he found himself feeling even more guilty. He had come to realize that she was everything he could possibly ever want. But she was not meant for him. And every thought of her was a betrayal of his brother.

Another sigh escaped him as he leaned on his elbows and stared out at the trees. He had tried writing a poem about the breeze blowing through the branches of the maple outside his window. The fruits of that labor were on the next page and he cringed slightly as he looked at them. It was a very rough attempt. He was rarely embarrassed about a poem he had written but that one...well it certainly wasn't something he was happy with.

"Kendrick-" He jumped at the click of the door opening. Quickly, he flipped the book before him closed so Edgar would not see what he had been working on, trying not to appear guilty as he turned around.

"What is it?" Something appeared to be wrong, judging from the concern on Edgar's face and Kendrick found himself immediately thinking of their mother. "Is everything all right? Is Mother all right?"

"What? Oh, yes," Edgar replied, momentary confusion flashing across his face before he shook it away. "It is this." He held out a letter to Kendrick.

Kendrick released a breath, glad that there was nothing desperately wrong. They did not have any distant family to concern themselves with. Therefore the letter could not bear any ill news.

Rather, it was another letter from Hazel and he hesitated before he began to read. It was clear from this letter that Hazel was still concerned about what had happened at dinner. And she wanted an explanation. In fact, she quite demanded it without outright saying so.

"It is not so bad as you may think," Kendrick finally replied, looking up at Edgar's relieved, though slightly guarded, face.

"You do not think so?"

"She is concerned that you do not approve of her. And she wishes to know what happened. But I have spoken to her, and I know that her mother has as well. We have all told her that you were simply nervous and that time will make things better for the both of you."

"Perhaps you are right."

"I know I am, I always am," Kendrick continued with a smile, in an attempt to lighten the mood. Edgar gave a weak smile but then returned his gaze to the letter.

"What should I do?"

"You should respond to her," he replied. "You can't ignore it like nothing has happened. She does deserve an explanation."

"Could you do it for me? You could write a much better letter than I and a good apology," Edgar attempted but Kendrick shook his head.

"Oh, no. I have done enough writing to Hazel on your behalf. I shall not do it again," Kendrick insisted.

"You are much better at it than I am. You know that I am truly sorry. It would not be a lie to tell her so," Edgar continued to wheedle, but Kendrick shook his head yet again.

"It would be if I were the one to say it. You are the one who needs to write to her this time. I feel badly enough for everything that I have already done."

"But you are a better writer than I am. I would be very grateful if you could help me."

"Edgar, it is you who needs to apologize to her for not paying attention. It is not me who needs to do this," Kendrick replied. He felt bad not helping his brother, but he would feel worse writing the letter.

"It would be best-" Edgar began and the door opened again. This time it was the both of them who turned guiltily to the door, though Edgar managed to school his features better than Kendrick.

"What is going on in here?" Their mother's voice was light and playful, the hint of a smile and a twinkle in her eye as though she had caught them at something. Though of course she could not know what she had caught them at.

"It is nothing," Edgar replied quickly. "Just silly things between brothers,"

"It is so nice to see my boys together again," she replied, "and getting along so well."

"We have always gotten along well," Kendrick managed, hiding his discomfort slightly. The fact that Edgar could not say anymore about him writing to Hazel now that their mother had arrived made him feel more at ease.

"Ah, you have mostly gotten on well, but I remember a time or two that you did not," she laughed at the memory. "The time that Kendrick managed to break your favorite saddle comes to mind," she said with a look toward Edgar. "Or perhaps the time that Edgar hid your poetry books."

"I do remember that. I'm still not entirely sure you gave them all back," Kendrick added with a mock glare to his brother.

"You will never know, will you?" Edgar teased and they all fell to laughing, at the memories.

"Where have you been to?" Kendrick finally asked, seeing the bright smile on their mother's face.

"I was just at Deighton Manor, visiting Hazel and her mother."

"Why did you not inform me that you were going? I could have gone with you," Edgar asked, and she shook her head.

"I wanted to see her alone," their mother replied. "I wanted to judge how things are going for myself and see how she felt about everything."

"And? How did she seem?" Edgar asked the question but Kendrick found himself leaning forward, wanting to know the answer.

"She seemed very well. And she looked quite beautiful this morning." Kendrick could believe it. She had looked very beautiful the day before as well, when he had seen her walking through town. Her beautiful red hair done up, her lovely dress complementing her bright eyes...He stopped those thoughts in their tracks, mentally shaking himself out of that reverie.

Hazel was Edgar's betrothed and that was all she would ever be. They could perhaps become friends again when she had come to live with them after the wedding, but that was all he should be thinking of her as.

"I have some things to take care of," Edgar finally stated, standing "Kendrick, if you could assist me?"

"Of course," he stood and followed his brother out of the room, leaving their mother to her own devices.

"I need your assistance, Kendrick. I cannot do this on my own," Edgar pleaded and finally Kendrick agreed. It was true that Edgar would have difficulty if he attempted to do it alone. And Kendrick really did want things to work out.

"Very well, but you will have to be part of this as well. We will make a plan for what to do." The two headed off toward the study, both thinking hard about what to do next.

As Kendrick sank down at the desk he thought he had an idea of something that would work. Of course, it would depend on Edgar as well, but he was certain that Edgar would do whatever was necessary to make sure everything was successful.

*Hazel,*

*I know that I have disappointed you in my behavior at dinner upon our first meeting. I was myself disappointed, though not at all with you.*

*You were exactly what I had thought you would be and so much more. You were lovely and kind and I was disappointed only in myself for my behavior.*

*I had wanted our first meeting to go so well and had been anticipating so much more. Yet upon arriving and seeing you at dinner I found myself overwhelmed and devolved into the strange behavior that you witnessed.*

*Everything that we had ever said seemed to leave my head as soon as I saw you. And everything that I wanted to say fell away.*

*There is no good excuse for the way in which I behaved, but I would like to hope that you will give me a second chance. And that you will understand that there was nothing about you that upset me in any way.*

*I hope that you will agree to meet with me, tonight. I will come to your window at midnight and I ask that you wait for me there.*

*It is best that we are able to speak in private, away from all of the others who would wish us well but may continue to overwhelm our meetings.*

*Yours,*

*Edgar*

Kendrick finished the letter, read it over once more, and pushed it over to Edgar. Upon reading it through Edgar looked a little concerned, as though he was not quite certain he was ready for such a big gesture. After all, meeting at midnight was certainly not something he had expected, Kendrick was sure. Still, he nodded his head in agreement.

"You will come with me, won't you?" Kendrick hesitated a moment but then nodded. It would be best if he did. At least that way he could help him know what to say to actually make things better.

"I will send this. Make sure that you are ready tonight. The betrothal will go on either way, but making Hazel happy is still important. You want your future wife to be glad for the match."

"I do," Edgar agreed. "And I will do what I can to make things right." Kendrick left the room to post the letter and returned to his own room.

It did not feel like this was the right thing to do. Writing that last letter did not seem like it was something he should have done. And going with Edgar tonight to talk to Hazel...that did not seem right either. But at the same time he knew that this was the only way that things would be fixed. It was the only way to make sure that Edgar said the right things and made Hazel feel better about the match.

With a sigh, he tried to mentally prepare himself for just what might happen that evening. It was going to be a long night, but with any luck things would be a great deal better after and the betrothal and wedding would certainly be more successful in the long run.

# CHAPTER 19

"My Lord, dinner is ready," he looked up in surprise at the voice. He hadn't heard anyone come in. And in fact, he hadn't realized it was so late. He was certain he'd only been in his room for a few minutes since leaving Edgar. But the sun sinking lower revealed that was not the case.

"I will be down directly," he replied and Andrew bowed and left the room. Kendrick turned back toward the book before him but the words escaped him now. With a sigh he set the pen down and closed the book, putting it away in the drawer before he stood and washed to go down for dinner.

Once he felt sufficiently ready he made his way down the stairs and into the dining hall. Fiona sat in her customary seat near the head of the table. Though she had taken over as head of the household when his father passed she had remained in her same seat at what would have been his left side.

Edgar had also silently accepted that they would continue to honor their father, continuing to use his own seat to the right of their father's side whenever he joined them for a meal. Kendrick sank slowly into his own to the left of his brother's customary place, wondering idly if he would be expected to sit at their mother's side or move down when Hazel joined their household.

"Ah, Kendrick, have you seen your brother?"

"When last I left him he was still working on business," Kendrick replied but he had barely gotten the words out when Edgar hurried into the room, just as the servants began bringing in the food.

"Sorry that I am late. I had just about finished some of the accounting." Their mother simply smiled and they all fell to eating with relish. Everything that Cook made was good, but her roast duck was one of the best things she ever made, and they were not about to waste a bit of it.

It was still quite early in the evening and Kendrick found himself wondering what he would do to fill the time until he and Edgar were to go and meet Hazel. He also wondered just what he was going to tell Edgar to say to Hazel when they arrived.

It was one thing writing out the letters. At least then he had time to think about what he was going to say and to change it if he deemed it necessary. In person he would have no second chance to change his mind once the words were out. And he had to hope that Edgar was able to convey the same sort of feeling that Kendrick himself had.

The room was actually very quiet, with each of them seemingly lost in their own thoughts. In fact, it was so silent that Kendrick feared even clanking his utensils too hard against the plate for it would break the stillness.

"Have you been alone all this time, Kendrick?" his mother asked, and Kendrick was pulled from his reverie rather abruptly.

"Aye, I was working on some poetry," he admitted.

"I should very much like to hear it," she replied and he only gave her a small smile but did not comment. He could never read poetry about Hazel to his mother. Even if he did not say who it was about it was clearly about someone and his mother would likely piece it all together.

"And what have you done to occupy your time today, Mother?" he asked instead.

"Oh, I spent the afternoon on some embroidery," she informed them, accepting the change of subject with no comment. Kendrick tried to act as though he were interested as their mother discussed the project she was working on, which was a gift for Hazel and Edgar for their wedding. But his mind was filled with other things.

What he and Edgar were to do this evening was certainly weighing on him. He wasn't sure why he felt so overwhelmed and so nervous. In fact, he was rather uneasy about the entire thing as though it were for him rather than Edgar.

Every time he thought of Edgar and Hazel being together, of their betrothal, he got the same sort of feeling in his stomach. There was a feeling of concern that he could not shake.

No matter how happy he wanted to be it seemed like all he could do was manage a smile when his brother looked his way, or an encouraging nod. But he couldn't bring himself to be actually happy for his brother. There was this...feeling, instead. A feeling that felt both beautiful and awful at the same time. For how could love feel anything but beautiful? And how could the thought of that love being for his brother's future wife be anything but awful?

"Shall you go to visit the duchess tomorrow again?" Edgar asked.

"Oh, I am sure there are some additional things that we will need to discuss. The wedding needs planning, after all." She was smiling that bright smile again and both boys could only return it, though each was nervous for their own reasons.

"The wedding shall take place soon?" Kendrick asked by way of filling in the silence.

"Goodness, yes. Fiona would like the wedding to take place as soon as possible. But of course, there's only so fast we can go and handle everything that needs doing." Hearing that the wedding was going to be coming up quick made Kendrick feel worse.

Whatever was happening in his stomach simply would not go away and he struggled to eat at least a bit more of his dinner. If he didn't then his mother was sure to be concerned. He would have a hard time explaining just what was wrong with him, especially when he didn't really know himself.

"If you don't mind, I shall excuse myself now," Edgar said finally, rising from the table. Kendrick quickly mumbled an excuse and followed him out. He felt bad for leaving their mother alone again, but he did not want to sit with her in that room and fight to keep his mouth shut about what they were going to do.

The longer he had to wait the more he wondered if it had been a good idea to make this plan in the first place. Maybe he had been wrong about this. Maybe a nice letter explaining his nervousness, or rather Edgar's nervousness, would have been better.

But it was too late now. The letter had been sent and there was no way to take it back.

"How shall we get to the estate?" Edgar asked as they reached the study.

"We shall have to ride. Mother always goes to bed at the same time. It should be easy enough to get downstairs and to the horses without her noticing. And once she is asleep she will not hear a thing."

"Good. That is good," Edgar replied, though he sounded distracted. "Are you sure this is the best way?"

"It is," Kendrick replied, with a great deal more confidence than he felt. It seemed to reassure Edgar however, as he gave a firm nod and pretended to go back to reviewing the ledgers and making notes.

Kendrick, however, found himself pacing the room, glancing over the shelves on the bookcase behind his brother. Occasionally he would stop and glance out the window then resume his pacing. Once he stopped and opened one of the books he found but he could not concentrate enough to read it.

"Why do I feel as though you are more nervous than I am?" Edgar asked finally.

"Perhaps because it is you who is counting on me," Kendrick replied and Edgar acknowledged the point.

"Aye. I know that you will help me through this. And that you will certainly not lead me astray." Kendrick would never *intentionally* lead his brother astray, but he worried that whatever he might choose to say would be wrong anyway.

"I will do my best," Kendrick promised, trying not to let his fear and anxiety creep into his voice.

"Of course," Edgar agreed nonchalantly. At least one of them seemed confident in Kendrick's abilities, he thought, still trying to decide exactly what they would do when they arrived. He needed to be prepared for what to say. But what did you say in a situation like this? How could he fix things for Edgar?

As the time slowly ticked by he found himself growing more and more restless, but of course, he could not show that to Edgar. Not when Edgar was counting on him and felt so unconcerned.

"You must be prepared," Kendrick finally told him and Edgar looked to him. This time he looked like he was actually listening and Kendrick took a breath. "There is much you can say to her, but it is best you know it beforehand."

"But you will be there," Edgar returned, nervously and Kendrick nodded.

"I will, in case you need anything. But if you know what to say it will be best."

"Very well," Edgar agreed and Kendrick paused a moment to think.

"It is good to tell her that she looks beautiful. She no doubt will be beautiful. She always is." A nod from Edgar and he continued. "You must apologize for what happened at dinner. She will be expecting an apology, even after the one that was written to her."

"What do I say?"

"Say that you are sorry for what happened. Tell her that you were very nervous. That seeing her for the first time made you so nervous you did not know what to say and you could not seem to remember anything at all." Edgar nodded again and Kendrick bit back a sigh.

He would much rather not go tonight at all. But Edgar might need him. And a part of him wanted to see Hazel anyway. And so he selfishly kept his mouth shut and continued to plan for himself to go as well.

"It is time," Edgar finally said, and Kendrick gave a short nod. He did not think his voice would hold up at this point. He was far too anxious and wanted to save whatever logical portion of his mind still remained for what they would do when they arrived at Deighton Manor.

This was a crazy idea and he wondered why he had ever thought of it. But once again he told himself that it was too late now to change anything. She would be waiting for them.

So the ride to Deighton Manor was quiet as both of the boys were lost in their own thoughts. But for Edgar it seemed a relatively peaceful ride and his thoughts appeared to be light in spirit. At least if his expression was any indication. Kendrick felt torn as to what he was doing, what he would say, and whether it was truly the right thing for him to be here at all.

The ride, for him, was tortuous as his mind continued to turn and his thoughts continued to be a jumbled mess. For a moment he would think that this was the right thing. Then he would think that it was most certainly wrong. Then he would wonder how beautiful Hazel would look tonight, and the next moment would scold himself for even thinking such a thing.

Once they arrived, they were met with the gates, which were of course closed for the evening, but Kendrick knew the best way in, so they tied off the horses and climbed over, near the side of the estate where there were few windows looking out.

"Do you know which window is hers?" Edgar asked and Kendrick nodded, still wordlessly, and led him around further toward the side of the house.

Hazel's room overlooked the gardens to the east of the house, with a lovely little balcony that had flowers and ivy growing on it. She had pointed it out to him once when they were children and he had never forgotten.

From there, he pointed Edgar to stand in the moonlight beneath the balcony, where she could surely see him if she looked out.

Edgar was able to walk straight toward the balcony, though of course avoiding the large window that Kendrick believed went into the kitchens. No one should be up at this time of night, but it was best to avoid sight as much as possible.

Kendrick, on the other hand, had to creep around even the small pool of light that spilled out of the house from candles in a few of the windows. Keeping to the trees he managed to skirt the circle of clear space where Edgar stood and into the bushes alongside the house.

It would not do for Hazel or anyone else to spot him and spoil the plan.

"Can you hear me?" he asked quietly and Edgar nodded. That was good. But Hazel should not be able to hear him from here. He was quite confident of that. Now all they had to do was wait.

Luckily, the wait was not long because even Edgar seemed as though he was starting to get anxious at this point. He was shifting his weight from one foot to the other, glancing around him then back up to the window every moment or two.

Kendrick tried to find a comfortable way to sit in the bushes where he could not be seen, and finally managed to figure out a way he could lean against the back wall when he heard the balcony door open.

It was only a faint creak and the only reason he even heard it was because there was utter silence otherwise, but both he and Edgar quickly turned toward the sound.

Hazel stepped onto the balcony and was lit slightly from behind by the light in her room. That first glimpse of her was enough to freeze him in his tracks a moment before he could even think to speak.

The green of her gown was a perfect look, and he wondered idly what she had told her maid about not wanting to ready for bed several hours previous.

Her eyes were bright but wary as she stood in the light, and Kendrick could see that she gripped the railing a little more tightly than necessary.

"Are you there?" Her voice was soft and a little uncertain and Edgar stepped forward more fully.

"I am," he replied. Her face broke into a polite smile at that, though the uncertainty remained.

"Tell her she looks beautiful," Kendrick instructed and Edgar quickly repeated his words.

"You look beautiful tonight," the smile on her face became broader at that and Kendrick could almost see the slight blush that he was sure lit her face.

"I thank you. You are quite handsome as well," she replied.

There was silence for a long moment then as Edgar opened and closed his mouth several times. He began to speak, though he faltered before it was even clear what he had been trying to say.

Hazel's brow furrowed as though she were confused, and perhaps not quite sure if she should remain on her balcony or retreat back to her own room.

For his part, Edgar looked as though he wished retreating to his own room were an option and Kendrick knew he had to step in.

"I tried so many times to write an apology for my behavior that was worthy of you, but I finally realized that I must do it in person," Kendrick began, and Edgar repeated his words, seeming immediately relieved. "I hope you do not think me too forward asking you to meet me here tonight."

"That depends a great deal on what you have to say," she replied, her tone slightly guarded again, as though she were worried that this would still not go as she hoped.

"I must apologize greatly for the way I acted. Tonight I come to you as myself, exactly as I am. As the one who wrote you those letters, and who poured out my heart and soul to you." Edgar cast a look in his direction that he disguised as a shy look toward the ground. That look said that Edgar wasn't entirely sure about this course, but he did continue to repeat what Kendrick said. "Your beauty the night of our dinner was not what I had expected. You were far more lovely than I had ever imagined and it stunned me that night.

"I was nervous to be myself and risk offending you or saying something foolish. But tonight I am here to say exactly what I feel and to let you see the real me."

"I must say that I am grateful you did not find me disappointing at our dinner that night," Hazel replied, her expression softened, greatly.

"Oh, no. Never that," That time Edgar did not need him to speak, but knew exactly what to say.

"Your apology is certainly accepted. I do hope that we can continue on from here in the same way as our letters." Her voice was slightly more eager now and Edgar returned it with a smile.

"As do I," he continued.

"I have written a short poem for you," Kendrick stated and Edgar hesitated the briefest of moments before repeating the line. Poetry was certainly not Edgar's strong suit, though he knew that Kendrick was good at it.

With that, he recited the poem he had created for this occasion. He had not intended to write a poem for his brother to tell her that night, but while he had been trying to fill the hours until midnight it had poured from him of its own accord.

The poem expressed his affection and his growing love for her. With a loving focus on the amazing qualities he had found in her, and his dreams for their future together.

Edgar repeated the poem after him, though he looked slightly embarrassed to be doing so. Hazel, on the other hand, seemed to appreciate every word.

"It is lovely," Hazel told him, her face practically glowing in the lamplight from her pleasure. It made Kendrick glow himself with pride that he could make her feel that way. Though he had to tamp down many of the emotions that he was feeling in that moment.

It was silly to feel such a way when he was only helping his brother to please his future bride. But still he could not help the strong rush of emotion and the smile that lit his face.

"I must go now," she said finally, "but I do hope we can meet again soon."

"Good night, Hazel," Edgar replied and she repeated the sentiment before slipping back inside the balcony. The light inside dimmed a moment later as she closed the curtains and Edgar and Kendrick made their way quickly back around the house and over the gate. It was only then that Kendrick felt ready to speak again. "It went well, right?" Edgar asked, his expression more confident now.

"Yes, yes that went well," Kendrick replied, partially to himself as he swung himself onto his horse. They headed back toward home, once again both lost in thought. And Kendrick wondered whether he was truly happy helping his brother to make amends with his future bride.

"All of those things that you directed at Hazel, is that what love truly is?" Edgar asked, seemingly deep in thought.

"It is what I believe that love is," Kendrick replied, refusing to look his brother in the eye as he spoke. It was good they were on horseback because it gave him something to focus on that would not betray his true thoughts.

"Your words were beautiful, indeed. But I cannot help but feel...sorry that such a thing is far from the truth."

"You do not love Hazel?" Kendrick managed to get out, trying not to sound like he was anxious about the answer.

"There is no need for me to love Hazel. Our marriage is simply a fulfillment of our duty to our families. She is a lovely girl, but there is none of the emotions that you express." They both fell silent after Edgar's matter-of-fact statement, though he was the first to break it again. "It is a shame, that I do not feel such things for her. I do wish that I did for her sake," he paused, "and perhaps a little for mine. That sort of love would seem to be a perfect thing to have in a marriage."

"It is all that I could want in a marriage," Kendrick replied, saddened even more that his brother was not at all in love with Hazel. He regretted that Edgar did not feel that way for her, since Edgar and Hazel would be wed no matter what.

But somehow, knowing that Edgar did not feel that way made him feel slightly less guilty for his own thoughts.

# CHAPTER 20

KENDRICK TOOK a deep breath as they continued on down the path. An uneasy feeling spread through him and though his brother had fallen into a rather easy silence, Kendrick could not do the same. Rather, his mind was racing. And his stomach was doing flips and making him feel a little strange.

The words that he had given Edgar to use tonight all echoed in his mind.

*'Tonight I am here to say exactly what I feel.'*

*'...Poured out my heart and soul to you'*

*'You were far more lovely than I had ever imagined'*

He could hear the words being said and could see Hazel responding to them. He could see her beautiful smile as she looked down at Edgar and listened to him profess his love for her.

It felt as though a bolt struck him in that moment and he knew what was wrong. Hazel. He was upset because he wanted to be with Hazel. Because everything he had told Edgar to say was what *he* wanted to say.

Praising her. Talking about her beauty. Reciting poetry. It was all what he wished he could do himself, rather than through Edgar. All those letters, they had made him truly fall in love with her. There was no more denying it. No use in denying it.

It was a good thing the horse knew the way to go, because Kendrick very nearly fell off him entirely as the realization fell over him like ice.

In love with Hazel.

But it was silly, of course. She was betrothed to his brother and there was nothing that he could do to change that. Nothing he would want to do that could possibly hurt his brother. But he still felt lost. And not just lost, but also guilty. How could he do such a thing to Edgar?

"Kendrick?"

He looked up, startled, and realized that they were stopped outside their own stables. Edgar had already stepped down from his horse and was waiting to lead him inside. His face was confused as he looked to Kendrick, still astride his own horse.

"I was lost in thought," Kendrick mumbled, sweeping himself from the horses back and gathering the reins. Edgar swept him into a hug instead.

"I have you to thank for everything that has happened thus far. For getting me to this point with Hazel. And for helping tonight as well." At that, Kendrick managed a weak smile, though he now felt even more guilty about what he had just realized. "I could not have done any of it without you, my brother."

"I am sure everything would have worked out," was the only reply Kendrick could muster, with a very small smile and a quick glance away. He felt flustered, gripping the reins even tighter and mumbling something about getting the horses in so they could get to bed.

The stable hands were there quickly to help with removing the tack and brushing down the horses. Peter and Jacob both slept in the stables and had heard the boys leave earlier. Luckily, neither of them would say anything to Fiona about their late night journey.

"It is late. We should be getting up to bed," Edgar stated, glancing up toward the house. "But I am grateful for everything."

"Don't mention it," Kendrick replied, wishing very much that he could forget it just that easily. Edgar didn't say anything else until they had slipped back in the front door and were heading to their own rooms.

"Good night,"

"Good night," Kendrick repeated, closing the door quietly behind him. Getting ready for bed gave him a few moments to think about what he was going to do, but of course, it wasn't as easy as that.

Far too many thoughts and ideas entered into his mind, but none of them would work, of course.

He thought of telling Hazel how he felt. But that was foolish because she had never even thought of him in such a way.

There was also a thought of telling her everything. But that was foolish as well because it would change nothing. And it would hurt Edgar.

He could leave, of course. But where would he go? And how would that really help anything?

With a sigh he lay down in bed and closed his eyes, willing his body to sleep. But it wasn't as easy as that either. Sleep alluded him and he found himself instead tossing and turning for what seemed like hours before he finally gave up.

Of course, as he rose from bed and gathered up his quill and diary he realized what had felt like half the night was actually only a few moments. But moments filled with torment that seemed to stay with him forever.

All he could think about was Hazel. And just what he was going to do about his feelings for her. Even though there was nothing that he truly could do.

*Hazel,*

*I do not know what else to do but to write to you here. Here where I can guarantee that you will never see it and never known how foolish I truly am. For I believe I have completely fallen in love with you.*

*It has been several months that we have been writing back and forth. But of course, you do not know that. No. It is Edgar that you believe has been writing to you and not me. But the words that I have written, and the words that Edgar has spoken to you are all from me.*

*It started as a favor to my brother. And I believed that I was doing something noble in helping him and you. I never expected that the letters that we wrote would lead me down a path that was wrong of me to follow.*

*I truly believed that the letters I wrote would be a benefit for you and for Edgar. And perhaps they were. For they caused both of you to care for the other. And they have furthered the cause of your marriage.*

*But I have fallen in love in the process. And it is I who shall be left out when your marriage comes to pass. I do not know what else I could do. Trust me I have attempted to come up with myriad options.*

*I have tried to find a way to right this wrong. To tell you how I feel. But there is no way to do so that will not hurt those who I would never choose to hurt. Yourself. And my brother.*

*And so, it is only here that I can write these words. Knowing that you will never see them. And I will never say them. Instead, they will waste away with the rest of my words. And I will wish you all the happiness possible, with Edgar.*

He sighed as he stared down at the words. It was a letter he could never send, of course. That was why he had chosen to put it into his journal rather than writing it in a way that he could send to her.

But as he read it over he still was not sure it conveyed everything he wished he could say. Hazel was everything he could possibly ever want in his own bride. She was beautiful. She was smart. She was funny. In fact, she was absolutely perfect. With a sigh he sank back down onto his bed.

The feelings he had were so strong that his chest ached as he thought of the fact that he could never be with her. She would always be out of his reach. Though she would be right here in his home in a short amount of time.

The thought made it harder to breathe and he clutched the diary to his chest as he lay back down. Perhaps now he would be able to sleep. Now that he had gotten more of those thoughts onto paper and out of his racing mind.

It still took quite some time before he was able to quiet himself enough to sleep. And even there he was overwhelmed by thoughts of Hazel.

*The sky was bright and blue overhead, while the sun shone on his back. All around was a sea of white. The petals of the multitude of daisies shimmering with the morning dew. The velvety softness practically calling to him.*

*But none of it called more brightly than the woman gradually coming into focus as she glided over the field. A woman with beautiful, long, red hair and bright eyes. Dressed all in white.*

*His mouth went dry at the sight of her. Hazel. Gorgeous in her white wedding gown. It was all over lace and silk. A beautiful dress that complimented her perfectly. One that he could not help but stare at as she came closer.*

*It was then that he realized he was dressed as the groom. His best suit and a flower in his lapel. It was the most elegant attire he had ever worn, and for a moment his heart swelled at the sight of her walking toward him. And then he saw Edgar.*

*Edgar who was also dressed as the groom. And who stood only a few feet away from him. Edgar who was also staring at Hazel with a mixture of pride and awe.*

*As Kendrick looked toward Hazel he saw that she was not looking at him. Rather, her gaze was fixed forward. On Edgar.*

*His heart sank as she walked right past him, never even glancing his way, joining Edgar. Accepting his hand with a brilliant smile that only served to make Kendrick's heart ache even more.*

*She had not chosen him. She had chosen Edgar. And he was alone.*

Kendrick sat up with a start and glanced around, still bleary from sleep. The sunlight shining in around the curtains told him that morning had arrived.

The blankets twisted and knotted around him said that he had slept fitfully. Though the memories of the dreams he'd had certainly attested to that.

With a sigh he dressed and ventured down the stairs. Edgar and his mother were already there, barely looking up as he entered the room so deep in conversation were they. And it did not take long for him to discover just what that conversation was.

"The wedding shall take place soon, of course. Rose and I have been in discussion about it."

"I would certainly be pleased for it to occur soon," Edgar agreed and Kendrick struggled to look away. The idea of the wedding happening soon was certainly not what he wanted. Rather, he wished that it could be put off indefinitely. But of course, that was not the case.

"There are still a good many things to do. But Rose and I have begun the plans, and I know she shall soon be approaching Hazel about her gown." The memory of Hazel's wedding gown in his dream caused Kendrick's heart to pang slightly again and he busied himself with the eggs that had been placed before him.

There had to be something that he could do, but he was still unsure what. After all, he could not bring himself to hurt Edgar in any way.

# CHAPTER 21

As she retreated back into her room Hazel took a deep breath and sighed. When she had first received the letter from Edgar to meet tonight she had been unsure. After all, meeting at midnight on the balcony was certainly romantic and something that the heroines of her favorite stories might do. But it seemed highly impractical and certainly inappropriate in real life.

Her teachers at school would have fainted at even the mention of such a thing. Though Louise would have found it a great lark and an adventure. Hazel herself had been torn between the two.

She was glad she had agreed to the meeting, however. It had certainly been worth the risk and had allowed her to get to know Edgar and his heart even more.

Another soft sigh escaped her and she sat before the looking glass. As she thought on the evening she absentmindedly picked up the brush that Trina had left on the dressing table, brushing through her long hair.

Edgar had seemed so perfect this evening. Everything that she could possibly want in a husband. He was sweet and kind and the words he spoke told her so much more of his mind. The way that he thought of things and the way that he saw the world as a true thing of beauty.

He was a gentle soul, and smart as well. In all, she was not even sure what it was she admired about him the most. There were too many wonderful qualities to even choose just one.

"Oh, goodness," the words escaped her softly as she glanced in the looking glass.

"My Lady?"

She jumped in surprise as the door opened and Trina stepped inside. "Are you still up and about? It is quite late."

"Aye, that it is, Trina. Why are you not abed at this hour?" she asked to deflect the attention from herself.

"I had chores to finish yet, Miss." Hazel felt a little badly that she did not even know what Trina did all day when she was not attending directly to Hazel. And that she was still up doing whatever it was at midnight.

"Well, I am off to bed," Hazel said finally, though her tone felt a little awkward and she turned away from Trina as she said it.

"Would you like help getting ready, Miss?" Trina did not ask why she was still up and about. She did not even ask why she was still dressed in her clothes from the day though of course Trina knew that she had not undressed her.

"That would be wonderful, Trina. Thank you." Having Trina to assist her was always a big help and she remembered all the times she had needed to prepare herself for bed or for the day alone while at school.

She wondered even more awkwardly if she should say something about why she was still dressed. But then, what would she say? And if she didn't say anything would Trina wonder? Would she mention it later?

Even worse, would Trina say something to the other servants? If she did it could get back to Hazel's parents that she had been up so late and they would certainly have questions. And of course she could not say what she had truly been up to.

Her parents would be most unhappy if they were to find out any of what had happened. Her mother might consider it harmless and only slightly inappropriate. She was sure her father would see it entirely differently, however. And the last thing she wanted was to make her parents upset.

Hazel watched Trina anxiously, trying to discern if there was any thought in her mind that something improper was going on. Or if there was anything in Trina's demeanor that seemed to indicate she would say something.

But Trina simply went about her business without betraying any glimpse of her thoughts.

Hazel allowed Trina to take charge, getting her prepared for bed and then leaving with all but one candle. The entire time she had still not said a word about Hazel's behavior or her dress or the late hour. She only bid Hazel good night before she left the room, closing the door softly behind her.

Yet, Hazel still felt too excited to sleep, and still somewhat anxious about what might happen in the morning if Trina said anything. Things had gone much better than she had even expected and she could not stop thinking about Edgar.

His words about her being beautiful, and about being overwhelmed by her rang in her ears. And the beautiful poem that he had recited was more than she could have ever imagined.

Yes, Edgar was going to be the perfect match for her. She could easily forgive his earlier nervousness now that she knew that was the problem. And she could certainly be pleased with whatever was to come.

Tonight she had learned more about Edgar. And she had been able to do it directly rather than through a letter. While she had always enjoyed the letters she did feel even closer to him now that she had spoken to him personally. Now that she had looked into his eyes — at least as much as she could from two stories above him — and seen the feeling there.

Especially after the poem he had recited to her. She sighed as she remembered his words and the soft tone that he had spoken with. The way he had talked of her beauty had helped her see that perhaps he really had been in awe of her — though she was not sure she believed her beauty was quite so awe-inspiring as all that — when he had met her the first time.

Edgar surely was talented in the way he put words together, and certainly he was very sweet and kind in the things that he said about her.

As she drifted off to sleep Hazel wondered just what she might learn next. And when she would see Edgar again. She hoped that it would be soon and that they would have a little more time to speak privately the next time.

# CHAPTER 22

KENDRICK FLED the dining hall as quickly as he could manage, certain that, if he stayed any longer, his family would learn his secret. No, it was better to stay away as much as possible. At least until he decided what he was going to do.

With a sigh he ventured outside walking to the stables but unable to focus enough for a ride. Instead, he absentmindedly fed some carrots to the horses and wandered back out of the building again.

What could he do? He was in love with Hazel. That much he had finally had to admit to himself. But there was nothing that he could do about it. Hazel was betrothed to his brother. He would not hurt his brother by doing anything about his feelings for her. It would not be right.

And who was to say that Hazel would be interested in him anyway? Even if he were to confess his feelings? It was certainly best to keep his thoughts to himself. For the sake of everyone.

With that thought he finally turned back toward the house. If he stayed out too long they would wonder where he was and that would only raise more questions he did not want to answer.

Though joining his mother in the drawing room certainly did not seem like a good option either. Unfortunately, there were no other options and he finally ventured in, sinking down into a chair near the window and attempting to appear as normal as possible.

It did not work with his mother, of course. She knew his thoughts and his moods far better than he would have liked and seemed to pick up on his poor mood quite quickly.

"Are you ill, Kendrick?" she asked, worriedly and he managed to shake his head.

"No, I am well." He was not quite well, but certainly he was not ill in the way she thought.

"There is certainly something the matter," she insisted.

"There is nothing," he countered but her gaze continued to search for an answer.

"That is not true, Kendrick. Come, tell me what is the matter," she sounded so matter of fact and part of him wished that he could tell her. He wished that he could confide in her the secrets of his heart the way he had when he was a little boy. And that she would be able to make everything all right again. Just as she had then.

But alas, that was not possible now. She could not make things better this time. Even if he were to confide in her, doing so would only put her in the middle between her two sons. And he would not do that to her.

"I am tired today," he said finally and her look turned even more concerned.

"Have you been having trouble sleeping?"

"Aye, for a short while," he admitted.

"I shall send for the doctor," she announced, already reaching for the bell to call a servant to them.

"No, no. There is no need for that," he insisted though she looked unsure. "I will be fine, Mother. I am feeling quite well."

"There must be a reason that you are not able to sleep."

"My mind is constantly working away at things. It is of no importance. I am sure it shall quiet again soon." He attempted to brush off her concern and it seemed to work to some extent. She still looked worried, but not quite as much as she had.

"Perhaps it is best if you go get some rest. If you do not feel better tomorrow, however, I shall send for the doctor." He finally agreed to return to his room, grateful for the escape.

Of course, there would be no rest for him. There was no way to rest with so many thoughts racing through his head. So many plans that would never come true. So many things that he wanted to say but couldn't.

Instead, he pulled out a piece of paper.

*It seems I am to continually be thinking of you and wondering if you would ever think of me in the same way. I am to be continually feeling such strong emotions that I cannot even find the words to fully express them.*

*I am in love with you. And I believe I always have been. Perhaps from the first day that we met. Do you remember when we were children together? It is something I shall never forget.*

*Each time I think of you I am reminded of those days together. Of the fun and the excitement of those early times. And I know that life with you would be everything that I have ever imagined and more than I could ever hope to deserve.*

*You remind me of sunny days and happy times. And I know that the beauty that you bring to every situation would only be magnified when we are together. We will brave every storm and create an amazing life together.*

*As I sit here, I can only think on the perfection of your smile, and the way that it brightens even the darkest of days. That smile, that look in your eyes that comes with each word is what shall get me through each day. I know I can never live without it.*

*I will cherish you from now until my last breath. And will always pray that nothing shall keep us apart.*

A knock sounded at the door and he was abruptly torn from the thoughts flowing out into the letter. In fact, he was startled to realize that the sun had sunk quite a bit lower, and it was in fact long past noon.

"Lady Fiona has requested you for tea," the butler announced and Kendrick nodded his head, setting the quill down and glancing once more at the letter on his desk. It felt good to finally get everything out, but he still felt ill at the thought of Hazel and Edgar together.

With a sigh he rose and followed the butler down to the drawing room. He would pretend that he had rested and now felt much better. Though how well he would be able to pull it off he was not sure.

"Ah, Kendrick, there you are." He gave a small smile and sat in his normal seat, accepting the tea cup she passed him. "Are you feeling better rested now?"

"I am," he replied, though he was not so sure he felt any better at all.

"Rest does seem to have done you good," she looked him over with a critical eye but seemed pleased with whatever she found in his face.

"What have you been about since I left?" Kendrick changed the subject and she allowed it, though that was only because she was very excited to talk about anything to do with the wedding. And of course that was what she had been thinking about.

"Oh, I am still working on a list of the foods to be prepared for the wedding, of course. We shall have all of the best items and we shall have Cook prepare roast duck. I hear tell that Rose's cook is quite good at game meats and so she shall be in charge of those. Then there shall be a series of pies and tarts. Your brother dearly loves apple tarts and so we shall be sure to have them. And we shall find out what Hazel prefers," she began.

"Plum pudding," the words burst out before he could think on them and his mother looked to him in confusion. "Hazel likes plum pudding. It is what she always selected first when there were parties while we were younger." He quickly glanced down at his teacup and selected a scone so that he could hide his face from his mother. He was not even sure where that information had come from, but it was something he remembered. One of many things he remembered about Hazel.

"Well then, we shall be sure to have it for her, of course." His mother continued on from there, listing out several different types of meat and treats that would be served, but Kendrick was only partially paying attention.

"Ah, I see you have had your tea," they both looked up, startled, as Edgar strode into the room.

"Oh, Edgar, I am sorry I did not call you down as well," their mother replied, frowning slightly.

"No matter. I have just finished some work and was looking for Kendrick."

"Well, I have some letters to write in planning for the wedding and so I shall take my leave of you." She bustled off and Edgar settled into her chair.

"I went to your bedchamber first looking for you and saw your letter."

"Oh?" Kendrick was not so pleased that his brother had seen the letter but chose to give very little response. It was best if Edgar did not realize it was so very important.

"I had it posted to Hazel," he explained, as though it were the most normal thing in the world.

"What?" Kendrick's eyes widened in shock and no small amount of horror. "Why would you do such a thing?"

"I assumed that it was to be sent to her. It was very similar to the other letters you had written." His tone was a little less certain now though Kendrick's was much more horrified.

"You should have asked first, before sending such a thing."

"Why would I? What is it that is so wrong with the letter?" Edgar looked concerned and Kendrick searched for a response.

"You did not read it?" Kendrick felt momentarily relieved, at least slightly, that Edgar may not have seen everything about the letter.

"I read the beginning," Edgar replied, defensively. "It was a love letter. Much like the others you had sent. I assumed it would continue what had begun the night before. What is wrong with it?"

"It is...the handwriting. I did not change my handwriting in the letter and Hazel may notice the mistake." Edgar brushed it off, immediately looking less concerned.

"There is nothing to that. She shall not notice such a thing. No one notices such minute details as all that."

"But if she does..." Kendrick trailed off, still concerned that Hazel was going to be reading the letter he had written. The one he had never meant for anyone else to see.

"It shall be fine. Do not worry so much," But Kendrick was not entirely certain he was worrying enough. If Hazel looked closely at the new letter...it could certainly mean trouble for him and for Edgar, no matter how dismissive he might be.

# CHAPTER 23

HAZEL STRETCHED her arms over her head and opened her eyes with a smile on her face. Things seemed so much better now. Last night with Edgar had certainly made all of the bad things seem like nothing more than a dream. And she was certainly glad that she needn't worry about it any longer.

Edgar had seemed just like the man she had been talking to for so long in their letters. In fact, he had seemed almost more the man she wanted him to be. Certainly nerves had gotten the better of him on their previous meeting. She believed it now. And last night he had been more open and caring than even before.

"Miss? Are you ready to get started for the day?"

She could not help the bright smile on her face as Trina entered. "I am, thank you."

It seemed that nothing could bring down her spirits today. Not even when Trina selected her favorite dress and discovered that there was a small tear at the back. Or when the ribbons that matched the second dress she selected were missing.

Hazel could only continue to smile and wait patiently while Trina bustled about trying to locate something that would fit together for the day.

"You are in a far better mood than the last several days," Trina observed and Hazel acknowledged that she was.

"I have had some good news," she replied with a sparkle in her eye and Trina looked intrigued.

"Aye? What is that? It must have come quite early. And before you were even out of bed."

"In fact, it came quite late," Hazel corrected, but she knew better than to tell Trina about her late-night visitor. It would not do for anyone to know that Edgar had been here at such an hour. Or that she had agreed to meet him.

Though the forbiddeness of it made their illicit tryst that much more exciting and romantic. And besides, nothing untoward had happened. They had not even been near enough for him to take her hand. So there could be nothing truly improper about it, could there?

She shook her head to clear the thoughts and noticed that Trina was still looking at her somewhat uncertainly, but whatever she thought did not much matter. Trina simply smiled and shook her head, continuing to lace the back of Hazel's gown and pin up her hair with the slightly different colored ribbons she had found.

Once she was ready Hazel descended the stairs for breakfast only to find that her father had already hurried off for some business. Her mother was waiting for her though and seemed quite excited.

"We shall be going to Aethelred for tea this morning," she announced and Hazel immediately felt pleased herself at the prospect. She would be able to see Edgar again and this time they would be much nearer than they had been the night before.

"Oh, I must have a moment to freshen up before we go."

"Dear, you have only just gotten ready for the day," her mother laughed as Hazel tried to eat both quickly and politely at the same time.

"Aye, but I must look my best to see Edgar again." The small helping of fruit was all Hazel could bring herself to eat.

Her mother laughed again but excused her to return to her room and freshen up again. Trina assisted her in brushing her hair and tucking it up into the customary bun that she often wore. This time with a few little curls to frame the look. Between the two of them they also brushed out the wrinkles from her dress and changed out the ribbons in her hair for new ones.

"Trina...how did you know to come to my room last night?" Hazel asked suddenly.

"As I said, I had things that needed to be done until late," Trina replied in the same calm tone.

"Things...like what?"

"A few things that needed taken care of in the kitchens, Miss," Trina replied and Hazel's eyes opened wide at the thought of the kitchens directly beside her own room, though on the first floor. The kitchens that would look out easily to where Edgar had been last night.

"Did you...did you happen to hear anything? While you were doing chores in the kitchens?" Hazel asked with bated breath.

"I may have heard some birds up and about a little late last night," Trina replied, finally looking up at Hazel. "But then again, I can't be sure. It was late, after all. And I was quite tired," Hazel sighed in relief. Trina certainly had seen and heard what was happening last night, but Hazel was just as certain that she would say nothing at all.

"I am sure those birds are grateful that you did not call someone after them last night," she added and Trina gave her a smile.

"I wouldn't dream of it," Trina replied. "Just so long as those birds don't get to chirping every night. We wouldn't want anyone else to hear them about." Hazel nodded and Trina turned back to smoothing her dress. "Now, are you quite ready to go?"

"Yes, thank you." She felt even more relieved now that Trina certainly wasn't going to say anything. And she was more than happy to get ready to get going to Aethelred.

By the time she was ready — or at least as ready as she could be when she was so excited she could hardly sit still — the carriage was waiting to take them to visit the countess.

"Ah, I had started to wonder if you were going to come along with me," her mother teased but Hazel was too excited and somewhat nervous to respond. She simply allowed Andrew to help her into the carriage and settled in across from her mother. "Dear, it is only tea. I know that things with you and Edgar did not go as well as you had hoped the last time," she began.

Hazel looked up and started to speak then changed her mind. No, she could not tell her mother about her conversation with Edgar and the way that he had resolved things.

"But it will be much better this time, I am sure," her mother finished and Hazel gave her a small smile. She expected that it would be much better as well, and she was most pleased with that realization. She simply couldn't wait to see him again.

The trip to Aethelred manor seemed to take forever, and Hazel couldn't seem to concentrate on anything. Even as her mother continued to try and speak about...well, anything, she couldn't focus. All she could do was stare out the window at the passing trees and road, smoothing her skirt repeatedly. But of course, that was only necessary because she kept rustling the fabric in between times.

"Hazel?"

"Hmm?" she looked up, still distracted and caught her mother's slightly concerned, slightly amused look. "We have arrived."

"Oh!" She noticed that Andrew was already waiting at the door, his hand held out for her, and she quickly descended the carriage. As her mother followed she smoothed her skirts one last time, approaching the door to the manor with the brightest smile she could muster through her nervousness.

"Your Grace, My Lady." The butler bowed to them both and stepped back to invite them in. "I shall announce you to Lady Fiona." They waited a moment in the hall while he did and then followed him back toward the drawing room.

"Ah, I had been waiting for you. Do you know that it is very nearly past the time I take my tea?" Fiona teased them and Rose laughed. Hazel only managed a weak smile as she glanced around the room for Edgar. But there was only Fiona.

"Well we had to be sure that we were ready, of course," Rose replied with a smile and a twinkle in her eye, but she did not say anything about Hazel.

As the three sat down at the table the tea things were brought in. At least having a cup of tea and a scone gave Hazel something to do while she was impatiently hoping that her mother would ask about Edgar. It would not do for her to do so. At least, she did not want to appear quite so anxious as all that.

"How have you been?" Rose asked finally, and Fiona smiled in response.

"I have been quite well. Though I must say, planning this wedding has been quite a feat for me," Fiona added.

"You are not planning it alone. I have also been making some plans for the occasion. And Hazel is set to go to the dressmaker in only a few days to get started on a design for her gown." This, at least, Hazel was interested in, and discussing some of her ideas for the gown — full but not too full, plenty of lace and beadwork, and a lovely train — drew her mind off Edgar. At least for a short while.

Once talk turned to the musicians for the occasion and which flowers should be brought in to decorate the hall she found her mind again wandering.

"Where are your sons?" Hazel's gaze immediately turned back to the two women when she heard her mother's words. She glanced eagerly to Fiona who smiled in response.

"They have gone out riding. In fact, they left quite early and have yet to return. I am sure that it shall not be long now," Fiona assured them both, but Hazel knew that both the boys enjoyed a long ride and wondered when they might really come back.

"Do you mind if I visit the library?" Hazel asked suddenly. Her mother and Fiona both looked up at her, startled and she knew that she had interrupted something that was being said. In truth, she had not been paying attention after she learned that the boys may not be back for some time.

"Of course, Dear," Fiona replied, ringing the bell at her side for a maid. "Could you take Hazel to the library, please, Mary?"

"Yes, My Lady," the girl curtsied to them both and Hazel followed her from the room and down the hall. It had been quite some time since she had been at Aethelred and she certainly did not remember where the library was, but once she saw it she was glad she had asked. The library here was at least as wonderful as the one at home. And she had not read any of these books.

"Thank you, Mary," she replied and the girl curtsied again.

"Is there anything else, Miss?"

"No, that will be all." With that Mary left the room and Hazel was granted free rein of the space.

It truly was a nice library, and so many interesting things were scattered about as well. This was not a library that was kept for showing off. This was a library that the family in the house liked to enjoy. She could tell from the books that were left on tables, some open, some stacked not so neatly, as though someone had been researching a topic. There were notebooks about, and little items scattered over the tables, revealing that someone had been there.

She strolled through the room, glancing at the covers of books that had been left out. Certainly at least a few of these were Edgar's and she wondered what he might be interested in.

Books about different parts of the world were surely his. And the atlas that looked well-worn seemed like another one that he would be reading. But there was a very small book on one table that did not have a title on it.

It looked quite worn, she thought as she picked it up. In fact, the cover was leather but soft like it had been handled quite a bit. And the gilt edges were lovely. This was a book that was certainly a favorite, but she could not tell what it was as there was no marking on the front cover. As soon as she opened that cover, however, she could tell what it was. A diary.

Hazel quickly closed the book and set it back down on the table, turning and walking away from it. It would not do to read someone's diary, after all. In fact, she felt anxious that she had picked it up at all and began browsing along the shelves looking for something to read.

But the book seemed to call to her. Even the slight glimpse that she had gotten showed familiar handwriting and she was nearly certain that it was Edgar who the book belonged to. Now she found herself glancing back over her shoulder again and again as she tried to look for a different book to read.

"This one," she said to herself, grabbing a book at random and taking it to a corner to flip through. But the book she had chosen did not catch her fancy. At least, not with that other book sitting on the table so near.

Hesitating even more she stood and slowly walked back to the diary. For a long moment she paused, looking down at the book and reaching toward it before pulling her hand back. But she could not stop herself and finally snatched it up again, flipping it open to a random page.

*It is a long day yet again. There seems always so much to do and yet not enough to do. Perhaps it is simply that the things that need doing are not the ones that interest me.*

*Rather, the sun on the petals over the garden is what entrances me, rather than matters of business or the manor.*

She flipped to another page, now so absorbed in what she saw that she did not concern herself with whether or not she should be reading the diary.

*Mother has had tea at Deighton again today, though she chose to go alone and not tell us of it until she returned. She had much to say about Hazel and I was certainly pleased to hear all of it.*

*She says that Hazel is a lovely young lady. That she is smart and beautiful as well. She shall make a wonderful wife.*

Hazel blushed at that and flipped to another page. Here and there she saw poems. Some she had never heard but a couple that she had. The ones that had been sent to her while they were writing letters together.

That meant the dairy was certainly Edgar's and just as she spotted another page with her name on it she heard a knock and the door began to open. Quickly, she shoved the book into her gown and turned toward the door. It would not do for anyone to know she had read the diary.

"Ah, Mother told me you had come to the library," Hazel smiled seeing Edgar walk in. The book weighed heavily in her skirts but there was nothing she could do. Learning what she could about Edgar would not be wrong anyway, would it? They were soon to be wed, after all.

Edgar still looked a little ruffled from his ride. His hair was somewhat windblown and his cheeks and eyes were bright. Yes, going for a ride had done him some good. He looked quite hale and healthy, though he had looked so at dinner that fateful night as well.

"Would you care to sit and talk with me a while?" he asked and she agreed easily, joining him on a couch in the room. This was the first time that they would be able to speak entirely privately. The first time they could be open with one another and that they were actually in the same room.

She was more than pleased to have the opportunity and reveled in the way he held her hand in his own as they spoke. Yes, this was exactly what she had always wanted for her future husband.

"What is it you like to do most of all?" Edgar asked her and she had to think for a moment. There were a great many things she enjoyed, but which was her favorite?

"I enjoy singing. My teachers said that I was quite good. And piano as well," she replied and he smiled.

"I should very much like to hear you sometime," Hazel could not help but smile as well, though she did not say anything further.

"What is it you enjoy most?" she asked instead.

"I greatly enjoy travel," he replied. "Though I shall have to reduce the amount of travel that I do as I begin to take charge of the estate." He seemed to be thinking hard as he said it, and she was certain she caught some disappointment in his voice.

"Shall you never travel now?" she asked cryptically, hoping that he would not plan to travel far from her.

"I shall still travel, only not so far and not for as long."

"I should like to travel," Hazel ventured and his eyes brightened further.

"I would be more than happy to take you along on my travels. There are so many wonderful places to see, and it shall all be much more pleasant if you are there with me." The fact that he wanted her to go along pleased Hazel as well, and she wondered at some of the places that they might go.

Another knock sounded on the door just as she was set to ask him where they would go to first. Both of them turned toward it and Kendrick entered, looking slightly embarrassed but with a smile as he glanced toward them then around the room.

"I am sorry to disturb you. I would like to just fetch my diary, if you do not mind." Hazel stilled at the words, keeping the smile frozen on her face. He could not be speaking of the little book in her pocket now.

Certainly he was speaking of a different diary because this one had to be Edgar's. It had the poems that Edgar had written to her. And the way it was written was very similar to the way that Edgar wrote to her.

"Of course," Edgar welcomed him into the room and Hazel managed a slight nod as well. But as Kendrick moved about the room, checking the books on the tables and desks it was clear that his diary was not there. His brow furrowed and he looked frustrated, and perhaps a little concerned, as he made his way around each of the spaces and did not find it. "Is something wrong?" Edgar asked, his own concern visible on his face.

"I was certain I left it in here when you asked if I would like to go riding. I was looking over some books and I thought I kept it on the table. But perhaps it was in my pocket. I do hope that I did not lose it on the trail."

"I am sure we would have noticed if it had fallen from your pocket while we were riding," Edgar assured him.

"You should have. You were behind the entire way," Kendrick teased and Edgar scoffed indignantly.

"Hardly. You were the one who fell behind several times." The brothers laughed but Hazel could only bring herself to smile slightly in response. If Kendrick was the one with the diary then that meant he was the one who had written to her. He had to have been. Why else would he have those poems in his diary?

She tried to piece together some explanation, any explanation, for why Edgar would have written poetry in Kendrick's diary. But there was nothing. And there was no reason that Edgar should have tried to pass off Kendrick's poems as his own. And what of the writing itself? That was certainly not right.

Her mind was whirling feverishly as she tried to piece everything together. No wonder Edgar had been so nervous and awkward at their dinner together. He had not known anything about what they had written to each other. Because he had not written any of it.

"I am sorry for disturbing you both. I shall have to look elsewhere." Kendrick seemed distracted again and he left the room and Edgar turned back toward Hazel.

"Are you quite all right?" he asked, his concern growing even more as he caught a glimpse of her face.

"I feel ill quite suddenly. Perhaps I could use some air," she managed to get out and he rose immediately, extending an arm that she accepted as gracefully as she could.

The diary in her pocket now seemed like it was on fire. She wanted to read it even more, to know just what it held and what else she might not know.

If this diary did in fact belong to Kendrick...it was too awful to even think about. If it was Kendrick's diary then it meant that they had lied to her. All of this time they had been lying to her because it was not Edgar who was writing all of those things to her. It was not

Edgar who even felt those things. How could they say that he did when he did not?

She could not believe that the two boys had deceived her in this way. How could they have done such a thing? To have Kendrick write to her from the very start...and now...was any of it real? Was Edgar anything like what had been written in those letters? She did not know what to think about any of it.

As Edgar escorted her outdoors she struggled to put one foot in front of the other. Nothing made sense. Nothing felt right. As he helped her sit on a bench at the edge of the gardens she barely heard whatever it was he said before quickly hurrying into the estate. He returned with her mother and Lady Fiona, who looked even more concerned.

"Hazel? Are you all right, Dear? What is the matter?"

"I feel quite ill all of the sudden, Mother," Hazel replied, managing to keep calm though she was feeling more than just ill.

"We shall leave immediately. Edgar, if you could have Andrew bring our carriage around, I believe I should take Hazel home now," her mother instructed, coming to sit beside her while Edgar rushed off.

"Would you like anything while you wait? Perhaps some water, Dear?" Fiona asked and Hazel managed to shake her head.

"Thank you, but I simply need to rest." The women fussed over her anyway until Andrew arrived with the carriage and they bid the countess and Edgar farewell.

# CHAPTER 24

HAZEL WAS quiet on the return trip as well, though this time it was not excitement that kept her from talking.

Her mother was also quite quiet, though hers was because she was worried about Hazel and just what might be going on.

"Shall I send for the doctor? You do look unwell," Fiona began and Hazel shook her head. What was wrong with her was not something the doctor could fix.

"No, I shall go and lie down and I am sure I will feel better soon," she replied, though she did not believe it. Her mother didn't seem as though she believed it either, pursing her lips and pressing a cool hand to Hazel's head.

"Are you sure, Dear?" she asked gently.

"Yes, I just need some rest." Her mother allowed her to hurry upstairs, though she called after that she was going to send Trina up with some tea.

In fact, it took only a few moments for Trina to appear with the tea and a few scones. But Hazel quickly sent her away again. She certainly wanted no company. Not even Trina who would not judge her for any of it. She tried a few sips of the tea, but it had no effect on her racing mind and she set it away.

All of this time she had been so sure that she was writing to Edgar, and that he was the one she was falling in love with. But she was falling in love with the person who had written her those letters. The person who wove such beautiful stories with their words. And as she gazed down at the diary she had pulled from her pocket she knew that was certainly not Edgar.

If the diary was Kendrick's then that meant the man she was actually in love with was Kendrick. Not Edgar at all.

She threw herself onto her bed and sobbed in a way she could not remember doing since she was a child. Though the broken-hearted feelings of a child were nothing compared to what she felt now.

Hazel was not sure how long she remained there before Trina returned. But she was aware of the fact that the day had started to fade and the shadows had begun to cross her room.

"Miss? Are you all right?" Trina seemed worried when she returned to the room for the tea things but Hazel barely even noticed.

"I am feeling unwell," she replied, though she knew that was still an understatement. She felt heartsick, betrayed, devastated. But there was no way to explain all that to Trina. Or anyone else. And she did not try.

Instead, for the next several days she told everyone that she was unwell. She told her mother when she came to visit several times a day. And she told Trina, who brought her tea and bowls of soup to try and coax her to eat. And she told the doctor who her mother insisted on calling after three days of her being sick and confined to her bedchamber.

It was the only way Hazel could think of to avoid seeing the Andertons again. She was sure that her heart could not take a visit. Not with Edgar and certainly not with Kendrick.

As she lay in her room she read through every bit of the diary. And when she had read it through she turned back to the first page and read it again.

It was practically filled with thoughts and feelings about her. The first were not as clearly romantic, but the ones toward the end were and she found herself very certain that Kendrick was in love with her as well. But how could he have done all of this? How could either of them have done it?

She felt foolish thinking of the letters she had received and the ones she had written. She had always known that Kendrick was the one of the brothers who enjoyed reading and writing. Edgar...well, she had never known Edgar as well, but he had not been as studious, even as a child.

"Miss?" Hazel turned toward the door as Trina entered with a letter in her hand. "This has only just arrived for you." She hesitated, but finally Hazel accepted the letter, noting the markings on the front that said it was from Kendrick. "Perhaps it will make you feel better?"

She doubted it, but Trina sounded hopeful, her face still clouded with concern.

"I shall look at it in a little while, thank you," Hazel replied and saw how Trina looked even more anxious at that.

"Are you sure you are feeling all right, Miss? I could send for the doctor again."

"No, thank you. I am only a little tired." It was far from the truth but Trina finally left the room and she was able to look at the letter again.

Part of her did not want to open it. Did not want to see what Kendrick had to say. Did not want to give him the opportunity to say anything. But she could not overrun the feeling of curiosity and finally she opened the letter.

*Hazel,*

*News of your continued illness has only recently reached Aethelred and we are most concerned for you. I am sending this letter hoping that you are already feeling better by the time it reaches you.*

*I wish you the best and hope that you will recover very soon,*

*Kendrick*

As she read through the letter she pulled out the diary again, looking from the diary to the letter in her hands. Yes, the diary was certainly Kendrick's. But then she hesitated before taking the box of letters from under her bed. Inside the box were all of the letters from Edgar. Or perhaps they were from Kendrick.

The last letter she had received was different from the others. She had thought so vaguely when she had received it but had brushed away any such thoughts. It had sounded like the others, and the difference, she had convinced herself, was minute. But the difference was certainly there. And that was confirmed now as she placed the letter beside the new one from Kendrick. The handwriting was the same.

Hazel sucked in a deep breath as she then turned to the other letters. The handwriting was slightly different on these, but there was still something very like that last letter, and the one from Kendrick. She could tell now that they were all written by the same hand. And that hand was not Edgar's.

A sob broke through as she looked over the letters again. She had been right. It was Kendrick from the start. All of it was Kendrick. And that meant he was the one she had been falling in love with all of this time. He was the one who had told her all of those stories and made her feel as though she was right there with him. Like they were meant to be.

There was no way she could marry Edgar knowing this. No way

she could possibly bring herself to be with anyone but Kendrick when she knew how she felt, and how he felt. But what could she do? How could she tell her mother the truth?

For several more days she refused to say anything. And refused to leave her room. The doctor was called yet again but could find nothing wrong with her. He simply provided a tonic for her nerves and said that she should rest. It did not please her mother to hear, but Hazel appreciated the fact that he wanted her to stay away from others. She couldn't have gone out amongst anyone anyway.

"Hazel? Dear, we need to talk now." She looked up as her mother entered her room, sitting on the side of her bed. "It has been over a week, nearly two. And you are still shut up in this room. There is certainly something the matter, but the doctor can find nothing wrong."

"I do not feel well, Mother. I do not know what it is." She did, of course. It was a broken heart that made her feel this way. But she still could not bring herself to explain it all to her mother. Not yet.

"Well, the countess is hosting a ball this weekend and we are all expected to attend. I cannot continue to make excuses for you, Dear. You must attend as well." Hazel still did not feel ready to face anyone, let alone Edgar and Kendrick. But then, she would likely never feel ready. It was best to simply get it done with.

"What is it that has been weighing on your mind and your heart?" her mother finally asked, and Hazel hesitated before shaking her head again.

"I am sure that it is nothing to be concerned about. I will feel better for the ball, certainly. And I will be most pleased to attend." It would be best to have it out with both of the boys at the same time. And what better place than at a ball like this one? She could be done and finally be able to move on. Though just what would happen next she had no idea.

# CHAPTER 25

THE SUN WAS SHINING BRIGHTLY through the window and Hazel found herself wondering just how the world could still be so beautiful with everything that was happening to her.

A ball would normally make her quite happy, but the thought of what was to come this time certainly did not. In fact, she was not quite sure how she felt about what was to come.

Would she even be able to do what needed to be done? She sighed again, climbing out of her bed and walking toward the window. Today was important. No matter what happened. She needed to get it done with. Even if that meant – but no, she wouldn't say it. Everything was going to work out fine.

"Good morning, Miss," Trina said as she opened the door and bustled into the room. She poured the fresh pitcher of water into the bowl near the dressing table and Hazel splashed a little water onto her face.

The cool water was refreshing and strengthened her resolve for what she would do today. Trina smiled and began to prepare her gown for the ball. It had only just been delivered the day before and she was excited to try it on.

"It looks lovely," Trina told her as she brushed out the folds of the dress so that Hazel could look it over. "It was good you chose the green to be made over," Hazel agreed. There had not been enough time to get an entirely new gown but she had selected one of her own to send in for some adjustments.

The green gown she had worn for the dance at school now looked entirely different. The bodice was trimmed in lace now and the buttons down the back had been replaced with mother of pearl.

Even better was the skirt, however, which was now even fuller and accented with a deeper green train that she could not help running her fingers over. The silky material felt wonderful.

"You shall certainly be the loveliest girl there," Hazel could only smile, her mood immediately brightened by the gown and the thought of wearing it for dancing.

As Trina helped her into the gown she realized that the neckline had also been changed slightly so that the dress just barely rested on her shoulders.

"Oh, it is the most beautiful dress I have ever seen," Hazel gushed over it, spinning in circles to see every bit in the looking glass.

"Aye, that it is," Trina agreed, smoothing down the lace and double-checking each of the buttons. It fit perfectly and was everything she could have ever wanted. There were even new ribbons to go with it, and slippers that were so comfortable she could not wait to dance in them.

If anything could make her feel better after everything that had happened it was certainly this dress. This dress that made her feel and look like a princess. At least she would look lovely as she confronted the two boys about what she had learned.

"Hazel? Are you finished, Dear?" She spun in front of the glass once more and hurried out the door to meet her parents.

"Thank you, Trina!" She called over her shoulder, stopping only once to let her mother 'ooh' and 'ahh' over the dress as well before they climbed into the carriage.

"Oh, you are simply beautiful," her mother smiled at her brightly and twirled her in a circle like when she was a little girl. "That was a perfect choice. Edgar shall not be able to take his eyes off you," she promised and Hazel immediately felt her mood sour slightly.

She tried very hard to keep her bright smile in place so her mother would not notice. But inside she was wondering just what would happen when she arrived at the ball tonight. And what she would do when she saw both Edgar and Kendrick.

As she settled into the carriage, she brushed her fingers carefully over the book she had slipped into her pocket when Trina wasn't looking. If she needed to, she would bring out the diary and show them what she knew.

For now, she would simply wait and see what happened. She wanted to know how far they would continue this charade. Would they actually never tell her the truth? Did they expect to lie to her forever? This time her sigh was audible and her parents both looked at her, concerned.

"I am anxious to be there," Hazel told them with a forced smile and both returned her look with an indulgent one of their own.

"It shall be a wonderful occasion," her mother replied. "I am anxious myself."

Once they had arrived, she took a deep breath and allowed Andrew to hand her out of the carriage, followed by her mother. This was it. This could very well be the night that changed absolutely everything about her betrothal. At least, the way she felt about it.

"Duke Radley Deighton and Duchess Rose Deighton. Lady Hazel Deighton." They were announced formally and proceeded to the ballroom where they immediately met Edgar.

His bow to her parents was polite before he turned to her.

"My Lady, would you care to dance?"

"I would be honored," she replied, wondering if this was the time she should say what she already knew. Or perhaps it was best to keep it to herself a little longer.

As Edgar took her hand to begin the dance she was momentarily swept away by the music and the experience of it all. She did love to dance. And dancing with her betrothed had something of a ring to it.

A smile graced her face for a moment and she could not even help the blush that spread across her cheeks when he told her that she was absolutely stunning.

"I have never seen a more beautiful Lady," he added, and she demurred politely, though she was still trying to decide what she would say to him, and when.

"You are very handsome, Sir," she replied with a slight smile and he returned it.

"Are you feeling much better now?" He seemed very concerned and she wondered if he was as concerned about the lies he had told her up until now.

"I am indeed. I feel perfectly well, thank you." He seemed relieved at her assurance and they fell silent a moment while the dance became more strenuous.

"I am glad you were able to rest and that you still were able to attend the ball tonight," he added, and she managed a small smile, looking over the beautiful suit he wore up to the soft curl of his blonde hair. His eyes were bright, like he was happy, but with a slight hint of concern. Or maybe it was just that he was anxious about this meeting as well. Maybe because of all of the lies that

were going on, she thought as she steeled herself a little more
against him.

"As am I," Hazel agreed. "Have you been busy the last few days?"

"There has been some business to attend to," he replied, "and I
have been riding with Kendrick quite often." At the mention of
Kendrick Hazel had to look away for a moment. All she could think
of was the diary in her pocket and how it felt like it was a rock
pulling her down. She had to do something. Had to say something.
But just how could she approach it? She felt far too hurt to be
tactful about uncovering the truth.

"Do you love me?" the words burst from her lips and she raised
her gaze to meet his. She held steady and saw the way that his eyes
revealed a slight panic at first as if he was trying to decide what
to say.

"I-you..." he trailed off a moment and she saw the resolve set in
his gaze finally. "I respect you. I shall always respect you. And I shall
cherish you for our entire lifetime. But I cannot tell you that I love
you now. It would not be true to say such a thing. I believe that love
will come as our marriage continues on," she was grateful that he
did not lie to her, and that he had determined to be honest now at
least, as she had been quite certain that he did not love her. How
could he have done what he did if he loved her? But that left more
to consider.

"Why did you tell me that you loved me when you did not?"

"I-when?" he stalled and she leveled her gaze on him again,
barely concealing her own anger.

"In the letters that you wrote to me. You said then that you loved
me," he faltered yet again and paused before speaking in a somewhat halting voice.

"In writing I often found myself creating letters that were more
poetic and perhaps I have said such things then. But I do not want
to lie to you. I wish to tell you only the truth of what I feel and what
our future together shall be." His tone was sincere, but it was clear
that he was nervous about what her reaction might be. His gaze
searching her own as he spoke.

"I thank you for your honesty," she told him, though her voice
was difficult to read. He seemed concerned that he could not tell
what she was thinking. His eyes still watching her, but she revealed
nothing.

As the song ended she curtsied low and he was forced to escort
her to the edge of the dancing area, bowing and excusing himself
from her side.

She knew that he was nervous to know just what she was thinking, but she did not want to say anymore just yet. Rather, she wanted to keep things to herself until she knew how she wanted to proceed.

~

Kendrick was standing by himself in a corner of the room, watching as Edgar and Hazel danced about the room. They moved so smoothly, and he found himself wishing that he could dance with Hazel that way.

But at the same time he could tell something was wrong. Edgar seemed troubled, and the stiff set to Hazel's back as she moved seemed to indicate more. Whatever they were talking about neither of them was pleased, though Kendrick could not quite determine what it was.

Of course, when the dance ended and Edgar left Hazel at the edge of the dance floor he tried to pretend that he hadn't been watching them. At least, when Edgar started toward him.

"How did it go?" he asked, pretending disinterest, but Edgar had a worried expression on his face. Certainly something seemed wrong.

"I think that she knows," Edgar replied ominously and Kendrick felt his stomach do flips, though he tried to pretend he did not feel anything.

"Knows what?" he asked instead and Edgar looked at him incredulously.

"About the letters. I think she knows."

"How could she possibly know?" Kendrick asked in shock. There was no way that she could know, was there? No way that she could possibly have figured out that Kendrick had been writing the letters.

"I do not know," Edgar admitted. "It's just...a feeling."

"Perhaps you should leave those feelings to me," Kendrick teased, but he felt uneasy at the same time, his gaze falling on Hazel as she was being led across the dance floor by another gentleman.

"There was something very...determined about her gaze today. It was very clear she knew something." Kendrick hesitated and watched Hazel a moment more. For an instant she glanced up and their eyes met. He could not help the slight thrill that went through him, but was startled by the slightest change in her own gaze. There was something there, though he could not determine what it was before she had quickly averted her eyes and continued on with the dance.

"I will go to dance with her when the next song begins," he told Edgar. "I will see what I can find out from there."

"Perhaps you will be able to learn more than I did," Edgar replied, seeming at least slightly appeased at the thought.

"Yes, perhaps I shall." But Kendrick wasn't entirely sure. He just knew that he had to try something and Edgar had no way to learn more.

The two of them remained side-by-side but silent as the song continued, each lost in their own thoughts as they watched Hazel. Once the song had ended Kendrick glanced over at Edgar and gave him a slight nod before walking toward Hazel.

He approached with a low bow and she inclined her head and curtsied in response.

"Might I have this next dance, My Lady?" he asked, and she gave him a polite smile and placed her hand in his.

"You may, My Lord," was her reply and the two moved to the dance floor.

"Are you feeling better after your bout of illness?"

"I am quite recovered," she replied but there was something off about her tone. It did not sound the same as the last time he had spoken with her. Still, he moved with her around the dance floor, grateful for the opportunity to hold her in his arms no matter the circumstances.

"I am very pleased to welcome you as my sister," he began, though the words hurt to say.

"Are you?" she interrupted. But there was something cryptic about her tone and he faltered a moment, stumbling in his steps, before continuing on.

"Edgar shall make an excellent husband for you. He is a good man. He cares for you greatly and will protect you all your life. In fact, I am sure the two of you shall make a perfect match." It was all for Edgar, he told himself. Edgar and Hazel. Because marrying Edgar would be good for her too. And so he pushed past the feelings that arose with each word he spoke.

"Edgar does not love me," Hazel replied, though she continued to move just as smoothly as ever. "And he may never love me. He has admitted as such."

Kendrick felt shocked at the revelation and the very droll way she stated things. But what could he do?

"I have always wished to marry for love and if Edgar does not love me...how could I ever marry him?"

"Edgar-Edgar is uncertain. He is nervous and anxious about his feelings and does not know how to express them. But he certainly does love you," Kendrick said instead, though he was not so sure himself. He was having difficulty remembering all of the steps he was supposed to be following as he continued to explain himself — or rather, Edgar — to Hazel.

"That is not true. He has told me himself that he does not currently love me. He thinks that perhaps it shall come, but what if it does not? What if as the years pass we do not come to fall in love at all? No, I could not possibly marry a man who does not love me."

"Edgar may have said such a thing but it is not true-" Kendrick began but now there was an angry look over Hazel's face. Her lips pursed together and her eyebrows drawn low over her eyes.

"I do not believe any of this. And how could I? How could I believe a word coming from your mouth when I know you to be a liar?"

His mouth dropped open at the harsh words and the tone with which she said them. "Hazel-" but the song had ended and Hazel left him there on the dance floor, never minding the propriety that would have bid him escort her away.

As his mind raced he hurried to leave the dance floor as well, though he had no idea what to do next when she was so furious. Would it be best to let her go? Or to follow her?

# CHAPTER 26

EVEN IF IT wasn't the best thing to do Kendrick had to follow her, and so he quickly tried to head her off at the other end of the ball-room. Certainly there had to be an explanation for what she had said, right?

But could she actually know? He tried to think of any reason that she would call him a liar and could come up with nothing. Unless Edgar was right. Unless she had somehow figured out that he was the one writing the letters.

"What do you mean by this?" He managed to get out, though the words came out harsher than he had intended. Hazel turned with her eyes flashing, angrily. She did not speak at first, merely pulled a small book from the folds of her dress and thrust it at him.

It took a moment for Kendrick to realize just what it was she had given him. But when he did he felt a rush of relief that his diary had been found, and then, almost immediately thereafter, a rush of shock, anxiety, nervousness, and so many other emotions at what she would have found within it.

"I have read it," she stated firmly, "And I know everything. I know that you are the one who has been writing to me all this time under the guise of being your brother. It is not Edgar who has written even a single letter to me."

He attempted to speak, but no words wanted to come out. And she did not have any interest in his speaking anyway. She continued on.

"You have deceived me. You and your brother both. And you have used me wrongly." Her voice practically shook with emotion, and her eyes continued to glitter brightly, "How could you? How could you be in love with me and yet encourage me to marry your brother? Knowing that I must love you, you who has been writing and making me fall in love with you all this time? I have never heard of anything so despicable in my life!" She did not shout it, but her voice conveyed as much emotion as if she had.

Rather, the manner in which she seemed to hiss the words through her teeth in order to not attract the attention of those around them only served to make it that much worse in his eyes. And then she stormed off before he could say another word.

Kendrick was left behind, his mouth gaped open in disbelief. Too many thoughts and emotions flitting through his mind. Shock that she knew everything about the letters and his being in love with her. And had she truly said that he had made her fall in love with him? Could it be that she loved him as he loved her?

But of course, that was still foolish and there was no reason for him to feel such a thing. It was still wrong of him. And he flushed at the thought that Hazel had realized that he was in love with her.

All the while Kendrick found himself rooted to the spot, unable to move. At least, until Edgar came to him and gently steered him to an edge of the room.

"What has happened? I could see the argument from across the room," he said quietly and Kendrick had to start and stop a few times before he could bring himself to speak.

"She knows," he managed finally and Edgar paled even further. "She knows all of it. Everything." With that, he regaled Edgar with the entire story and everything that Hazel had said. He did not leave anything out, though he was not sure he could have if he wanted to at this point. He could not lie yet again.

"Do you truly love her?" Edgar asked quietly once he had finished. There was nothing to say to that. At least, nothing that Kendrick could bring himself to say to that. He did not want to admit it. But he could not lie either and so he simply looked away in silence for a long moment, leaving that to answer Edgar's question instead.

"I should not be here. In London. I cannot stay and see you married away to Hazel. And I cannot stand in the way of your marriage either. Rather, I will leave and things will begin to be much better for yourself and Hazel. I am the reason things were so strange to begin with and the reason that everything fell apart that way," Kendrick replied wretchedly. He felt awful at everything that had happened and the way that he had ruined things. After he had only meant to help to have it all go such a way...

"You can't leave," Edgar replied incredulously.

"It would be best for everyone. Best for you. Best for me. And certainly best for Hazel."

"You've lost your mind. I do believe it would be good for you to travel outside of London. There is an entire world out there. But not because of this."

"Edgar-"

"No," his brother replied firmly. "You certainly have a way with words but if you do not move from words to actions you shall never get the girl you love."

"What are you talking about?" Kendrick asked and Edgar shook his head with an exasperated look.

"You love her, right?"

"Yes," Kendrick admitted, though he paused a moment before he did.

"And she loves you."

"She said she did," he admitted again, her words echoing in his mind. *'knowing that I must love you, you who has been writing and making me fall in love with you all this time?'*

"I do not love her, Kendrick. It is possible I might someday learn to. She is a wonderful girl, after all. But I do not love her now and that someday may well never come. Our marriage was arranged. And I was more than willing to fulfill my duty to marry her. But if you love her then I could never marry her. I could never cause my brother that kind of pain for a girl who I feel little more than an obligation toward."

"But the marriage-"

"You are being foolish, Brother. You love her. It is clear in the things that you have written. So step up and be the man I know you can be. You will need to take action, and quickly. Before it is too late." Kendrick paused a moment, looking across the room at Hazel and realized that his brother was right. This was his chance. His only chance, and he stood up straighter at the thought.

"You are right. I cannot give up on her. Not until I have tried everything."

"Good. Now go to her." Kendrick quickly strode across the room to Hazel, reaching out his hand toward her.

"Please, Hazel-" but she simply turned away from him, walking to another and taking his hand to join the couples on the dance floor.

All Kendrick could do was watch miserably as the two danced and Hazel studiously avoided meeting his gaze.

# CHAPTER 27

SHE HAD NOT EVEN WANTED to dance, let alone with Lord Henry, and her eyes teared as she tried to remember the steps to the dance as they made their way around the dance floor. But she had needed something to get her away from Kendrick. After all, she had already said too much about her feelings to him.

How could she love him? How could she feel anything but anger toward him after what he had done to her? After the lies and the way that he had wronged her? All she wanted was to be alone.

And so, she begged off a second dance, telling Lord Henry she needed some air. But it was only part of what she needed. Venturing out onto the balcony gave her a chance to gulp in some of the cool night air, but it did nothing to quell the strong emotions that were rising up.

She grasped the railing of the balcony and was finally unable to bite back the sobs that threatened to truly overwhelm her. The thought of just what was happening was far too much. How could she be in love with one man and destined to marry another? How could she possibly marry Edgar knowing what she did about Kendrick? And knowing how she felt about him?

"Hazel?" the soft voice made her stiffen instantly, because she knew exactly who it was. Kendrick stood in the doorway between the balcony and the ballroom and she had to steel herself to respond.

As she quickly, and somewhat roughly, brushed the tears from her eyes she refused to turn around.

"Leave me." But there was no response for a long moment. She thought at first that perhaps he had left, but then his voice began again, this time slightly closer.

"Please, Hazel, give me just a moment of your time. Let me explain." Begrudgingly she turned around to face him, though she tried hard not to feel too kind toward him.

"What is it then?"

He came closer then, reaching out like he wanted to take her hand and then thinking better of it.

"We did not mean to deceive you. Neither of us did. It all came about entirely by accident." He paused a moment and then continued. "Your mother and mine set the betrothal. Edgar was not even returned from his trip yet and of course you were still in Bath.

"I had no idea how I felt about you at the time. I had not seen you in so long and I agreed with our mothers that it would be an excellent match for the both of you. I had no reason to believe otherwise."

He stopped and Hazel simply waited for him to go on. Thus far there was nothing that said she should forgive him for what he had done.

"Our mother told Edgar that he should write to you. That it would help you both to get to know one another. But Edgar is awful with letter writing. We only rarely would get letters from him while he was away and when we did they were hardly worth reading most of the time. He sent them as an obligation, merely to let us know he was still alive. When he asked me to write letters for him...I thought that I was helping my brother by doing so. I thought that I would write a few letters to help you understand him better, and to help him get to know you. I never expected to fall in love with you. When I did...I felt awful. I knew that it was wrong of me. You were set to marry Edgar. But I could not help it."

He took a pause and continued, "And I certainly never expected that you would fall in love with me." He seemed to be waiting for a response but she did not give one, save for looking away from him as tears threatened yet again. "But love is not something that we can control. It is something that simply happens on its own. Without our say so."

She did not want to admit anything to him just yet, but there was truth in what he said. Just in the way that he told his story she could tell that he was being honest with her.

"We never wanted to hurt you." He continued, pleadingly. "We never thought that there would be anything wrong with my writing the letters. We only wanted to make this match work."

She opened her mouth to speak but then thought better of it, closing her mouth again and turning her head away from him.

"I am sorry, Hazel. So sorry for hurting you." It was just then that her mother made her way out to the balcony.

"Whatever is happening here?" she asked, though it was clear that she had heard at least part of what had just transpired.

"I cannot speak of it now," Hazel replied and her mother set a hand on her shoulder, looking deeply into Hazel's eyes with the same soft look she had used when their puppy died when Hazel was only six. Or the time that Hazel's tutor had left abruptly to elope and had never even said goodbye.

It was a look Hazel knew well, but she was not about to sit and be comforted by her mother this time. This was too much, too hard.

Hazel started for the doorway, but Edgar was there before she could escape yet again.

"Hazel...please do not punish Kendrick for my mistakes. I asked him to write those letters. And he was trying to be a good brother. But he loves you. I know that he does. The things he has said to you, the things he has written, I did not know that he felt them for himself. If I had, I never would have let this go on as long as it has. I would have ended it all so much sooner," Edgar pleaded, but Hazel ignored him, brushing past him to the ballroom.

Even this did not deter Kendrick, however, who had apparently waited as long as he was prepared to. Instead, he followed her, boldly grasping her hand to force her back toward him. And then, right there in the middle of the ballroom, with everyone turning to stare, he dropped down to his knee and continued his pleading in a much louder voice.

"I am in love with you, Hazel. Perhaps I always have been, since we were young. But now I know that it is so much more than it ever was before. I know that the feelings I have for you are strong and they are true. And they will never fade away. And I may have done you wrong. I know that I have. But I love you and I shall always love you. And if I must I shall spend the rest of my life making things right to you."

Hazel stood completely still, frozen, stunned at the declaration. Kendrick still on his knees before her; his face turned up to gaze into her eyes. And his own showed nothing but kindness, care, devotion. It was overwhelming, as was the feel of his hand holding hers. So she looked away.

Edgar was standing completely still and silent in the doorway of the balcony where she had left him. Though he had turned around to face them. She was too nervous to give more than a quick glance to the other people in the room who had all fallen silent themselves and turned to stare.

Fiona was near the opposite wall, her hand pressed to her mouth in surprise, as though she were trying to determine just what was happening, her gaze moving between her two sons.

Hazel did not see her father at first, at least not until another gentleman moved and he was revealed only a few feet away from her. His gaze was difficult to comprehend, but it seemed he was quite confused by what was transpiring as well.

Only her mother moved, approaching Hazel slowly and setting a gentle hand on her shoulder.

"You are the only one who can choose your path," Rose told her softly and Hazel's eyes returned to Kendrick's. "Follow your heart, Dear."

"I love you as well," Hazel finally admitted and Kendrick's face broke into a broad grin, his eyes sparkling with happiness and his mouth stretched wider than she had ever seen it.

He stood immediately, pulling her into a hug that very nearly knocked the breath out of her. Everyone around them cheered and laughed, clapping and exclaiming over the wonderful news. Even Edgar, who was the first to approach, seemed very pleased and had no ill words for either of them. Expressing his happiness at soon gaining a new sister.

It was more than she could have dreamed of, and far better than she had expected when she set out that morning. Who would have thought that things could turn out so well?

# CHAPTER 28

ONE END TO THE OTHER.

16 steps from the edge of the dictionary shelf to the end of the row.

25 steps from the end of the row to the window seat.

8 steps from the window seat to the table.

20 steps from the table to the edge of the dictionary shelf again.

Around and around Kendrick paced.

And he counted each of his steps as he did.

He had thought the library would make it much easier for him to write out his vows. And yet...it certainly did not seem that way. Rather, he felt overwhelmed and more nervous than ever.

Each time he tried to put his pen to the paper he found himself only more frustrated with the words that spilled out onto the page. Nothing was right. Nothing seemed enough to convey the emotions and feelings he had for her.

With a sigh he sank into the chair again, pulling out his diary and turning to a fresh page. But even as the words fell from his pen he knew they were not right. Not enough. A frustrated groan escaped him and the library door opened.

"Darling, what are you doing?" his mother asked, and Kendrick turned toward her with a frustrated look.

"I am attempting to write my vows."

"And how goes it?" Edgar asked, though they should have been able to tell quite clearly by the expression on his face.

"It is not well," Kendrick replied anyway, his frustration leaking through into his voice.

"Ah, Kendrick, you worry too much. I am sure that your vows

are just fine and that Hazel will like them. After all, she has liked everything else you have written" Edgar replied, but Kendrick shook his head.

"It is not enough to simply have something that is 'fine.' These are the vows to the woman that I love and they must be perfect." Both Edgar and his mother laughed lightly, though not cruelly.

"You are a writer. I am sure that you will be fine creating the perfect words for your vows," Edgar added

"I would wish that being a writer would make me better at writing my vows, however it does not seem to be helping me in the least," he replied with a grumble. "I must get to work as my vows must be just right."

"My dear, do not overtax yourself," his mother replied, brushing her hand over his hair and forehead as though to detect a fever. The way she had when they were both young.

"I want my vows to be perfect. The way that Hazel deserves." His mother and brother gave him indulgent smiles at that.

"Nothing is ever perfect. And that is fine. Do you expect her vows to you to be perfect?" Edgar asked, trying to make his brother feel better.

"No," Kendrick replied.

"And Hazel will not expect perfection from you. Do not strain yourself. The words that you want to say will come to you," Edgar said.

"Perhaps," he agreed, though he wasn't sure he really believed that."

"Now, we need your thoughts on some of the details of the wedding,"

"I am happy with whatever Hazel wants," he replied and his mother smiled.

"You have no opinion on the food to be served? Or the flowers to be used?"

"Hazel should choose all of those things. I wish that she will be happy with our wedding." The words still sent a thrill through him when he thought about it. *Our wedding.* It still seemed so strange to think that everything had fallen into place just like that.

"You are far more than smitten already," Edgar teased and Kendrick could not help but smile.

"I love to love. And love to show my love. Now please, leave me to my writing so that I can create the vows that my Hazel deserves," the words were bouncing back and forth through his head, and he was sure he was on to something now.

"Do not put too much pressure on yourself," his mother instructed. "Hazel would not want it."

He gave a brief nod, but he was already drifting further into his own mind. His mother brushed a hand over his hair again and smiled at him once more. With that the two left the room, leaving Kendrick to his own thoughts which suddenly seemed so much clearer.

"Thank you," he managed to get out, though he was distracted by the placing of his pen on the paper before him.

The words he wanted to say suddenly flowed through him as if of their own accord and he could not wait to share them with Hazel.

As she entered the dressmakers Hazel had to take a deep breath to steady herself. The very first time she had entered this shop it had been to begin the gown she would wear to marry Edgar. But everything had changed now. Including the dress.

When she had begun her plans for her wedding, she had been very in love with the idea of being married and the gown she had chosen reflected the fluff of a schoolgirl. But now...now she wanted something simpler and more elegant. Something that was fitting of the man she was to marry.

"This is the silhouette that I have in mind, from you description," the seamstress informed her, presenting a lovely gown with a fitted waist and a modestly large skirt. "It will have a long train, as you requested, made with silk to give just the right look as you walk through the church."

Hazel could not help the brilliant smile that spread across her face at the thought of it and, as she slipped into the gown so her measurements could be taken yet again, she luxuriated in the image of the dress that began to build in her mind.

"Now, the wedding trousseau?" her mother began as Hazel slipped back into her own gown, the seamstress carefully setting aside the sample gown, now filled with pins.

"Yes, of course," the seamstress replied.

"She shall have five everyday gowns and two new ballgowns." Hazel's eyes widened in surprise. Seven new gowns was quite a lot, but her mother insisted that she enter into her marriage with everything she needed. "We shall spare no expense for our only daughter," she replied as Hazel protested.

"But it is so much,"

"It is what our daughter deserves. And of course there shall be nightclothes as well. You should take extra care with those," her mother smiled and the seamstress nodded with a knowing look but Hazel blushed scarlet.

"Of course. We have some lovely materials that have only just come in, and a bit of lace would also do wonderfully," the two women nodded and Hazel looked away, feeling embarrassed at the thought of her nightclothes and just why they needed to be 'taken care of' at all.

Once her mother and the seamstress had finished discussing everything, Hazel and Rose left the shop, preparing to go to the shops closer to town where she could select the bedclothes that were needed for her trousseau as well.

As soon as she stepped outside, however, her eyes lit immediately on Kendrick. He was just leaving the tailor down the street and she knew that he must be getting his own wedding attire ready. It was as though they were already drawn to each other because his eyes rose to meet hers at the same instant she saw him and a smile spread across both their faces.

"Ah, Hazel," he approached quickly, not even trying to seem less than ecstatic to see her. She felt the same as her heart began to flutter wildly in her chest. "It is lovely to see you. I had not hoped to catch you in town."

"We have just come from the seamstress," she replied, though that was obvious as she had barely left the front stoop of the shop, though her mother remained inside.

"And I have only just left the tailor,"

"Have you gotten your wedding clothes then?"

"We have been finalizing the look of things," he replied and she nodded in agreement.

"As have we."

"Have you written your vows?" Kendrick asked and Hazel blushed slightly and nodded. The vows had been difficult to write. Not because she was not excited to marry Kendrick, but because none of the words that came to her seemed good enough. Still, only this morning the words had finally righted themselves and the vows seemed everything she wanted.

"I have, and I cannot wait to share them with you."

"Aye. I have only just finished mine and am anxious to share them with you as well," he agreed.

"Ah, Kendrick," He turned toward the voice and bowed immediately to her mother as she walked from the shop. "It is lovely to see you."

"The pleasure is mine, Your Grace," he replied and Rose gave a smile between him and Hazel.

"Well, Hazel?" she led.

"We must be going," Hazel said quickly, "We have much more to do to prepare for the wedding," she wished she could stay and speak with Kendrick all the rest of the day, but of course it could not be. They needed many more things before the wedding, and there was not a lot of time to get it all done.

Kendrick looked as disappointed as she felt, though he hid it well enough as he bowed to each of them.

"Of course, I shall leave you both to your day. Perhaps I could call on you tomorrow?"

"That would be wonderful," Hazel replied, excited. She was already looking forward to it and the bright smile on Kendrick's face said he was as well.

As the two parted ways Hazel could not shake the smile from her face. All she could think of was Kendrick, and how wonderful their life together was going to be.

# CHAPTER 29

THE REFLECTION in the looking glass did not look like her at all. Or rather, it looked like the very best she had ever looked, and then some. Hazel had not even known she could look so beautiful and she didn't even need anyone else to tell her that she was. Though of course, there were plenty of people who did tell her.

"Oh! You are positively radiant," Louise exclaimed as she walked through the door and Hazel jumped up excitedly at the sight of her.

"I thought you would not make it!"

"I could not possibly miss the wedding of my best friend. Oh, but with the rain and traveling through the mud I was not sure either," she admitted. The two girls hugged tightly, though Louise stepped back quickly so as not to wrinkle Hazel's gown.

"Today is the day."

"It certainly is. The day you shall marry the true love of your life. I suppose you shall not be setting me up with Kendrick after all," Louise's eyes sparkled and Hazel had to laugh as well.

"No. I shall keep him for myself."

"Ah, well, I may still be the one to marry the Earl, only it shall not be the one that I thought." They laughed and Hazel wondered if Louise could possibly be the right fit for Edgar instead. But the thoughts flew from her mind almost immediately as Louise gathered up her veil.

"Is it time already?" she asked with an anxious but excited smile.

"It is," Louise replied. "As I said, I very nearly did not make it. We must get you finished right away." As Louise tucked the veil in around her hair both girls could only stare into the mirror. "You are a vision. Kendrick is certainly lucky to have you as his bride."

"I cannot wait to marry him," Hazel replied.

"Are you nervous?" Louise asked and Hazel shook her head.

"Not at all. When you are marrying the one you love there are no worries." The two girls stared into the looking glass for another long moment before the door opened again. This time it was her mother standing in the doorway.

"Oh! Hazel, you are lovely," she was teary-eyed as she approached, her hands gently brushing over Hazel's veil and her gown. The sweet touch and the softness of her mother's voice made Hazel tear up as well and practically fall into her mother's embrace.

"Mother! I am so excited for today."

"I am excited for you, Dear. And yet it is bittersweet for me. I shall lose my daughter today, as she truly becomes a woman, marrying the love of her life."

"You shall never lose me, Mother," Hazel insisted, tightening her hold for a moment before stepping back.

"Aye, that is true. Married you may well be, but you shall always be my daughter, and the most wonderful thing to ever happen to me."

They shared another hug and her mother gave her another long look before she finally straightened.

"I have come to tell you that it is time. Everyone is assembled, and we are only awaiting you." This was it. The moment she had been waiting for all of her life, though of course this moment was so much more than she had ever expected it to be.

As she left the room the Duke approached from the hallway, smiling brightly at the sight of her.

"You are lovely," he stated rather formally, but his gaze betrayed an entirely different emotion. The slight tearing in his eyes and the way that his mouth softened into a smile as he looked at her said that he was very pleased. But also perhaps a little more emotional than he wanted to show. She shared a smile and a hug with her father as well. This was it. This was the start of her entirely new life and she could not wait to see what was in store for her. As she and her father entered the church and began to walk down the aisle all eyes turned toward them. But the only eyes she saw were those of Kendrick, standing at the end, waiting for her.

His eyes grew teary even as she watched and she knew that hers had done the same. The thought that they were about the stand before all of these people and pledge themselves to one another was more than she could stand. It was, quite simply, everything she could have ever wanted.

When her father had left her beside Kendrick she had a

moment to glimpse Edgar standing beside him. He was the best man, opposite Louise who now stood behind Hazel.

It was clear from the brilliant smile on his face that there was no ill will on Edgar's part that he was not the one getting married today. Rather, he seemed genuinely pleased for his brother, and for her as well.

"Lord Anderton, you may recite your vows," the reverend began and she turned toward him even more fully.

"Hazel, I once saw you as a friend. One with whom I could run, play, and perhaps engage in mischief alongside. Yet, even then, I believe I knew that you would be so much more to me. You were my friend and my confidante even then. And now, you are so much more. I stand before you today, more than ready to take the vows that will join us together forever. I stand before you, ready to become your husband and to love and cherish you for the rest of our lives."

She was absorbed in the words that he spoke, and the way that his voice was so sweet and gentle as he did. His hands holding hers were soft. Everything was silent as he spoke, save for the soft rustling of clothes as their guests moved slightly, and the sound of the candles flickering around them.

"I am yours in every way and shall spend my life making yours everything that you want it to be. I know that you shall be my everything and you shall make each day sweeter and more fulfilling than ever before. I cannot wait to begin to make yours even the smallest bit of what mine shall be with you at my side." The look of his eyes in the candlelight was beautiful, and she could see the slight glint that said he was tearing up as well.

Hazel could not help the tears that welled over as she listened to Kendrick speak the beautiful words he had prepared for her. As she thought of just what amazing and wonderful things were coming for the both of them, as they joined their lives together, she was overcome with happiness. In fact, she was so overcome that she very nearly forgot every word that she had planned to say herself.

"Lady Tumbler, you may recite your vows," the priest stated.

"Kendrick, today, I stand before you ready to take my vows and to become your wife. I stand here, beside you, as I shall from this day forward, in everything and in every way.

"You, my husband, shall be my everything, my world. And I shall spend each day striving to show you how I feel and how much I love and cherish you. I shall spend each day as your wife feeling honored that you have chosen me and that I am the one that gets to be there with you for the rest of our lives together."

Kendrick looked as though he was about to cry as well when she was finished and he took her hands gently in his own as the reverend continued with the ceremony. But she barely heard a word of it.

All she could focus on was Kendrick before her. His hands holding her own. His gaze fixed on hers. It was everything she could have ever wished for and she did not think anything could ever compare to this moment.

At least, not until she heard the reverend conclude his sermon.

"I know pronounce you to be man and wife. May I present, Lord and Lady Kendrick of Aethelred." Hazel felt the tears truly falling at that. She was now truly married. She was joined to Kendrick forever and the two of them would be spending the rest of their lives together.

He gave her a sweet kiss and the two led the way out of the church to the cheers and well wishes of all of their family and friends.

Her father had prepared a wedding breakfast that was open to a large crowd of their loved ones. But it did not matter who was there. Hazel and Kendrick had eyes only for one another as they made their way by carriage back to the manor.

The Duke and Duchess had spared no expense in making sure that the manor was decorated to welcome their guests. And they had ensured that everything looked absolutely gorgeous for their daughter.

But Hazel could hardly notice. All she cared about was making her way to the table that had been set for them all. The table where her father had, for the day, relinquished his seat at the head so that Kendrick could sit in the place of honor. And beside him, at his right hand, was Hazel.

The breakfast was filled with all of their favorite treats and each ate more than their fill. Though Hazel was not sure how she even ate anything at all. The food tasted wonderful, but it paled in comparison to how she was feeling in this very moment, looking into Kendrick's eyes.

Once the food was finished the guests all spilled into the ball-room and Kendrick and Hazel were able to venture about, greeting everyone and thanking them for celebrating this wonderful day with them.

Even still, the two could not bear to be separated for even a moment, holding hands and moving together through the room.

"Ah, young love. You two are a beautiful couple," one of the guests remarked and Hazel could not help but smile and blush slightly at the compliment.

"Aye, so lovely," another added.

"It is Hazel who is so lovely that anyone in her glow would seem perfect as well," Kendrick replied and the people around them smiled even brighter at his compliment of her.

The evening seemed interminably long and short at the same time. While she enjoyed greeting each of their guests and meeting with the people she loved, it seemed like they would never have time to themselves.

And yet, at the same time it felt as though the time was passing so quickly and before she knew it the light outside the windows was beginning to fade as it neared on tea time.

As she spoke with another of their guests her eye caught on Edgar across the room. He was speaking with someone, though at first she could not tell who the lady was. At least, until she caught a better look at the pale lavender gown and realized with a start that it was Louise!

She could not see Louise's face as they spoke, though the relaxed manner of her stance said that she was comfortable enough with the conversation. And Edgar was leaning toward her as he spoke. His face animated and bright.

It was clear they were enjoying each other's company and she could not help but smile at the thought. Edgar had not been the one for her, but she certainly wanted him to be happy. And she most definitely wanted Louise to be happy. If they could find that happiness in each other...it would be even more remarkable.

"It is time for us to be going," Kendrick said finally and Hazel smiled at him yet again. It was time for their honeymoon, which they would be spending in the country.

All of their things had already been sent ahead, and there was nothing else to do but take their leave and bundle themselves into the carriage, which they did quite quickly.

"Goodbye, Mother," Hazel said as she gave her parents a quick hug and a kiss. This would be the last time that she would leave their home as a resident of it. From now on she would be only a guest. This would no longer be her home.

The thought was bittersweet on its own. After all, this was the house she had grown up in and had lived in all her life, other than when she was at school, of course. To be leaving it was sad.

Yet she was excited to begin the new future that Kendrick and she had discussed. And so she left through the front door with a broad smile and an air of excitement about her.

# EPILOGUE

HAZEL OPENED her eyes to bright sunlight streaming through the window. For a long moment her dream clouded her mind and she wondered at the window being on the wrong side of the bed. It seemed like it was only yesterday that she was waking up in her room at her parents manor. But it had been a year since she had last woken in the large four-poster bed that had been hers since she was a small child.

"Ah, you are awake." She turned with a smile toward the door, and Kendrick who had just entered it with a breakfast tray. As her hands strayed to her rounded stomach she could not help but smile broadly. Yes, everything was so much better now than it had been even those happy days a year ago.

Her childhood had been wonderful. And her life in Deighton Manor just as lovely. But nothing could be better than the life she had now. With her adoring husband and her unborn child.

"It is too lovely a day to be sleeping in," she replied, sitting up in bed while Kendrick readied a small table with their fare. When he returned to the bed it was to give her a gentle kiss on the forehead, followed by a second kiss over her belly.

"Aye, it is certainly a lovely day," he agreed as he did. She laughed in response, her hand reaching out to lovingly stroke the side of his face.

"Is it me you love most? Or our unborn child?" He placed his own hand over hers and smiled.

"I love you both equally," he replied. She did not doubt it. He was always showing her just how much he loved her and ever since she had announced that she was pregnant he had been overjoyed about the prospect of a child. "Come now, it's time for breakfast."

He poured out their tea for breakfast and filled her plate before his own. Kendrick was always attentive to her needs and always so sweet to her. In fact, in a year he had never said a cross word to her and she smiled as she thought of all the things that could have vexed him.

But he seemed to have endless patience and she loved that about him. It would serve him well as he became a father as well. With another loving touch to her stomach, Hazel stood and went to the table he had set.

"Edgar is set to come home today. I was in town yesterday and they said that the ship had berthed three days prior, right on schedule."

"It shall be nice to have him home again," Hazel replied with a broad smile. Edgar had left shortly after their wedding, on a shorter voyage this time. Though he had seemed perfectly happy at the wedding and had said he had no regrets about the dissolution of his own betrothal Hazel thought that perhaps he was a little sad.

After his life of traveling and being alone perhaps he had been happy at the idea of someone to share his life with. But he had wished them both well, and his mother who had been even more saddened by his departure, and taken his leave of them, promising that he would not be gone long.

"He has only been to the continent this time. A short voyage to be sure for him." Kendrick smiled and picked another scone from the tray.

"I had asked him to bring back something special," Hazel replied and they both smiled, thinking of just what he might be bringing back with him.

"I do hope he will be pleased with the state of things."

"You have done an excellent job running the estate while he has been gone," Hazel assured Kendrick. "He will be most pleased with what you have done."

"Eat a little more," Kendrick said instead of replying, putting another slice of sausage onto her plate and another helping of eggs. "It is good for you and the baby." She laughed at that but did not protest much about eating more. It seemed she was always hungry these days.

"What time shall he come?"

"There is no way to know. If he helped oversee the offloading of the supplies he may not have left until late. In which case he may not be here until end of the day. Though if he has ridden all night through, he could be here quite early."

"Well then, we shall have to get everything ready for him in case he is here early," Hazel instructed, ringing the bell at the side table to call for Trina.

"Yes, My Lady?" Trina asked, entering the room and surveying the sweet scene before her.

"Edgar may be home at any time today. We would like everything to be prepared for his arrival."

"Of course," Trina replied. "I'll make sure the staff are aware. But I am sure they are already quite ready. They have been talking of it for days as well."

"I am glad everyone is excited for my brother to return," Kendrick said with a smile.

"They certainly are," Trina agreed. As she showed herself back out Hazel turned toward Kendrick again.

"I can't believe it has been a year already that we have been married."

"Neither can I. It feels like only yesterday that we first married." He smiled at her fondly, his hand on hers on the table.

"And soon we shall have a little one to join our perfect family."

"That we shall. I hope that it shall be a little girl with her mother's beautiful eyes and lovely smile," Kendrick replied and Hazel could not help but smile in response.

"And I hope it shall be a little boy with his father's sweet nature," she told him. "A young poet just like you."

The two sat in silence for a long moment, holding onto one another and smiling, thinking blissfully of the future that they would have with their little one very soon.

"Oh, we must get moving. Edgar could be here anytime and I want to be sure that everything looks just right."

"He shall not be concerned about the house," Kendrick laughed. "He has always been happy enough with the state of things when he returns."

"Perhaps, but this is the first time that he is returning since we have been married. I want him to see that I can care for things well in his absence."

"He does not doubt you, I am sure," Kendrick replied. "And our mother also does not expect you to run all of the household."

"Does she feel that I am overstepping my place by taking charge so?" Hazel asked, concerned, and Kendrick laughed again.

"No, of course not. She is more than happy to have someone else to share in running the household, but she does not wish you to feel overwhelmed or overburdened by such things."

Hazel heard his assurances but they did not help her when it came to her own thoughts. This was the first time she had been even partially in charge of running a home and she wanted to do it properly.

As soon as she was fully dressed and prepared for the day — Trina came back to help when Kendrick took the breakfast things away — she hurried downstairs to meet with Fiona.

"Ah, there you are. And how are you doing this morning?" Fiona asked kindly. Hazel smiled in response.

"I am doing quite well. And the baby seems to be having a bit of a rest this morning which has made it a little easier. Oh, but there is so much to do today to prepare for Edgar."

"Things will get on quite well. They always do. You should take some time to rest."

"Oh, I couldn't," Hazel replied even as Fiona led her toward the couch in the sitting room.

"Just for a moment, Dear. I do not want you to overtax yourself. And Edgar would not want it either."

"I do not want him to think that I am not fulfilling my role here," Hazel protested.

"Your role is to be his brother's wife," Fiona said gently. "It is not your job to run the household. That is mine for as long as Edgar lacks a wife of his own."

"I do not mean to take your position," Hazel's eyes widened in surprise. She had certainly not meant to make Fiona feel badly.

"No, Dear. I do not worry about that. I do not mind having a little help with the things that need done. But I do not want you to feel as though I am expecting you to handle everything. It is certainly not your responsibility. And it is not what either Edgar nor I expect of you."

"But I would like to be of assistance. I do not like to be idle."

"Then we will find things for you to do, of course, but in your condition it is best that you are idle more often than not," Fiona insisted.

Once Hazel had agreed to take it easy and to be sure to take plenty of rests, Fiona gave her the job of checking in on Cook to be sure that dinner was progressing well, and making sure that the maids were getting Edgar's rooms ready the way he preferred.

It was at least something to occupy her time, which otherwise seemed always to be spent in a lazy fashion, reading or sewing something for the baby.

She did not mind spending her time in pursuit of tasks for the baby, but often she felt that she was being too idle and would find herself bored. It was just at that time that she heard the front door open and a great deal of excitement followed.

"Ah, Edgar!" Fiona was certainly overjoyed to see her son and the rest of the household quickly came to greet him as well.

In no time he had been escorted back to the sitting room where Hazel was waiting. She stood quickly to welcome him with a smile and pressed her hand to his.

"It is so nice to see you again."

"And you as well. It seems there is much that I have not been told," Edgar teased, taking in Hazel's rounded stomach. "Am I to be an uncle already?" He smiled broadly at the thought and she could not help but smile even more in return.

"You shall. Quite soon as well." He gave her a hug as Kendrick walked into the room.

"It has been too long without you, Edgar," Kendrick said, taking his turn at a hug from his brother.

"Let us all sit and you can tell us about your travels," their mother replied, helping Hazel back to her seat on the couch. Everyone else fell into their favorite spaces, though they tried to be as close together as possible.

"This has been one of my shorter trips, but I must say it was an exciting one as well. Travel to the continent is not so difficult as one might think. In fact, Kendrick I believe you should take your wife and your child there when they are able."

"Perhaps I shall," Kendrick agreed and Hazel smiled broadly at the thought of traveling.

"Much of the area is like what we are used to here. Though some areas have even more parties and celebrations than even we are used to," Edgar acknowledged.

As they fell into their discussions of Edgar's travels and everything that had happened at home since he had been gone it felt just like everything Hazel had ever wanted.

Being here, in this room, with these people, was everything she could ever have imagined. It was home. As much as her family at Deighton Manor had ever been. And she was overjoyed to share in life with all of them.

# EXTENDED EPILOGUE

I would like to thank you all from the bottom of my heart for reading my book "*The Lord Behind the Letters*"!

Visit a search engine and enter the link you see below the picture to connect to a more personal level and as a BONUS, I will send you the Extended Epilogue of this Book!

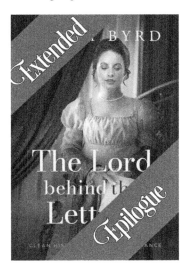

http://edithbyrd.com/AmB020

I would be honored if you could spare a little time to post your review!

## A MESSAGE FROM
## EDITH BYRD

Thank you all very much for reading my book to the
  end!
  I strongly believe that every story needs to be told, but it is truly
a great story if it is worth reading. I really
  hope mine was worth your trouble!
  I would like to thank from the bottom of my heart my friend and
colleague Fanny Finch. I had been her fan for a long time before
she gave me the opportunity to work alongside her as a beta reader,
and later she in-
  spired me into taking up writing.
  She was gracious enough to help me start my career as an
author with our cowritten novel and my debut and
  for that I will be forever grateful!
  As a parting gift I offer some advice: if writing is your dream, it
is never too late! All you need is the will to take a risk and good
people around you to nudge you on and never let you quit!
  Faithfully yours,

# ABOUT STARFALL
# PUBLICATIONS

Starfall Publications has helped me and so many
others extend my passion from writing to you.

The prime focus of this company has been – and always will be
– *quality* and I am honored to be able to publish my books under
their name.

Having said that, I would like to officially thank Starfall Publications for offering me the opportunity to be part of such a wonderful,
hard-working team!

Thanks to them, my dreams – and your dreams — have come
true!

# BE A PART OF EDITH BYRD'S FAMILY

I would like to thank you all for supporting me in my
first steps as an author.
If you're not a member of my family yet, it's never too late! Stay up to date on upcoming releases and check out my website for exclusive gifts, romance suggestions,
and lots of surprises!
Social Media:
Facebook
Goodreads
Bookbub
Amazon

## ALSO BY EDITH BYRD

Printed in Great Britain
by Amazon

87249946R00122